THE PARIS DECEPTION

THE PARIS DECEPTION

THE FRASER AND COOK HISTORICAL MYSTERY SERIES, BOOK TWO

DAVID O. STEWART

ePublishingWorks!
love what you read.

Book design by eBook Prep
www.ebookprep.com

Cover Art by Justin Stewart
Justifii.com

June, 2020
ISBN: 978-1-64457-169-9

ePublishing Works!
644 Shrewsbury Commons Ave
Ste 249
Shrewsbury PA 17361
United States of America

www.epublishingworks.com
Phone: 866-846-5123

ACKNOWLEDGMENTS

Though the writer's life is a solitary one, he never writes the book alone. I'm very grateful for the support and guidance of my editor, John Scognamiglio, and of Will Lippincott, my agent and friend. I was fortunate that two excellent readers, Gerry Hogan and my wife Nancy, cast their critical eyes over the manuscript. It benefited greatly from their attention. My friend Rich Zweig helped me think about how a physician might respond to the extreme stress of caring for so many grievously injured and sick patients.

My greatest fortune is that Nancy's still sticking with me. The least I can do is dedicate the book to her.

To Nancy

FOREWORD

BY MARY K. TOD

People read novels for enjoyment, but with historical fiction they also read to understand and learn. According to historian Margaret MacMillan, author of *Paris 1919*, "history can offer us instructive analogies. It can help us to formulate useful questions about our own times. And it can provide warnings: we are on thin ice here, there are dangerous beasts over there." *The Paris Deception* prompts us to think not only about the past, but also about today. Through the characters of President Woodrow Wilson, French Premier Georges Clemenceau, and British Prime Minister David Lloyd George we gain insight on the conflicting values of countries, on the complexities of building peace, on the weight of great responsibility. We see the United States in its ascendancy, Britain as its empire begins to fade, and the total collapse of Germany.

From 2014 to 2019, governments and citizens from around the world looked back on World War One, commemorating the beginning of that dreadful conflict, the seminal battles where thousands died for minimal gains, the final days of struggle, and ultimately, the peace that followed. We observed the pageantry, listened to leaders lament unbelievable losses, and read true stories of bravery and daring involving everyday people. Authors released new WWI novels: stories of families torn apart, the chaos and horror of war, the ineptitude of leaders, the longing for home; stories of intense camaraderie, unfaltering duty and heroism; stories of tragic loss and lives forever and devastatingly altered. I've written three such stories and read many, many more.

But what do we know about the peace process that followed WWI? Which leaders led the way or blocked the path to some sort of justice? Which borders changed and why? Which new countries were created? Which special interests were served? How did the conditions of peace sow the seeds for WWII? *The Paris Deception* by David O. Stewart is this novel. In addition to Wilson, Clemenceau, and Lloyd George, we meet Lawrence of Arabia, Prince Feisal and Rabbi Stephen Wise who seek decisions for Palestine and the Arab people. We also meet lesser known figures such as Allen Dulles future CIA Director, US Secretary of State Robert Lansing, and German politicians attempting to salvage their country. All had important parts to play.

Through the fictional characters of *The Paris Deception*, we experience the war in flashback, understand the devastation brought about by the Spanish Flu, and feel the agony of having a son go off to war. In one chapter, Joshua Cook who served with the Harlem Hellfighters, an African-American infantry regiment, relives the trauma of battle:

> "The hard part was the bombardments, huddled in trench muck, water up to your knees, while shells rained down, hoping not to be shredded by shrapnel or vaporized by a shell blast, hoping not to disappear without a trace, leaving no more evidence of your death than of your life."

The experiences of Joshua's character also remind us of the racism that was rampant at that time and still infects our world. *The Paris Deception* – history that is highly relevant for today.

M.K. Tod's World War I novels include *Lies Told in Silence*, *Time and Regret*, and *Unravelled*, which was awarded Indie Editor's Choice by the Historical Novel Society. In addition to her writing, Mary blogs about reading and writing historical fiction on www. awriterofhistory.com, reviews books for the Historical Novel Society and the Washington Independent Review of Books, and has conducted four highly respected reader surveys. She lives in Toronto, Canada.

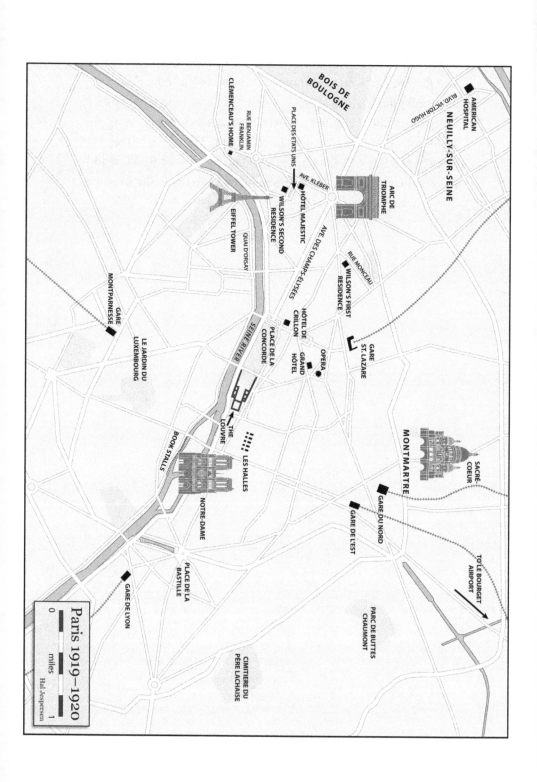

Paris 1919–1920

0   miles   1

Hal Jespersen

ONE

Friday, December 13, 1918

Major Jamie Fraser could barely breathe as the packed Metro train lurched out of the station for Les Sablons. A hard object—an umbrella handle? –threatened to perforate his left kidney. He squirmed to ease the pressure. The crowd, on its way to greet President Wilson's arrival in Paris, was too buoyant for Fraser to complain about a mere kidney. He had another. The air in the car sagged with the smells of sour tobacco, recent soups, and layers of unlaundered clothes.

It wasn't even five weeks since the armistice ended the war to end all wars, the one that President Wilson promised would make the world safe for democracy. The slogans hadn't entirely lost their power over Fraser. They were why he signed up to be an army doctor at his advanced age. Or part of why. Over the last ten months in Paris, working fourteen and sixteen hours a day, his sense of mission had shriveled. In its place were the mangled and dying soldiers, their wounds beyond the reach of his skills.

He had helped those he could, avoided those he couldn't. At mealtimes, he picked at bad food. Late at night he used bourbon to dull his senses—the sights and smells that assaulted him in every ward and examination room—accepting a hazy doze in lieu of actual sleep, grateful when no agonizing dreams startled him awake. The tide of blood and pus and putrefaction swept in from the stinking trenches in northern France to the cavernous American hospital in Neuilly. That tide washed away many of Wilson's slogans.

When the armistice stanched the flood of new casualties, Fraser's mind began, tentatively, to recall why he came to France. As it cast about for those reasons, there were the slogans. Today he would celebrate the war's end with the heaving mass of Parisians. Together, they would cry out fervent hopes for a new world.

Climbing the steps from the Concorde Station, Fraser squinted into a gray sky. On his rare ventures out of the hospital, Paris weather seemed to hover within a narrow range. On some days, sharp chills rose from pavement wet with recent drizzle. On other days, the air felt raw with rain about to start. If a bold scrap of sunbeam burst through the clouds, it soon faded like last night's dream. For him, the City of Light seemed more the City of Frowns. Distant German guns boomed day and night, occasionally raining shells onto the city, which sometimes cowered, sometimes raged, and sometimes just accepted destruction as part of its life.

Hundreds of those hated German cannons were standing cheek-by-jowl across the cobbles of the Place de la Concorde. The guns, finally silenced by the armistice, were prized prisoners of four years of slaughter over scraps of muddy ground.

Fraser stood still on the plaza and looked around. He wanted to notice everything, to remember it for the letter he owed to his wife Eliza and daughter Violet.

The crowd strolled in every direction, some in groups or pairs, some alone, but all together in their hearts. The dim weather dampened no spirits. Bitter memories were banished for the day. Paris was choosing to be gay. Flags of every nation in the victorious alliance fluttered from lampposts and buildings. Boys sprouted on tree branches like overgrown fruit. Discarded newspapers and crumpled cigarette packs cushioned the plaza's uneven stones, which more than a century before ran with the blood of a king and queen who lost their heads to Dr. Guillotine.

A sturdy middle-aged woman with apple cheeks stopped before him. She looked into his face. Her smile was sad. She took a step and embraced him through their overcoats, then pulled back and looked down. A tear stood on her cheek.

He gripped her shoulders and leaned down. "Peace," he said, more urgently than he intended.

She pulled a wadded handkerchief from her sleeve and snorted into it. When she walked away, he noticed the tricolor flag on a stick that trailed from her other hand.

The soldiers who swarmed the plaza were immaculate in their uniforms, French blue jackets and scarlet trousers mingling with American olive. The khaki of Britain and Australia receded from the eye when a Sikh platoon marched by with gleaming ivory turbans and extravagant whiskers. A Greek officer in blinding white and a pleated skirt nodded to a soldier sporting a fez and a jacket of red and green embroidery. The soldiers strutted like peacocks, men who had survived the firestorm that killed millions in shin-high mud.

An unshaven man swung by on crutches, his rhythm steady. Fraser had grown used to empty trouser legs, armless sleeves, faces rearranged by bullet or blast. An overage gendarme waved a baton in Fraser's direction. He wanted the crowd to climb out of the street back onto the curb. Wilson's procession was getting close.

Fraser shrugged helplessly. Too many bodies pressed behind him. The gendarme shrugged back, then walked on. Rising on his toes to peer over the crowd toward the Champs-Élysées, Fraser noticed a woman behind him with each arm over a small child. He gestured for them to move in front of him for a better view. The children slid efficiently into place. The mother nodded thanks as he took a half step back.

Cannon erupted, a steady pounding of the great guns that Fraser never wanted to hear again. The crowd had no such feeling. Their cheers began to the right of him and surged across the plaza. Outstretched hands waved silly small flags. The people around him picked up the cry of "*Vive Weel-SONE.*"

With only a few military vehicles in the vanguard, the procession slowly made its way toward Fraser. Without a thought, his arms shot up and his voice joined the thundering, wordless shout. They were shouting victory. They were shouting survival. For months, his smiles had been only sympathetic or sardonic. He broke into a boy's carefree grin. Months of fatigue lifted.

The president stood easily in an open car, hailing the crowd with waves of his glossy top hat. He acknowledged the cheers with a broad smile, teeth glistening like rows of fresh headstones. Turning from side to side, he and the crowd were two poles of a giant magneto. Energy surged from one to the other and back. Wilson, square-shouldered, seemed inflated by this welcome worthy of an emperor returned from conquest.

The car drew even with Fraser. Wilson's eyeglasses reflected the silver sky as he pivoted Fraser's way. An ocean of sound burst around them. It was hope. Fraser shouted louder. He strained forward, reaching to the tall, graceful man.

Wilson had used intoxicating words to promise peace. In his glorious Fourteen Points, he proclaimed rules for the postwar world. Secret diplomacy must end. Individual citizens and communities must determine their own futures. Arms races must end. People must be free to trade with each other. All nations must join in a single organization that would guarantee peace and independence to great and small states alike.

Some reacted skeptically to this storm of American idealism. Georges Clemenceau, premier of France, noted drily that God made do with only ten commandments.

But Wilson's words promised that the years of carnage were not simply one more spasm of butchery by a species addicted to violence, nor yet another greedy scrabbling after wealth and power. His words made the war almost holy, a testing that would redeem every ghastly sacrifice, that would lead to true and lasting peace.

And on this day of December 14, 1918, huge crowds shouted that his words were true. The enemy was vanquished. Right had triumphed. It ever would triumph. Paris loved him for it. Fraser loved him for it.

In the lobby of the Hotel de Crillon, which fronted on the plaza, bright light refracted through crystal chandeliers then reflected off diamond-patterned floors and marble pillars. After the melee on the plaza, the buzz of lobby talk soothed Fraser. He paused in the warmth to gain his bearings.

A dozen knots of men huddled in urgent conversations around plush chairs and settees. Their bright costumes transformed the lobby into an elegant caravanserai for those who held the world's power and those who craved it. Three men wore red fez caps with suits that even Fraser knew were out of fashion. In a far corner, turbans and mustaches recalled the proud Sikh warriors on the plaza. Two Africans looked like kings in flowing gowns of vivid prints. Europeans and Americans had their own costumes. Long, high-buttoned suit coats announced serious purposes. Tailcoats radiated formality and social position. Vested suits with unbuttoned jackets suggested a bit of dash. The newspapers said the American government was bringing five hundred experts to help Wilson make the peace. The British brought even more.

Fraser gathered himself and strode to the concierge desk. In clumsy French, he asked for the office of Colonel Edward House.

"Colonel House?" The concierge's English was solid. His eyebrows rose to express raw skepticism. "Does he know you?" With a flourish, the man produced a sheet of names in a white-gloved hand. "Are you on the list?"

"Well, he doesn't actually know me, but I am to attend a meeting in his office...."

The concierge held out the list again.

Fraser sighed. "James Fraser. Major James Fraser, US Army Medical Corps."

The concierge placed the list on the desk. "You are not on the list."

"But I'm expected." Fraser made a face. "Can you call up to the room and see if Admiral Cary Grayson is there? And tell him that I'm here? He's the man I'm supposed to see. Admiral Grayson." He said the last name very slowly and with emphasis.

The concierge pondered the situation, then lifted the receiver and requested a number. He turned his head so Fraser couldn't hear him.

After muffled talk, he replaced the receiver. "Room 201," he said, then turned to another guest.

Grayson greeted Fraser warmly at the open door to Colonel House's suite. "Come." He led Fraser inside. "You must see the European decadence to which we Americans hope to grow accustomed."

The room fell into a hush—thick carpet and thicker walls—as soon as Grayson closed the door behind them. Two silent workers sat at elegant writing desks with filigreed accents. The United States government had taken over all of this former royal palace for the duration of the peace conference. Colonel House, the president's closest adviser, occupied what had been the king's own suite of rooms with a commanding view over the Place de la Concorde.

Grayson said nothing as Fraser took a few hesitant steps and goggled at the luxury. The furniture was sumptuous, though all for business—desks, conference tables, and large chairs clustered in conversational groups. The decorations were overpowering. Every surface was carved or beveled, crested or gilt-encrusted. Creatures, mythological and real, frolicked on mantels, window frames, and doorways.

"It's rococo or baroque or some darn thing," Grayson said, walking to a small interior room that shared the sixteen-foot ceilings of the rest of the suite. "I stop noticing it after a while, which seems exactly not what the builder intended, but what the heck. We're all hayseeds here."

"The colonel has done well for himself," Fraser said.

They sat in armchairs that were nowhere near as comfortable as they looked.

"You should have seen Lansing when he took a gander at this. Green with envy, he was. Even though Lansing's own suite is pretty darned regal, even for a Secretary of State." Grayson was fortyish, compact, with sharp features and a ready grin. He had the bounce of a gymnast. He was President Wilson's personal physician and had summoned Fraser for a meeting on his first day in Paris.

Fraser still had no idea why Grayson had summoned him.

"Major," Grayson began, "I wanted to see you because of the influenza. Before we left, I spoke with Dr. Echols at the Rockefeller

Institute. He says you studied influenza in New York before you joined the army. What they're calling the Spanish influenza?"

"Yes, they are, but not for any particular Spanish quality of it. My research didn't cover this strain of the disease. I was already here in France before any of this strain broke out."

"Echols said that you're the army's best man on the disease."

"Heaven help us if that's so."

"This is no time for false modesty, Major. The army confirmed Dr. Echols' opinion. They say you lecture other doctors on the influenza. Echols tells me you're first-rate. On influenza, who's better than you?"

Fraser crossed his legs. "Admiral, we're all pretty terrible on the subject of the flu. You know this from all the flu deaths—back in the States and here in Europe. Even the Germans haven't figured it out. It may very well have cost them the war. If I'm the best you can find, it's only a measure of how little we know."

Grayson tapped a foot nervously. "Major Fraser, I have a single patient, the president of the United States. In ordinary times, that's a heavy responsibility, but these are no ordinary times. This president, despite appearances, has never enjoyed robust health. In fact, he's had many physical setbacks that the public doesn't know about and need not know about. The health of this president over the next weeks and months"—he paused for emphasis while he seemed to inflate to a larger version of himself — "well may determine the fate of the world."

Fraser, not entirely comfortable with this enlarged version of Grayson, nodded.

Grayson leaned forward. "Right now is the most pivotal moment in history for at least a century. All the nations of the world are in Paris, right here, within a mile of this building. They're here to decide what the world will look like for our children and grandchildren and their children. Why, they'll decide what to do with Germany, with the German colonies in Africa and Asia, what to do with Austria-Hungary and the Turkish Empire. It's the most monumental moment.

"And"—Grayson pointed in the direction of the plaza outside— "you saw the special position that President Wilson holds. He's something the world has never seen, a leader who wants only good. He holds the power

7

to make good into something real. The British and French want to return to the old ways, to imperialism and competing armies, all that medieval nonsense that led to war in the first place. Wilson is different. He's no mere politician. Do you know he never asked a man for his vote until he was fifty-four years old? Today he has the power to transform the world. He can make it so right triumphs over might, and will ever after."

An hour before, Fraser had experienced a sort of ecstasy over the president's ability to remake the world, but now he drew back. Right has triumphed over might, he thought, because several Allied armies engaged in four years of uninterrupted killing and dying. "How can I help?"

"I've tracked the influenza in America. You're right about that. Of course, it's been catastrophic. Why, we had almost 50,000 cases in Philadelphia alone. Many thousands have died. Many, many thousands. I have to protect the president from it if I can, and I must know how to deal with it if that becomes necessary. Tell me about the influenza in Europe. Its etiology, its course, its prevalence. What prophylactic measures are prudent. What therapies are available."

Fraser told him what he could, embarrassed by how little he could relate. Quarantining flu cases from the healthy population did seem to limit its spread, but no one knew how the disease got started. No one knew how to treat it. None of the available drugs made much headway with it. Like in America, a significant percentage of those who got the flu then died from it. They died, gasping in agony, sometimes bleeding from every orifice.

Millions he added, had died around the world.

TWO

F raser, not a particularly social animal, actually volunteered to represent the Medical Corps at the American Embassy's party to welcome the president. He craved a closer look at Wilson. Grayson, supposedly a man of science, had described Wilson in terms suitable to a messiah, if not a supernatural being. On the Place de la Concorde, Fraser had responded ecstatically to the president's arrival. Somehow events had placed Wilson at the center of the world's hopes. It was impossible not to be curious about him.

Entering the main reception hall, Fraser was surprised that he didn't experience the vague disquiet and awkwardness that most formal affairs brought on for him. His army uniform was entirely acceptable, even without a riot of medals on his chest or a shiny sash of office. He accepted a glass of champagne from a waiter and enjoyed its fizzy amiability.

He exchanged small nods with other military men in the room. None of them, he assumed, had faced enemy gunfire or gone over the top in one of the mad rushes on German positions. They were the old men who sent young men to die. What, he wondered, if officers could know which

9

soldiers would die before they sent them off? Would that change their decisions? Fraser felt no guilt about his own role. The front lines were no place for men in their mid-fifties. Or men who had recently been in their mid-fifties. In any event, during the flu epidemic, he had faced death every day. Hundreds of doctors and nurses died from the disease. Fraser did his duty, too.

These thoughts were dragging down his mood. Each passing minute offered fresh evidence that he knew no one in the room. Shying from striking up a word with the august personages swirling around him, he pretended to study the paintings on the wall. They were largely nymphs and satyrs and mythical creatures. He found none to be of the slightest interest.

"Major Fraser?" A younger man with close-cropped hair bowed slightly. Fraser missed his name as it flew by. "Colonel Siegel said you'd be coming. He asked that we look after you."

"Very kind of you, but I don't think I need looking after."

"Perhaps you'd like to meet Mr. Lansing, my boss?" The young man indicated a small group underneath a precise rendering of nude figures gamboling in pastel woods.

From news photos, Fraser recognized Robert Lansing—erect, slender, white hair and mustache. He looked like Fraser's idea of a banker and Princeton man. After living in New York for almost twenty years, Fraser had an idea of what bankers educated at Princeton looked like. He followed his nameless guide.

"Major," Lansing said after the introductions, "what's the spirit of our wounded men?"

"Well, I suppose it varies from man to man, based to some considerable extent upon how badly hurt they are."

"Eager to get home, are they?"

"All of us, sir. We hope the peace will come quickly and will be a just one."

Lansing's face slid into a fish-eyed stare. The pause was awkward.

"I'll drink to that!" The cheerful voice came from a young man on Fraser's right. He had been introduced as Lansing's nephew, but Fraser had missed his name, too.

Fraser felt hopeless. He tapped glasses with the nephew, who looked a younger, less constipated version of his powerful uncle. The same lanky build, even features and trim mustache. The younger man had an appealing ease and confidence. "Uncle Bert," he called over, "won't you drink to a speedy and honorable peace?"

"Really, Allen," Lansing said with a trace of irritation, "I pray for it with every breath I take." He turned to Fraser. "If you will excuse me." Lansing nodded toward the entrance to the room, filled now with President Wilson, his tall and sturdy wife, and their attendants. "Duty calls."

"You must overlook Uncle Bert's manners," young Allen said in a soft voice. "He finds it tedious to be a bit player at the Second Coming."

"Was the president in Paris on an earlier occasion?"

Allen laughed with delight and turned to the enchanting brunette on his arm. "We're in luck, Dorothy. Our doctor is a droll one." Allen gathered their empty glasses and set off in search of a waiter with full ones.

Dorothy, Fraser learned quickly, worked as a typist with the British delegation. The champagne began to make him animated. Good God, it was a tonic to talk with a pretty woman who was dressed for a party. She was a few years older than Violet, he guessed. Her perfume drew him closer. He leaned near to taste the damp aroma. It was more intoxicating than the champagne. He complimented her gown, a blue satin brocade with a square neck that stopped just short of daring.

"The French, you know," she said, holding the skirt to the side and letting it fall. "They understand how to dress in a way that we British never will."

"I've had little opportunity to observe that, given our hospital schedule. But it would do wonders for my patients' morale if the nurses wore such lovely frocks."

A look of slight concern crossed her face.

His smile felt foolish. Was he playing the aged lecher? He straightened and asked about Allen's connection to the peace conference.

"Oh, you don't know?"

Fraser shook his head.

In an exaggerated whisper, she said, "He's a spy."

"Shouldn't that be a secret?"

She smiled. "Not if I know it."

On cue, Allen's good humor burst upon them. His hands wedged three full champagne glasses in a precarious triangle. "Fetching drinks effectively is a low skill, but a useful one."

After a few minutes of banter, Fraser, emboldened by alcohol, mentioned that he had thought of inviting the president to visit the American soldiers at Neuilly Hospital. There were more than a thousand there, and nothing would be better for their spirits.

"Why, you clever chap!" Allen took Fraser's arm. "We must go at once so you can extend your invitation. Dorothy, you sweet girl, come with us. Your presence increases my social appeal immeasurably."

Her smile made clear that Allen's brand of lechery caused her no dismay at all.

Aware of being light-headed, Fraser lagged behind them, steering carefully around the obstacle-strewn floor. Grande dames swished, men in white tie and tails swerved unpredictably, waiters sought out the thirsty, and furniture reared up from the floor at unpredictable locations. The champagne worked more quickly than the bourbon he was used to. He arrived at Wilson's side a full minute behind Allen and Dorothy.

Lansing stood on the president's other side with a look of escalating indigestion.

"Mr. President," Allen cried out, "Allow me to present Major James Fraser of the medical corps, who has an intriguing proposition to make."

With a mild smile, Wilson extended his hand. His grip was firm. He looked straight into Fraser's face.

Based on news photos that highlighted the president's rigid posture and pursed-lips grimaces, Fraser expected a pompous prig. But Wilson didn't seem pompous or priggish. With a champagne-lubricated tongue, Fraser said his piece.

The president listened with bowed head. "Yes. Yes, of course. Mr. Dulles"—he turned to Allen— "can you arrange this with Colonel House? We should have some time in the next few days. I would like to do this very much. Mrs. Wilson, too." The president dismissed Fraser with a nod and a quick thank-you.

As Fraser and the others retreated from the president's party, a fierce-looking man with dark hair accosted them. "Sir, we must speak," he said to Allen, intensity radiating from his deep-set eyes. His strong jaw seemed to bite off his words.

"Ah, Rabbi Wise, allow me to introduce you to my friends." Imperturbable smile in place, Allen Dulles—*that* was his name—showered social niceties on the rabbi.

"See here, Dulles." The rabbi was not much impressed by good manners. "We must discuss Palestine. I've been talking with Colonel Lawrence. We're in agreement that the president has an opportunity to bring real peace to the Arabs, but that he must be very strong in doing so."

"I'm so grateful, Rabbi, that you and Colonel Lawrence have been willing to resolve this problem for us. That will make our lives much easier." Dulles smiled at Fraser. "You're familiar with the challenge that Rabbi Wise and his British friend have resolved for us?"

"I fear not," Fraser said, his mind still replaying his successful conversation with Wilson. The president's voice had been pleasant to the ear, a resonant tenor that carried well in the noisy hall, yet seemed to involve little effort to project.

Dulles grinned broadly and gripped the winsome Dorothy's hand as it rested on his arm. "The British, it turns out," he said to Fraser, "have done something naughty, really very naughty."

Wise began to speak, but Dulles held up a finger to stop him. "Ah, a man of the cloth like yourself cannot condone the duplicity of perfidious Albion." He spoke like a schoolboy gleefully correcting the teacher. "There are many portions of the map to be rearranged due to the collapse of the late, unlamented Turkish Empire. Our English-speaking cousins have been very busy. They promised the lands of Syria and the Trans-Jordan to their brave Arab allies and our Jewish friends, to share in perpetuity and monotheistic brotherhood. But"— his finger went up again— "they also promised much of the selfsame lands to the French, to enjoy in perhaps slightly less than perpetuity. Both promises, of course, involved the British retaining a delicious slice of that territory for themselves. Actually, the British slice might even have deposits of petroleum which would fuel the Royal Navy for generations. A most definite moral quandary, don't you agree, Rabbi?"

"Not at all," Wise said. "As a moral matter, you merely look at the strength of the claim of each party. The French would be mere colonialists on those lands, while the Arabs and the Jews have occupied the lands for millennia."

"Millennia, Rabbi? I thought the Emperor Hadrian dismantled Judea in the second century after the death of our Lord. The Jews have been a bit thin on the ground there ever since." Dulles' expression turned less playful. "And as for your Colonel Lawrence, as an officer of King George's army he would be well advised to concentrate on assisting his own government in choosing which of its solemn promises it will honor, rather than providing advice to the American government."

Rabbi Wise was unimpressed. "We are riding the tide of history, a tide that President Wilson is at the very crest of. You cannot resist this, Dulles. That tide will ensure these precious biblical lands should be shared by the Jews and the Arabs."

"You misunderstand me." Dulles seemed again relaxed and happy. "I resist nothing. I merely anticipate that the president will very much value hearing what the British intend. Perhaps his majesty's government would also benefit from your moral vision. You might share it with them."

As they walked away from Rabbi Wise, Dulles apologized for the intrusion. "He's a tiresome windbag, of course. Really, the Hebrews have been insufferable since Jeremiah. With them, self-righteousness never goes out of fashion. It's their great misfortune, and thus is ours."

"That's not been my experience," Fraser said, unable to keep the stiffness out of his voice. "Several excellent Jewish doctors gave their lives while treating our soldiers here in France."

"Yes, very commendable, I'm sure." Dulles flashed a smile that made Fraser feel patronized by a man thirty years younger. "Dorothy and I must be off. She insists that we dance to that orchestra at the British hotel, and I am powerless to resist. I will be in touch about the president's visit. That was a brilliant stroke, Major."

Fraser patted his jacket pockets. "I have no business card with me. Let me write out my address and telephone."

"Not to worry," Dulles said. "I'll find you."

Outside the embassy, Fraser paused at the stand of taxis and limousines, then decided to walk to the hospital through the chilly air. He set off at a brisk pace down Boulevard Victor Hugo, elated by the evening. The street lights sparkled. The stone buildings lining the road seemed eternal, unassailable. Droning motorcars impatiently pulled around horse-drawn wagons. Paris was shedding the leathery hide of war and mourning and fear. He wondered about New York, whether it had grown the same sort of hide so far from the battlefields of France. He hadn't thought about New York for months. His family was there—a wife who had run short on love, a daughter whose social ambitions made him feel an alien in his own home.

Fraser slowed his pace. He felt a headache coming on. He looked for a taxi, but there were none.

Sunday, December 22, 1918

"Hello, son." The president paused at the foot of a bed in the ward for gas victims.

The sixty beds usually hummed with conversation and movement, but today all attention was focused on the man in a formal suit buttoned to his collarbone, both hands holding his hat by the brim. Those patients who could walk were clustered around him. Some wore uniforms for the first time in weeks or months. Others were in standard-issue pajamas and robe. Those who could see guided the blind ones.

"Where are you from, soldier?"

The man on the bed moved his head, then moved his lips, but nothing came out.

"Bobby can only whisper," said one of the hangers-on.

Wilson stepped around to the side of the bed, shifting his hat to a single hand that dropped by his side. The blanket over the soldier was rough gray wool, clean and pulled taut, tucked in on both sides to impress the president. He leaned over and said something to the soldier, patting his arm. The man nodded. Wilson straightened and looked back at Fraser, who gestured toward the door.

The president took a breath and shook his head. He turned to the next bed. "Hello, son," he said, leaning over this time.

They had been at it for three hours. When he arrived, Wilson said he was going to see them all, except for those with infectious diseases. Admiral Grayson had barred him from seeing anyone who might be contagious. A bit past halfway, Wilson had seen much of the hospital's horrors. Men with bullet wounds. Men peppered with shrapnel. Men with parts blown off by cannon shells or rotted off by trench foot. Men without ears or noses.

After another fifteen minutes in the gas ward, they retired to the corridor where Wilson's two aides loitered. Mrs. Wilson had already departed for another soldiers' hospital.

"Would you like a break?" Fraser asked the president.

"No. I should keep going. Dare I ask how much more?"

"There are the shellshock wards. Some of those men will always need to be in a hospital. They can be...difficult, troublesome—"

"I'll go there, Major."

"And four more general wards."

Wilson nodded.

"President Wilson!" The voice came from an approaching wheelchair occupied by a red-haired man whose legs ended at the knees. He held his hand out. "I'm from Georgia, outside Augusta."

"Well, sir, Augusta was my home, too, though I was only a boy there." Wilson flashed his smile as the two shook hands.

"I know it, sir. That's why I wanted to tell you, so's you'd know that at one of the hospitals I was at over here, they mixed the colored and white troops together."

Wilson turned to Fraser. "Is this true, Major?"

"I can't say, sir. Close to the front, when men are wounded and dying...."

"Not this hospital, of course," said the soldier in the wheelchair. "There's no colored here. But I thought you should know."

"Thanks, soldier. I'll look into it," Wilson said. "Perhaps you can tell me something. Why do there seem to be so many soldiers with leg wounds in this hospital?"

The man in the wheelchair gave the president a searching look, then shrugged. "Well, sir, the boys who got wounded higher, not many of them got this far."

The silence was awkward. "Of course," Wilson said. He bowed slightly. "Thank you for stopping to see me."

As the wheelchair rolled away, the hinge of Wilson's jaw bulged with tension. "I sent these men to war, Major. These are my fellows. They've made terrible sacrifices. I must use all the moral force I can summon to give meaning to their sacrifices, though it means remaking the world. I will see it through. You may rely upon that."

THREE

Monday, December 23, 1918

I n the hesitant morning light, Joshua's eyes traced the cracks in the
ceiling plaster of what had once been the dining room. The cracks
formed a spider web of decay and fatigue. Some were wide enough for a
fingertip. After four years of occupation by the French Army, then by the
American Expeditionary Force, the chateau's owners soon would recover
a husk of what was once a sumptuous home. Their decision to settle
close to the border with Germany had been a mistake. Some of the
trenches were no more than twenty miles away.

The guards from the Negro soldiers' lockup—a glorified tent enclo-
sure—had brought Joshua in early. His trial would end that day in the
makeshift courtroom. His defense lawyer wanted to talk with him about
what to expect. Not so much a conversation, Joshua figured, as a
warning.

One of the guards at the door cried out, "Attention!"

Captain Chadsworth Nash waved for Joshua to remain seated, then
extended his hand. He turned a chair to face Joshua and sat with a groan.
For an officer and a lawyer, he wasn't so bad. For a soldier, he was short
and stout.

Skipping social niceties, Nash reviewed the day's schedule, beginning with the closing arguments. He nodded toward the officers at the table that served as the judge's bench. "I know they look stuffy up there, but three of the five were combat officers. They'll appreciate that you're an educated man, a college graduate, and your record as a platoon leader. They know that you and the Ninety-third were in bad places and that you fought well. We've got testimony on that."

"You mean we took a lot of German lives."

"Yes, that, but also that the men followed you, you led them well." Nash was giving Joshua his earnest look, the one he used on the judges.

Joshua was tired of it, tired of being on trial for desertion. "I was thinking about that last night, taking lives," he said. "One minute they had their lives. Then we took them. What did we do with them? We had no use for them."

"They were trying to kill you."

Joshua smiled with the corner of his mouth. "Yes. Some were."

Nash shifted in his chair. "Sergeant Cook, this isn't the moment for philosophy."

"Sir, I still think we should have testimony from the French officers. They know my fighting better than the Americans do. Hell, we wore French helmets and carried French guns."

"I'm afraid this court wouldn't care much what some French officers said. I've seen it in other trials. The British, either." Nash made as though to stand. "Listen, I need to go over my argument."

Left alone again, Joshua's mind wandered. He couldn't stop it. When he was first arrested, two months before, he raged over the stupid charges. It was incredible really, to be accused of desertion after the fighting he had seen. As the legal process ground forward, blithely indifferent to his innocence, his rage could slide into terror that he would be officially labeled a coward, then shut up in prison for years. Since the trial began two days before, he had sunk into passivity. Nothing he did seemed to matter.

He had started remembering the fighting. Not in any coherent pattern, just patches and moments.

The feelings. Terror. Chaos. Decisions based on hunches, guesses that saved your life or gave it away. Go forward. Turn back. Take shelter. Help a wounded man. Not that one, he's dead. That one'll die soon. Save yourself. That was the voice that never stopped. Save yourself. It made for bad sleep, no sleep. He sometimes dropped off, only to wake up after ten minutes, or an hour, or two hours. Never more than that. He could lie there and smoke and lose track of time. It was the best he could do, but it wasn't sleep. Once he woke to find himself curled up on the floor of his cell.

He saw a man do that at the front, curl up, right there in the trench. Some ran. Joshua wanted to, but he couldn't. The men in his platoon watched him. Some of the guys were brave, some were sorry specimens. But they all watched him. He was supposed to lead them. So he couldn't run.

The men liked having guns in their hands. All the colored soldiers did. French or American rifles, they didn't care what. Most wanted to fight, fight someone. The hard part was the bombardments, huddled in trench muck, water up to your knees, while shells rained down, hoping not to be shredded by shrapnel or vaporized by a shell blast, hoping not to disappear without a trace, leaving no more evidence of your death than of your life. There was no safe place, less dignity. Jefferson was blown up emptying latrine buckets behind the front trench. It was like playing Russian roulette with a revolver that has cartridges loaded in every chamber.

Joshua spent so much time waiting to die, waiting for the bullet or the shell. Five minutes of bombardment could last forever. The fighting ebbed and flowed, but it never ended. There was always somebody, not far away, trying to kill him. Even dozing, upright, mud to his knees, his brain listened to mortar bombs and rockets and shells, flare guns and rifle fire, gauging the risk, deciding whether to dive on the ground or huddle in a dugout.

At first, he thought that patrols and attacks would bring relief. It would be movement, finally doing something. But they were worse. It wasn't just the artillery and mortars and gas, but also machine guns and riflemen. You were out in the open where they could aim right at you. It was even easier to get killed out there.

The prison camp hadn't seemed so bad at first. At least his men weren't watching him anymore, looking to him to have some sort of secret, to know how they could survive.

Joshua realized that Nash was back, shuffling papers next to him. The prosecutor was seated at the parallel table. The guard called out again. The room stood to attention as five white officers walked purposefully to their seats behind the table. The windows behind them overlooked the chateau's semicircular front drive. On a signal from the presiding officer, the prosecutor began his final argument.

He was hanging it all on the two MPs who arrested Joshua. They were a couple of prize crackers, not interested in a word Joshua said. He found it hard to listen to the prosecutor. So much he said was wrong. The man's heart didn't seem to be in it. The war, after all, was over. Even if Joshua had been hiding out from the front line, even if he was the worst coward in history, what could it matter now?

"Gentlemen of the court." Nash's voice snapped Joshua out of his reverie. "Sergeant Cook served as a brave soldier for five months of hard fighting. He was wounded twice, and both times returned to the front." Nash's voice was low, nearly conversational. He didn't gesture a lot. Yet he conveyed, in a controlled way, that he believed in his case, in Joshua.

Joshua appreciated that.

"Sergeant Cook's company had been advancing for six days, through miserable weather. They took two villages from the Germans and a hill that was a powerful stronghold. They were too successful, advanced too far, got out beyond their supplies. They hadn't received provisions for all six days. If it hadn't been for food they took from the Germans, they would have starved. If they hadn't found a well at a farmhouse, thirst alone would have stopped them. But still they advanced, never really sleeping, never really resting, driving the Germans before them."

Nash paused. "And then his commanding officer, Lieutenant Markham, made a decision. They couldn't last without provisions. Someone needed to go get them. So he chose his best non-commissioned officer, Sergeant Cook, a man he had placed in the front of several attacks. He told the sergeant to take two soldiers and go to the rear. Markham told Sergeant Cook to find food and water, and bring it back.

When the sergeant reached the rear, he could see the problem. All was confusion. Thousands of men, separated from their units, wandered here and there. The roads were clogged. Supplies stalled, went to the wrong place, and were just plain lost. There was no order."

Joshua could see one of the officers nod in agreement. It had been pandemonium. Trucks stalled on one-lane roads while horse-drawn teams tipped over, spilling their loads. Other trucks pulled around, then sank in mud up to their hubcaps. MPs screamed. Horns blared. Voices shouted. And always the artillery boomed. It was amateur night at the vaudeville show. It had been better when the Ninety-third fought with the French. At least the French knew how to feed their own soldiers during a battle.

"My colleague," Nash waved a hand at the prosecutor, "complains that Lieutenant Markham didn't write out his order to Sergeant Cook. He complains that the two men with the sergeant didn't hear the lieutenant give the order. He complains that the lieutenant cannot confirm the order in this trial because he lost his life shortly after ordering Sergeant Cook to retrieve provisions."

Lost his life, Joshua thought. Careless.

"We wish that the lieutenant, a valiant officer, was able to testify in this court. Nevertheless, gentlemen, this was the middle of the decisive battle of the war. Orders are shouted over blasts of artillery and machinegun fire. Grenades explode. Written orders are a luxury that frontline soldiers like Sergeant Cook don't often enjoy.

"My colleague, though, has no explanation for a key part of the testimony given by those military policemen who are the key to his case. When Sergeant Cook was arrested, he and his men each carried two haversacks jammed with food, enough for an entire platoon. If they were running away, if they had decided to flee danger and abandon their comrades, why would they carry heavy loads? Why wouldn't they travel as light as they possibly could and get away as fast as possible? And why would all three of them stay together? Had they split up, each might have fallen in with some stevedore unit or a trench-digging unit. Several colored units were working behind the lines in that sector. After all his time at the front, Sergeant Cook certainly knew how to avoid battle if he

22

wanted to. But that's not what he was doing. He was gathering supplies, desperately needed supplies, for his comrades.

"The prosecution of this fine soldier doesn't hold together. It's contrary to his record and it's not supported by the evidence or the experience of war. I urge the court to return a verdict of not guilty and send Sergeant Cook back to the duties he performs so well."

The guards took Joshua outside while the judges conferred. He was grateful for the chance to smoke. War had taught him the virtues of tobacco. It can be smoked most anywhere. It never loses its power to distract from the unpleasantness of the moment. During a shelling, burrowed into a dugout, he could focus his entire mind on the rising smoke from a cigarette tip, its lazy, curving ascent a graceful helix just inches from his face.

He indulged in a trace of a smile. In fat times and thin, cigarettes deliver the same subtle message: the world is unchanged, whatever you experienced before is the same. He remembered what Nash had said. Not the moment for philosophy. What was the moment for?

It wasn't more than fifteen minutes when word came to return to the courtroom. Nash had said a quick verdict would be a good one. Joshua pinched off his cigarette. He pocketed the stub.

After the court delivered its verdict of acquittal, after he stood at attention and saluted the judges, Nash sat him down again. Neither man was smiling.

"You remember what I told you," the lawyer said.

"General Parkman."

"Right. He reviews the verdict, and he's the worst son of a bitch in the army. He can sustain it or vacate it and order a retrial."

"You think he'll vacate it?"

"I do, sergeant. He's death on deserters and just itching to make another example. And he's no friend to the Negro soldier."

"Then I get retried again?"

"Yup. But without me. They're shipping me out next week." Nash started to stuff his papers into a valise. "Even if the Germans don't sign a peace treaty, the army figures it doesn't need a lot of lawyers over here anymore." He sat back and passed a hand over his short brown hair. He looked like his stomach hurt. "Listen, after eighteen months I still haven't got the army figured out. But I'm going to tell you that something bothers me. I don't know anything specific. It's little things. The way people in my office act, the way they talk to me about your case. I don't think we were supposed to win today." He looked up directly at Joshua. "I'm sorry, Sergeant. I wish you luck."

Tuesday, December 24, 1918

Joshua was glad to have any visitor on Christmas Eve, even a stranger like Sergeant Virgil Carr. Though Carr was also from the Ninety-third Division, Joshua didn't know the name.

Last Christmas had been miserable enough. They had been on board a converted freight ship so decrepit that it had to return to port twice for repairs. Out on the Atlantic, he had expected any minute to head to the bottom of the ocean, courtesy of a German U-boat or maybe the simple disintegration of the ship. This Christmas promised to be worse.

He shivered once as he waited in the tent used for visits. His greatcoat was heavy, but there wasn't much heat in the camp, certainly not in the tent he shared with seven other prisoners. A guard stood on either side of the tent's entrance, facing him.

A dark-skinned man came through the tent flap. Grinning, he tossed over a pack of Camels. Joshua caught it. As a Christmas gift, it wasn't the worst he'd ever received.

"Now I know you want those," said Carr, "but I got more than that." He pointed to a chair on the other side of the tent and one of the guards shrugged. Carr dragged it over next to Joshua, lit his cigarette, then one for himself. "Colonel Hayward sent me."

"Have you and I met?"

"I'd be surprised. I've been playing in Captain Europe's band, setting these Frenchies on fire. They can't get enough of us. I'm on cornet."

"I heard you guys. Back in Spartanburg."

"Spartanburg." Carr shook his head. "I guess those people back there weren't *all* bad."

"Yes, they were."

Carr burst out laughing, the kind of snuffling, eyes-crinkled-up laugh it was hard not to join. He smiled at the tent roof after taking a long drag on his smoke. "Yeah, they were."

"Playing in the band. That's good duty."

"Damn right it is." They smoked for a minute, then Carr put his cigarette out on his boot sole. "So, Colonel Hayward sent me here with your medal. D'you hear about the medals?"

"Come on. I'm a deserter."

"That's bushwa. Everyone says so. I'm not talking about any American medals. These are from the Frenchies. The Croix de Guerre!" He savored the French words, gargling the r's. He grinned again. He reached into his pocket. "They passed them out to the whole damned division, the entire Ninety-third! Nothing the US Army could do but grumble in its beer."

Joshua took the medal, still in a box, lying on a black felt bed. It was a bronze Maltese cross intersected by two swords, suspended from a green ribbon with vertical red stripes. The dates 1914 and 1918 had been inscribed at the center. He stared at it in his hand. It looked small. Suddenly he couldn't speak. He wasn't ready for the emotions. Finally he said, "Thanks."

"Thank Colonel Hayward. You know, he's all right." Carr began to stand up. "Hey, I'll tell you a rich one. They just started training us for combat. Sent us to the front last spring without even target practice. Now the war's over, so they decide it's a good time to train us. Rich, ain't it?" He pulled his cap on. "Also, to make up for the medals, they cancelled our holiday rations. Just the Negro troops. Merry damned Christmas."

Joshua tore his eyes from the medal and looked up at Carr. "I won't say I wasn't tempted that day." He shook his head. "I won't say I wasn't tempted that once I got dry socks and ate some warm food, let someone else die instead of me. But we weren't running. We knew the boys were thirsty, near crazy with hunger. We got the food and water. It was for them. I didn't linger. I didn't."

"'Course you didn't. You got the medal that says so."

FOUR

Saturday, January 18, 1919

The difference was the tapestries on the walls. To Dulles' eye, the tapestries, their colors still vibrant after centuries on display, gave the Quai d'Orsay its distinction. Europe had plenty of barny old palaces stuffed with friezes, ceiling frescoes, and echoing marble corridors. Most of those drafty warehouses of history and pride bristled with lush scarlet curtains and chandeliers that blazed against the darkness. Interchangeable, really.

But the home of the French Foreign Ministry, overlooking the stately River Seine, had the tapestries, old and priceless, proudly blazoning France's ancient wealth and greatness. Far more important, their playful scenes conveyed a rollicking sense that life was to be enjoyed. What's the point of being king, they whispered to Dulles, if you don't have some fun in the evenings? Henry IV, from the look of tapestries, lived that way three hundred years before.

Dulles loitered near the guttering tea-urn, waiting for President Wilson to arrive. He and the old boy were getting along better than he had expected, certainly better than Uncle Bert predicted. Dulles found the president mostly levelheaded, which wasn't easy when a man was drenched with adoration in France, then in Italy, then in England. Wilson could be a bit vain and peevish, but no more than any other Savior of Mankind. Probably less.

"Eight-to-five we don't do any actual work today, either." The benign face of Mark Sykes was before him, his bushy mustache hovering over a cup of tea nearly white with milk.

Dulles gave a theatrical sigh for the Englishman. "The president's only been here a month, you know. These things take time."

"Yes, well, we don't have all that much bloody time. We hang about here, having neither war nor peace, not knowing whether to send the troops home or not, not even quite convinced we really won the war. The world is bloody falling apart while we listen politely to tales of woe from every slapped-up tribe of unhappy people in the known world."

"Speaking of tales of woe, Mark, I still would like to have a word on Mesopotamia."

"Ah, yes, oil. Eh?"

"America cares a great deal about the self-determination of peoples, and the peoples in that region are as entitled to self-determination as everyone else."

"Yes, quite. Also, we all think there's a honking great pile of oil there."

"As it happens."

Sykes finished his cup of tea and set it down on a side table. "Allen, dear chap, I fear my masters find it awkward to imagine discussing Mesopotamia with America, which didn't even trouble itself to declare war against the Turk. How could you expect to be part of the self-determination of the peoples of the Turkish Empire?"

Dulles was ready. "Having also won its own independence from a particularly violent and repressive monarchy, America deeply shares the experiences of those oppressed peoples. Indeed, our history gives us a special responsibility to assist all oppressed peoples in achieving self-determination."

Sykes laughed delightedly. "Oh, you are the most dangerous tribe of all. All that greed wrapped up in virtue. It's really a lethal combination."

The buzz at the doorway alerted them that the Big Four—Wilson,

Clemenceau, Lloyd George of Britain, and Orlando of Italy—were arriving, their entrances carefully timed so none would have to wait for any of the others. With mutual nods, Sykes and Dulles separated to serve their respective masters.

A senior British delegate handed his top hat to an aide. "Such a fuss, these top hats," he said to Premier Clemenceau of France standing next to him, "but I was told I had to wear it today."

"Yes," Clemenceau replied with no evident expression. "That's what they told me, too." With a flourish, the Frenchman removed his bowler hat. As the two men moved toward the presiding table at the end of the room, Clemenceau asked, "What of the Czech prime minister? Will he live?"

The Englishman smiled. "Most extraordinary. The bullet hit his wallet in his jacket pocket, so his injury was really quite slight."

"Ach, lucky for him, bad for me. My wallet is always empty."

"Honesty is its own punishment."

Dulles watched President Wilson intercept Clemenceau, then glided over to join them, standing at a respectful distance—close enough to hear, but not to intrude. The clean-shaven Wilson was taller, Clemenceau broader with a white walrus mustache and the soft gray gloves he always wore, indoors and out. Dulles knew he was standing at the fulcrum of the peace conference. Wilson and his idealism were the irresistible force of the new twentieth century. Clemenceau's old-style diplomacy, based on balance-of-power calculations among Great Powers, was the immovable object. Clemenceau's excellent English, mastered during four years in America and many more married to a New England woman, gave him a key advantage in the negotiations. So far, the immovable object looked entirely immovable.

When the leaders separated, Dulles retired to his seat behind the president and Uncle Bert. Lansing leaned back and asked in a whisper, "What were they discussing?"

"Who will preside in the chair. The president had already decided to concede it to Clemenceau as host."

"Ever gracious, aren't we?" Lansing allowed a trace of annoyance to pass over his face, then mastered it. "Look around this room, Allen. Then tell me what's missing?"

Dulles scanned the room quickly. The Big Four were all there. So were their various aides and retainers, not to mention the day's schedule of petitioners from small countries and from places that yearned to become small countries. He wasn't sure what his uncle meant and said so.

"The Germans, Allen. The Germans. All we have here are the winners and their friends, grunting and squealing like pigs at a trough. I've negotiated treaties in my time, but never without talking to the other side."

Tuesday, January 21, 1919

"Where the devil is he?" Lansing was tetchy after a full day of hearings followed by several hours of meetings with American staff members. Gallivanting with his two nephews through the Hotel Majestic headquarters for the British delegation, was not high on his list of preferred evening activities. He didn't care for the Negro jazz that welled every few moments from a floor below, as though a door were opening and closing. That music made him nervous. He was the Secretary of State, for heaven's sake, and didn't appreciate being kept waiting by anyone, much less a presumptuous English army officer below the rank of general. "You said he'd be easy to pick out."

"Now, Uncle Bert," said Foster Dulles, "give it a minute. Colonel Lawrence is short, you know." Slightly taller than his younger brother, Allen, Foster combined the same lean frame with the permanent expression of a man whose shoes pinched. "They say he's utterly without polish. Simply says what he thinks."

"There he is," Allen cried out, leading them through the lobby. A small, pale man in British khaki stood at the crest of a half flight of stairs, his Arab headdress setting him apart. It was green silk with tassels of deep red. He bowed to the Americans as they approached and indicated a seating arrangement in a quiet nook. There were no handshakes.

"Colonel Lawrence," Lansing began when they were seated, then was interrupted by a waiter.

The Americans ordered coffee. Lawrence wanted nothing.

Lansing started again. "What can we do for you, Colonel?"

"You know of my involvement with the Arab cause, Mr. Secretary?"

Lansing nodded in assent.

"I wanted to speak with you about how essential it is to recognize the legitimate claims of the Arab people. They fought the Turks for their independence, and they must have it. Prince Feisal, who led them, is the only true and legitimate leader in the region. He's reached an agreement with Weizmann and the Zionists to provide an area for Jews to settle in Palestine. President Wilson, in view of his support for self-determination of all peoples, can play a major role in fulfilling this destiny."

"Excuse me, Colonel," Foster broke in. "Do you speak for the British government in this matter? I have reviewed the Sykes-Picot treaty between your government and the French in 1916, and it divides that region between those two nations. It says nothing about an independent Arab state, nor of Jews in Palestine."

Lawrence showed no expression. "Sykes-Picot is rubbish. A stupid scrap of paper scribbled out to hurry the end of the war. Even Sykes thinks his own treaty must yield to the commitments that His Majesty's government made to the Arabs." His eyes were a disconcerting blue, a rich cobalt, yet he never looked directly at the Americans. His voice was both low and filled with power.

"Awkward, isn't it?" Lansing said, "that His Majesty promised the same lands to two different parties?"

"Scraps of paper cannot withstand history. The French have no legitimate claim to this land, which is truly the land of the Arabs and the Jews. The Arab people fought for their independence, and it would be an historical wrong to deny it to them."

"I'm sure the president will study this situation most carefully," Lansing said, pausing while the waiter delivered three cups of coffee to a low table before him. "If I might offer a bit of advice, Colonel. Your advocacy might better be directed to your own government, as Mr.

Wilson will be particularly interested in how our ally, Great Britain, interprets its various—some might say inconsistent—commitments in that region."

Lawrence was quiet for a moment. "Prince Feisal will arrive shortly to explain his rights and those of his people, and I hope you will take the opportunity to consider them." He stood abruptly and bowed slightly from the waist. "Gentlemen, thank you for your time."

Lansing picked up his coffee and sat back. "What a remarkable person," he said, nodding to Allen, "just as you suggested."

Foster picked up another cup. "He does make an impression."

"Yes, but not a good one. What can he be thinking? There's a great deal of petroleum under all that sand, petroleum that's needed to fuel the world's navies. The Arabs and their camels are hardly fit stewards for that kind of wealth."

"I can't see why the British wouldn't abide by Sykes-Picot," Allen said. "It's quite straightforward. The French get their bit—though Lawrence is certainly right that they have no decent claim to it—and the British get the oil in Mesopotamia."

"Ah," Foster said, "it needs to be a bit more complicated than that. The United States must have a share in this business or else why did we send our troops across the ocean?" His usual sour expression deepened into a scowl. "There's no reason we can't find some opportunity here. Mr. Cromwell agrees we should be able to retrieve something from the frightful hash the British have made. Uncle, how do you think Mr. Lloyd George will dance through this minefield of his own creation?"

"You know what a slippery number he is. He'll say anything to anyone. Actually, he and Clemenceau have already been at each other's throats over this business. The French are having a spell of seller's remorse over Sykes-Picot. They fear being left out of a great petroleum bonanza. The great danger is that Lloyd George starts listening to that blue-eyed Bedouin." Lansing nodded to the chair where Lawrence had sat. "Lawrence has become quite the hero in Britain."

"Indeed," Foster agreed, "the prospect is more dangerous when you add in our high-minded president, who despises anything that smacks of actual American self-interest, and who will have his Hebrew friends pouring Zionist propaganda into his ear. There's no way to know how it will all end up." He looked across to Allen. "You'll have to keep a special eye on the Middle East. Mr. Cromwell can brief you. I'm afraid I'm going to be fully engaged with the reparations and financial settlement with Germany."

"How does that go?" Allen asked.

"It's a full-time job keeping up with this Maynard Keynes fellow on the British side. He's two or three times smarter than everyone else, but distinctly bolshie. Not sound at all."

"What do you mean?"

"Well, for starters, he actually agrees with Mr. Wilson that the victorious allies should be charitable toward Germany in order to establish the League of Nations."

Lansing snorted his dismay.

"Now, the League is fine as eyewash for the public, but it's not really a serious proposal, and the serious men here know it. Certainly Clemenceau doesn't take it seriously. I fear that our overwrought theologian in the White House will sacrifice America's future on the altar of his pipe dream. You can't play by rules of your own choosing while everyone else follows the old rules."

"Foster." Lansing put down his cup. The coffee was tepid. It would probably keep him up, anyway. "What conversations are going on between your group and the Germans?"

"None that I know of. It's a bit tricky, as you know, figuring out *which* Germans to speak with. They've thrown all their energy into crises and street riots—socialists one day, Spartacists and anarchists another, out-of-work soldiers the next. Nothing but strikes, rebellions, murders. I imagine most Germans are missing the Kaiser."

"In any country," Lansing said, "the banks and the businesses don't change. German banks have always been run by sound men. We must find someone sensible to speak within Germany."

"Perhaps Mr. Cromwell can help. The law firm did have a number of German clients before the war."

"You must tread carefully, Foster. Until very recently, these people were killing Americans in large numbers. It wouldn't do for word to get out that we were having back-channel chats with Germans."

"Of course not." Foster sipped his coffee with a self-possession that Lansing found unsettling in someone barely thirty. Evidently evening coffee didn't keep him from sleeping.

FIVE

The dockside tumult in Brest made it easy for Speed Cook to jump ship for the second time in a week. He shouldered his suitcase the way a stevedore would carry passenger luggage. Once off the gangplank, he swung the bag down and carried it civilian style. Then he kept walking. The fog and drizzle helped. With a wool cap covering his gray hair, he drew no notice.

The ship's captain got a fair deal: Cook's free labor in return for hauling him across the Channel at a time when getting to France wasn't easy.

Cook had used the same device to get from America to England. With so many sailors siphoned off onto navy ships, merchant captains asked few questions of possible crew members. Which meant that he would be one of the few Americans at the Second Pan-African Congress in Paris. That prospect put some juice in his stride.

His path to the activist life had been improbable. He had been scuffling for dollars, promoting Negro baseball games up at Olympic Field on 136th Street in Harlem. The ticket sales weren't much, but he did all right with some smart betting on the side. During one game, he recog-

34

nized the famous Dr. W.E.B. Du Bois in the stands. He introduced himself and they hit it off. Dr. Du Bois could be highfalutin with his New England ways, but underneath the superior veneer, the man had the same rage Speed had, that every Negro had. The thing with Dr. Du Bois was that he had thought through his rage. He could explain it, trace out where it came from in history. He could point to ways Speed could put it to work to make things better for all colored people. So Speed signed up with Du Bois and his NAACP, stopped scuffling for dollars and joined the cause, the movement, something bigger than himself.

In Paris, he would meet the leading colored people on the planet, ones from Africa and Europe. The other Americans who meant to go, the ones who formed that International League of Darker Peoples, they weren't going to make it. They couldn't get passports. The US government didn't want a lot of darker peoples walking around Paris, reminding folks that America still had lynchings and the Ku Klux Klan and no voting by colored folks. That would be embarrassing when President Wilson was bringing democracy to the world, at least to those parts that had white people. Du Bois had managed to get an actual passport—he was too prominent to be turned down—but no one else could. The others wailed with disappointment at being left behind, something they hadn't much experienced in their doily-covered, froufrou lives.

Cook hadn't moaned and groaned about the injustice of Wilson's government. He dusted off the seamen's papers he had from years back, then signed on to a terrible old rust bucket that was carrying wheat to the folks starving in Europe. It wallowed to England in only nine days. And now he was in France, jumping his second ship.

Before going to Paris, he had something important to do. American soldiers, waiting to embark on the voyage home, crowded the streets near the Brest waterfront. He bulled through them, which was easy for a big man like him. The cobbled streets were slick from recent rain. The sky was threatening. It felt cold enough for snow. Stone walls near the port looked centuries old. He checked his bag at the railroad station, struggling with the language. He asked a doughboy for directions to army headquarters. Drizzle started as he walked five blocks to a large stone building that stood comfortably away from the mayhem on the docks.

He pulled off his cap as he stepped to the sergeant at a desk in the center of the entranceway. "Sir, I'm hoping to find the 369th infantry regiment."

The sergeant wore a broad-brimmed hat with crisp creases and a sparkling braid at the base of the crown. He ignored Speed for at least a minute, not moving, staring at papers spread before him. He called over a guard standing at the foot of the staircase. "Take this to Colonel Davison." After handing over an envelope, he returned his attention to the papers on his desk.

Cook shifted his weight and strained to keep his voice level. "Excuse me, Sergeant, I just need some directions and I'll be on my way."

"Uncle, do I look like I don't have nothing better to do than sit around and chin with you all day?"

"I'm looking for my boy, he served with the 369th. He was at the front, but we haven't heard from him for too long. Army can't seem to tell us where he is. I need to find him. His mother needs to know. I don't even know if they're here in Brest, but it seems worth a try."

The sergeant took a deep breath, then pulled a sheet from a drawer. "The camp for nigger soldiers, let me see." His finger traced down the page. "It's over the east side of town." He looked up and pointed to his left. "That way."

"What's the best way to get there?"

"Shank's mare, uncle. You look a strong feller."

Speed swallowed the bile that still rose in his throat, even after so many years.

He passed taverns and cafés, ones that doubtless catered to soldiers and sailors but were buttoned up tight in the ugly morning. Whoever pocketed the dollars and pounds and francs from the men who passed through Brest wasn't investing it locally. The street cobbles tilted at treacherous angles. The buildings slouched wearily, paint peeling from woodwork and wood sheets hammered in place of glass panes.

Cook felt the familiar sense of dread come over him, the tingling at the back of his neck. They had no word from Joshua since September. The boy's last letter had the usual reassuring words for Aurelia, but if you read between the lines, you could tell he was tired. His spirit was tired. From his work with Du Bois, Cook knew that the army worked hard to ruin the lives of colored soldiers. It wasn't enough to send them out to get killed. They had to be insulted and humiliated, too, made something less. Always less.

He and Aurelia waited anxiously through those last weeks before the armistice, when the fighting was at its peak. They made excuses for Joshua not writing, for the army not getting letters out of France. But when the armistice came, the silence stretched on. Cook tried the army offices in New York, but had no luck. He wrote to Joshua's commanding officer. He got no response. He tried to work through some politicians he knew in New York. They were precinct hacks but they might have known someone who knew someone. Still nothing. He even asked Dr. Du Bois to see what he could find out, but he learned no more. Aurelia grew more and more alarmed. Their daughter Cecily scoured the lists of the dead in the newspapers. When she saw a Joshua Clark listed, Aurelia wondered if it might be a mixup, that it was supposed to be "Joshua Cook," but then they found out that Clark was from a white regiment.

It got so they couldn't talk about it anymore, but they couldn't talk about anything else. Aurelia blamed him for Joshua going in the army. If something bad happened, and something bad must have happened, she might never forgive him, or herself. Dr. Du Bois had pushed the idea that Negroes should join the army and fight. That way, he argued, the race would show it was worthy, worthy of fair treatment. Its young men, standing shoulder to shoulder with white soldiers, would finally change things.

It sounded good in their living room on 127th Street. It sounded good to Joshua, who went down and signed up, didn't wait to be drafted. After that, it started to sound a lot worse. Now it was about his own son, not other people's boys. And now, now they knew it hadn't changed a thing, and it probably wouldn't ever, not the way they treated the colored soldiers.

Cook judged he'd walked a mile and a half, maybe more. He saw a colored soldier "Hey, son," he called. "Where can I find the 369th?"

"Straight ahead, sir. Sinking into that swamp over there." The soldier pointed down the road Speed was on.

"Thank you, son."

Speed's steps came faster. Soon, he would know something. Maybe in a few minutes. Maybe an hour. Not more than that. He didn't let himself think about what that terrible news might be.

A large tent had a handwritten sign stating "369th." It was warmer inside, the space lit by bare electric light bulbs that dangled from wires. A few colored soldiers sat to one side. He guessed they were messengers.

Snatching off his cap, he wrung it out on the dirt floor. He approached a table created by boards set across stacked crates. A white clerk looked up at him.

"Excuse me. I'm looking for information about my son, Sergeant Joshua Cook."

A flicker of recognition passed over the clerk's face.

"Do you know my son?"

"No. No, I don't."

"Can you tell me anything about him?."

"That's really a matter for Colonel Hayward. He's due back in an hour. You can wait over there." The clerk nodded toward some flimsy-looking chairs along the tent wall.

"Can I look around for my son?"

"He's not here."

"Where is he? Where's my boy, Sergeant Cook? Is he hurt?"

"You have to wait for Colonel Hayward."

"Listen. I've been waiting for almost four months. I know Colonel Hayward." Cook leaned forward across the makeshift table. He itched to grab the clerk and shake him.

A hand clapped down on his shoulder, hard. Cook spun around, shrugging off the hand of a guard.

When he turned back, the clerk had stepped back and was holding his hands out, palms down. "You have to wait. It won't be long."

The minutes crept by. Then they moved slower. Then they got down on their bellies and lay completely still. Cook kneaded his wool cap, twisting it and untwisting it, punishing the soggy, scratchy fabric. He thought he would explode. Or scream. Or hit something.

A man who had to be Hayward pounded through the tent flap. He pulled off his hat and shook the moisture off it while walking past the clerk and behind a canvas divider that hung across two-thirds of the tent. The clerk followed him without looking at Cook, who was already out of his seat. The clerk returned and waved him forward.

Hayward came around his makeshift desk when Cook entered his space. They shook hands.

"Colonel, we met in New York."

"Yes, I recall."

"I need to know what's happened to my son Joshua."

"Your son's alive, but he's got troubles. Please sit down."

Speed felt shaky as he dropped into a chair. Hayward took a chair next to him. His strong, blunt features included a deep cleft in his chin. He looked Cook in the eye and described the situation.

Cook's relief turned to disbelief, then anger when he heard that General Parkman had reversed Joshua's acquittal. "Colonel, what can I do? How can I get him free?"

"Mr. Cook, that retrial might be happening right now or very soon. If I were a cynical man, I'd say they delayed it until the infantry was sent here to be shipped back to the States. That way, none of us can testify. Several of our officers testified for him at his first trial, about him being a good soldier." Hayward held out a pack of cigarettes from his breast pocket.

Cook declined the offer. Hayward lit one. He took a deep drag.

"Where is he?" Cook asked.

"Still near Chaumont, the army headquarters."

"Then I'll go there." Cook's leg was jiggling up and down. He wanted to get on his way, but Hayward had been decent for a white man. Cook didn't want to be rude.

Hayward chewed his lip for a moment. "You might not want to go there first. You might think about starting in Paris. If you know any officers in the army, anyone at the peace conference, even someone in the French Army, maybe you can persuade them to help. General Parkman has been implacable, but your son's case can't be that important to him. Somebody above him might be able to fix this." He sighed and put his hand on Cook's arm. "I'm sorry for this. Your son's a good man. Most of them are. Don't believe anyone who says anything else. It's been my privilege to go to war with them."

When Cook stepped out of the tent, he barely noticed the rain. He made it back to the railway station without noticing anyone or anything. He had no plan. He needed a plan. He thought of Aurelia and Cecily. He couldn't write them with this news. It was too terrible. He'd write when he knew more. When he had a plan.

SIX

"I tell you, Jamie, I can't stand this." Colonel Jerome Siegel burst into Fraser's office through the open door. He threw a stapled, multi-page memorandum on Fraser's desk. The distinctive HQ format was unmistakable.

"First we're supposed to prepare for an advance into Germany. Then, it's all about supporting the Army of Occupation in the Rhineland. Now it's demobilize, demobilize, demobilize, fast as you can." He stalked over to the lone window in the office and jammed his hands in his pockets. "And tomorrow, goddammit, it'll be something else entirely."

Fraser got along fairly well with his commanding officer, a quiet, curly-haired doctor from Massachusetts. Siegel had risen far enough in the military bureaucracy that he hadn't actually treated a patient in five years. Though he was an army lifer, he didn't resent physicians like Fraser who parachuted into the army from lucrative private practices. He was glad to have good doctors, even wealthy ones with silk hat backgrounds, as long as they did the job for the men.

"So, what's the drill now?"

"Send everyone home in ninety days. Ninety days! Wilson and his buddies downtown haven't even begun to work out a peace treaty and we're supposed to make plans to send all of these patients, all of our personnel, and all of our equipment home by May first." He shook his head and threw himself into a visitor's chair. "Imagine how screwed up the Germans had to be to lose to us."

"They'd been fighting for three years before we got here. We might give the French and the British and the Russians some of the credit."

"Thank God for all of them." Siegel began to stroke his chin. "So, Jamie, I need you to work your magic again. A full plan for demobilization—every patient, every staff member, on a ship headed home—by May Day."

"Pretty crazy."

"Especially since there's no report of any real progress from the peace conference. I know you've been gaga over our commander in chief since he came through here, but he'd better saddle up and finish this business."

"Did you see his speech yesterday?"

Siegel sat back with a smile on his face. "Nope, but I get the feeling I'm about to hear part of it."

Fraser reached behind him and grabbed the morning's paper, which he had folded to Wilson's speech. He used his finger to scan the text. "Here. Here he says it. 'We are the masters of no people but are here to see that every people in the world shall choose its own masters and govern its own destinies, not as *we* wish but as *it* wishes.'" Fraser put down the paper and looked at Siegel. "Can you imagine an Englishman or a Frenchman or a German saying that?"

Siegel smiled. "You forget, sir, that you're talking to a New England Republican. We're congenitally unable to applaud statements by Southern Democrats." He shook his head. "I hope what he says is true, Jamie. For all our sakes, especially those poor bastards who did the dying."

Fraser leaned forward. "When do you need this new plan?"

"Suppertime?"

Fraser smiled and raised an eyebrow.

"All right," Siegel said, "just this once, you can have until Thursday morning."

"It doesn't have to make sense, does it?"

"How the hell could it?" Siegel stood and walked to the doorway, then turned back. "And Jamie, one more thing. I'd like you to be in the last contingent to leave, with me. Sorry, but I don't want to try to run this operation without you."

"Of course, Jerry."

"Thanks."

Fraser stood and took the place before the window. The courtyard view was simple and stark. No snow. Bare trees that weren't prospering. A few stone planters with scraggly plants. A gray sky above. He thought about preparing a plan to send everyone home in three months. Demobilization could never happen so fast.

The prospect of home didn't cheer him. These months in France, for all the gore and death and slaughter, had been a respite for him, a respite from the life that had been running off the tracks. He remembered a saying from his childhood. If you want to make God laugh, tell him your plans. Fraser had kept Him amused.

He thought rarely of his first marriage to Ginny. Sometimes he couldn't even summon up the image of her face. Their life together, one that seemed happy at the time, had disappeared into the roaring void of the night when she'd died giving birth to their baby boy, who also died, the pathetic Dr. James Fraser unable to save either.

Eliza, he had thought, would bring him back to life. From the start, he had known she was a stretch for him. He was a country doctor, a widower, a hick from eastern Ohio. She was a glamorous figure, beautiful and poised, a former actress who deftly moved into theatrical management with all the skills of a professional performer. The first few years were wonderful. Their daughter Violet was a blessing. Fraser began to make his way in New York medical circles, learning to be a better doctor than he thought he could be. The chance to participate in research at the new Rockefeller Institute was more than he had ever hoped for.

Yet he never lost his self-image as an overachieving bumpkin. He felt no surprise when Eliza tired of him and sought more diverting company. She tried to argue with him, to tell him what was wrong with their life, but he wasn't any good at arguing. They were one-sided arguments. He couldn't think of what to say until hours after she went to bed, long after it was too late. He began to work later and later at the lab, avoiding home. She was discreet about her gentleman friends, mostly. Fraser didn't ask. The cuckolded husband is such a ridiculous figure. It was better not to think about it.

The experience of an unhappy marriage was such an appalling mixture of the infuriating and the trite. How could a person marry someone who made him unhappy? It seemed so simple. Marry a person who makes you happy. Marrying wrong was bad enough—after all, it made him unhappy most days—but piled on top were the embarrassment and the anger at himself for doing so. Yet all around him were people who made the same mistake. It was cold comfort. It only cheapened his own blunder, reducing his exquisite pains to the moral stature of a hangnail or a blister. They were all ridiculous, all of them.

Then Howard, an actor, entered the picture and stayed far too long. He turned Fraser's embarrassment into mortification. If Howard was what Eliza wanted—with his vanity, his good looks, and his empty head—Fraser had misjudged his wife from the start. When the war came, Fraser leaped at the chance to join the Army Medical Corps, an honorable way to stop having to share his home with a woman who seemed a stranger. The army was a refuge from his life.

His father had served in the Thirtieth Ohio Volunteers during the Civil War, coming home from the Vicksburg campaign a sick and emaciated man who lingered at the edge of life for a few more years. By joining in this new war, Fraser could honor his father. He might even do his country some good.

Now, though, his time in refuge soon would end. He was going to have to face Eliza. Face his daughter. Face his life.

He turned back to his desk and sat down. He could get a jump on the demobilization plan if he started before morning rounds.

SEVEN

When Prince Feisal stood to approach the podium before the Peace Council, an electric charge flashed through the ceremonial conference room of the Quai d'Orsay. His black hair and black beard contrasted with his silvery turban. His flowing robe of soft gray silk was edged with scarlet. His dignity and calm suggested the quiet of empty spaces. He glided to the front of the room and began to speak in soft Arabic. Though none of the delegates understood the language, he commanded the room, casting a spell with unexpected glottal stops and gentle susurrations.

Allen Dulles thought of the tales of Scheherazade.

But the magic of the moment dissipated as the young prince had to pause for translation. An earnest interpreter rendered Feisal's remarks into French, then a second interpreter restated them in clotted English. When Feisal began again, his Arabic had degraded from spellbinding to incomprehensible. Impatience and boredom built in the hot, high-ceilinged room.

Allen Dulles, feeling trapped, sat in his usual place behind the principal delegates arrayed on one side of a vast table. Near each delegate was at least one interpreter, leaning forward vigilantly, ready to mutter clarifications into a master's ear lest an offhand remark be lost in the soup of unfamiliar languages. Behind Dulles' row came the secretaries, striving to suppress the signs of their near-terminal boredom.

Heavy curtains blanketed the tall windows, closing off twilight on the Seine. The conference's familiar smells, tangy ink and heavy central-heating lingered in the air with a hint of violet hair wash from the French delegation. The principal delegates favored heavy black suits with brilliant white cuffs. Military advisers in blue and khaki and olive broke the visual monotony, as did the crimson drapes and green baize blotting pads before each delegate. An approaching messenger's progress could be tracked through hushed footfalls on carpet and staccato bursts on parquet flooring. The cane seat of Dulles' chair felt brittle. His mind strayed to the vixen he had met the previous night at El Sphinx, an establishment offering the sort of sensual Xanadu that could be found nowhere in North America. He wondered for a moment about tonight's minx, Lady Florence. Inevitably, she would be more conventional. Unlike last night's companion, though, she offered the enchantments of an estate in Surrey and properties on the Italian Riviera.

Of the few spectators present for the prince's appearance, one group stood out. Colonel Lawrence, green-tasseled headdress in place, burning blue eyes contrasting with a vague and insincere smile, watched his robed protégé from the second row of gilt chairs. Next to Lawrence were the heavy-featured American rabbi, Wise, and that hard-charging British Jew, Weizmann. Conference staff joked about Weizmann's resemblance to Lenin, the Russian Bolshevik, but in truth, the two men could have been twins.

Clemenceau decreed a break between the prince's talk and questioning by the delegates. To rally his spirits, Dulles moved directly to the tea table in the adjoining room.

The large Colonel Boucher, never far from Clemenceau, approached with a plate stacked high with brioche and macarons. "Monsieur Dulles. You must assist me with these."

"Solely in the interest of amity among allies." He selected a brioche and bit through its crisp shell into its buttery center. He heard a low moan, realized with surprise that it came from him.

"You have the brioche in America?"

Dulles swallowed quickly. "Pale imitations, Colonel. Wicked ones, to be honest, which should be illegal."

"I am glad we can save you from such sins." Boucher made short work of a macaron and held a brioche at the ready while he swallowed.

Dulles, toying with the idea of a second brioche, nodded toward the prince and his knot of colleagues. "Tell me, Colonel, what do you make of that rather motley collection?"

Boucher looked troubled. "Motley?"

"You have a Jewish chemist who invented explosives for the British, an American cleric of the Old Testament, and a glory-mad English soldier and archaeologist, all sponsoring a descendant of the prophet Mohammed."

"That is what *motley* means?"

"Perhaps I should simply say *unusual*. But what do you make of them?"

Boucher licked his fingers and again offered his plate of treats. Dulles decided on a macaron. In Paris, he had concluded, the only crime was saying no.

"I think," the Frenchman said, "we should not think of them as unusual. They are something with which to be…coped, is that right? Your president, I am told, has many Jewish friends, as well."

"Not so many."

"Perhaps they seem like many to us." Boucher shrugged and placed the plate on the table. "You know, we enter the war. We talk to our allies, the British, on what will happen in Syria and Jordan when we win. We agree with our allies and write down the agreement. Then, we win. Wonderful, we think. We shall have peace on the terms already agreed. They are, after all, written down. But this group, this *unusual* group"—Boucher loosed a theatrical sigh—"they do not like those terms because they have agreed to other terms with England. Colonel Lawrence prefers those other terms. The newspapers have great love for Colonel Lawrence, and Mr. Lloyd

George reads the newspapers very carefully. The newspapers make Colonel Lawrence very strong. Suddenly our agreement—poof!" He lifted a cloth napkin from the serving table and used it to dab his lips and brush crumbs from the front of his tunic. "Perhaps your Mr. Wilson can use the shame to persuade Mr. Lloyd George to honor our treaty?"

Dulles snorted. "Shame the British? You can't be serious."

"Perhaps not."

"Really, Colonel. Can the French be shamed?"

Boucher smiled. "Quite impossible."

Allen Dulles, uncharacteristically early for his evening date, noticed the Arab party in dining room of the Hotel Majestic. Despite the influx of foreigners for the war and the peace conference, headscarves and robes still were conspicuous in a Parisian restaurant. The prince seemed to be something of a cut-up, entertaining his laughing companions. Evidently in the Arab world, as in the West, jests by the powerful are unfailingly funny.

Rabbi Wise waved Dulles to their table and had another chair brought over. Dulles, with Lawrence translating, told the prince how fine his presentation had been that afternoon and what a strong impact it had on the delegates. Feisal waved off the compliment, which had been entirely insincere.

Lawrence related that the prince was explaining that his family had no interest in being called kings. Because Feisal was a descendant of the prophet Mohammed and because his ancestors had been Sharifs of Mecca for 900 years, kings were far beneath his family. The prince smiled happily as Lawrence spoke, his composure before the Peace Council having slid into genial affability. He promptly directed a new story at Dulles.

Again, Lawrence translated. "In the desert," Lawrence said for Feisal. He seemed to know where the story was going. "Out in the desert, it is the custom to tie camels head to tail in a long row. That way they stay together in case of high wind, when the sand blows and it is possible to become lost. The camels are very strong but not so smart. No camel is fit to lead the other camels. He might simply lead them all in the wrong direction. So, it is the custom to put a little donkey at the head of the row, and the little donkey will lead. He is not strong, but he will go straight."

Feisal waited for Lawrence's translation to catch up with him, then started again.

Lawrence continued. "The Arabs did the same when they fought the Turk."

Feisal spoke again, speaking a short phrase that ended with *Lawrence* and extending a hand to the Englishman. Lawrence didn't bother to translate, since the table was already guffawing at the explanation that he had been the Arabs' little donkey.

Dulles grinned, thinking the story managed to celebrate and belittle Lawrence.

Lawrence, whose face showed no reaction, said softly, "A private word?"

Dulles nodded.

In Arabic, Lawrence excused them from the company. After Feisal's response, Lawrence reported that the prince wished Dulles' business card. Dulles presented it with as much formality as he could muster in a hotel dining room.

Feisal produced a pen and wrote on the card, then handed it to Lawrence, who read out, "I agree to all of Feisal's demands."

Feisal let out a great belly laugh, then bowed his head as Dulles said farewell.

Lawrence led them to a quiet alcove in the lobby. The man was only a little older than Dulles—at college, he would have been a senior when Dulles was a freshman—yet he had an ageless quality.

Becoming a legend in your twenties must do that, Dulles thought, even if you're short and odd-looking.

"Mr. Dulles, I understand you've become an adviser to the president." Lawrence appeared for all the world to be speaking not to Dulles, but to the armrest of Dulles' chair.

"Mr. Wilson has many advisers."

"Let's not waste time. The president holds the hopes and dreams of the Arabs in his hands. The Arabs are great people. They invented algebra and installed indoor plumbing at a time when Europeans were still chanting around open fires. Arab religion and literature are deep expressions of the human soul, and their civilization goes back millennia."

"This is all most educational, Colonel—"

Lawrence held a hand up but still did not look at Dulles. "They joined us in striking down the Turk, and they must share in that victory or they will become our adversaries for generations. It's that simple. I have lived with them. I understand them. If we fail in this, we will trigger an era of mistrust and hatred that may rival the Crusades." Still no eye contact. "I hope you can explain that to the president." Lawrence nodded, rose, and walked off.

Lawrence was a man of passion, Dulles thought as he sat back in his chair. That passion could be both appealing and disturbing. Certainly he wasn't an altogether trustworthy fellow.

Dulles found that dinner and dancing with Lady Florence were very small pleasures. No expanse of prime real estate could compensate for her sluggish conversation and deficit of sensual feeling. He ended the evening as quickly as possible.

Noting the light shining under the door to Uncle Bert's suite at the Crillon, he rapped on the door. When he entered, his uncle sat stripped to his vest in an overstuffed armchair, a stack of papers on the side table next to him with a glass one-third full of golden cognac.

"I warn you, Allen, that I'm in a foul humor. You might do better to pass on to your room."

"Cognac?" Dulles nodded to a bottle on a low coffee table.

"Serve yourself."

"The foulness in your life?"

"This wretched conference."

"Ah."

"Ah, indeed. Our sainted president is leaving to go home to deal with

Congress. Of course, he never should have come in the first place, which I told him in no uncertain terms, thereby beginning my exile to the outer regions of the universe. Also, Lloyd George is leaving for London to deal with his Parliament, his unions, his Irishmen, and I don't know what else. Before they depart, the single thing they will have agreed to is the Covenant for the League of Nations. Not a bad thing of itself, but hardly a worthy output for the immense leaders of the world who have stopped everything else in their respective countries for a two-month period. They will not, Allen"—Lansing pointed an accusing finger at him—"decide on another goddamned thing before they leave."

Dulles concentrated on pouring his drink. His uncle had discerning taste in liquors.

Lansing continued. "The world wants peace, Allie. But Mr. Wilson wants his League of Nations, so the world will have to wait for its peace. We'll keep just enough troops here to enrage the people back home, disappointing the soldiers who are so homesick and disgusted that they go AWOL on a daily basis. And that will also be just enough soldiers to fail utterly to intimidate the Germans. It's a masterpiece of a muddle."

"Mr. Wilson will come back to finish the treaty, of course."

"Oh, yes, but this will add at least a month's delay, so time will be very, very short upon his return. Revolutions are breaking out around the world while we prance through broad statements of principle for world peace."

"World peace isn't such a bad thing. Perhaps Wilson and Lloyd George will return to Paris more highly motivated after talking with the people back home."

They sat quietly for a while. Dulles took a swallow of the cognac. It burned sweetly, then warmed him. One more reason to admire the French.

Lansing tapped a finger on the side of his glass. "Allie." Lansing leaned forward slightly. "I must know what is going on with Wilson. I must have additional sources of information. Day to day, I'm completely in the dark. I had no idea about this trip back home. Even Colonel House doesn't know what's going on over at that palatial residence Mrs. Wilson flutters about in."

"Uncle Bert, are you suggesting that we should spy on our own president?"

"That's a crude phrase, Allen. Gratuitously so. We should think of it more as an effort to enhance consultation at the highest levels of government."

"How exactly do you propose to enhance consultation?"

"That's the sort of thing you're so good at, Allen, you and your clever brother. I'll leave it to you."

EIGHT

Monday, February 17, 1919

"**M**ajor?"

Fraser looked up wearily at the speaker.

"There's a patient you should see in the gas ward." It was the dark-haired nurse with the overbite.

There must have been a time when he could remember their names, but he couldn't even remember when that was. She wouldn't come for him now, at the end of the day, unless it was important. Still, he didn't stand.

She interpreted his lack of response as disbelief. "We agreed that you should see him."

Ah, it had been a corporate decision of the nursing staff. No medical director could afford to ignore that.

In the gas ward, the nurses had placed screens around the patient's bed. Infectious. Fraser instantly hoped it was pneumonia, not influenza. There were reports of new flu cases in the city. In the autumn, the epidemic started with the soldiers and spread to civilians. It exacted a hideous toll before petering out. He didn't want it back.

The patient was Gunnarson, a pale boy from the Midwest who was missing one leg below the thigh. His lungs were already compromised.

"He complained of a headache," the nurse said. "The fever came on this afternoon."

Fraser went through the steps. He listened to the boy's heart and lungs. He looked down his throat and inside his nose. The examination told him nothing he didn't already know. After the first five hundred cases of influenza, he could diagnose it from across a crowded room. There was a miserable look, a flush combined with a gray cast of the eyes.

"Private Gunnarson?"

The boy looked at him dully.

"You're coming down with a fever. We're going to put you in a ward for special care. I hope you'll respond well there."

The boy nodded.

"Nurse Callahan." The name just came to him. The key was not thinking about it. She was from Philadelphia. Or something like that. He kept his voice low. "Take him to the green ward. Keep him comfortable. And please put masks on, for everyone."

"The masks scare the patients, Doctor."

"Better scared than sick. I'm not going to lose any more nurses—or doctors, either. Also, shift the beds so the patients are head-to-heel, like we did last fall."

"In all the wards?"

Fraser sighed. "Yes, I guess so." Moving the beds was hard work. There weren't enough orderlies so the nurses had to pitch in. And then it would be inconvenient for getting to the patients. He ordered it because it might help suppress the spread of the disease. So little did.

On his way back to his office, he stuck his head in the doctors' coffee room. "A definite case of flu in the gas ward."

"Jesus, not again." O'Connor, the only one in the room, stood at the window. He looked unhappy, offended.

Fraser liked that about him.

"You're sure?"

"Yup."

"How bad?"

Fraser shook his head. "I'm going to call the general. Spread the word, okay?"

"Shit. Is it the same stuff?"

"Hard to say. I've only seen the one case, but it looks the same. It's not been that long, so it probably never went away."

"Maybe it won't be so bad this time."

An hour later, after Fraser described the new case to the appropriate officials of the Army Medical Corps, a rap sounded on his office door. It was after six, long since dark in early February. He called for the person to enter, then looked up at Lawrence in a heavy overcoat and military cap. Without his Arab headdress, his hair showed as a sandy color. Though somewhat dazzled by his famous visitor, Fraser chose not to rise. It was late. He was tired. It was his office.

"Major Fraser?"

"Yes. What can I do for you?"

"I'm Colonel T.E. Lawrence—"

"Yes, I know. We met."

"Did we?"

"At the American Embassy. The party to welcome the president."

Lawrence gave no sign of remembering. "I'm terribly sorry to impose on you, but I've come about a friend, Mark Sykes, who seems to have come down with the influenza. He's at the Hotel Majestic—"

"What the devil is he doing at a hotel? That's a splendid way to spread the disease."

Lawrence looked uncertain for a moment. "He's just fallen ill, grievously ill, and it's moved very fast. We didn't think to move him right now."

Fraser gritted his teeth and shook his head slowly.

"See here," Lawrence picked up, "you've been pointed out as the man who knows the influenza best, and I've come in the hope you might see Mr. Sykes. There's a car waiting for us at the door."

Fraser tried to dismiss the subject with a backhand wave. "There are plenty of doctors in Paris who know this flu. It's one of the advantages of an epidemic. Everyone treats it."

"Doctor, I could try to impress you by explaining that Mr. Sykes was critical to resolving the future of Arabia, which he is. But that matters not a fig to me, nor should I expect it to matter to you. I say only that he's my friend. I would count it a great kindness if you would see my friend. Perhaps I should have gone to another doctor, but here I am and I'm afraid for him."

Unhappy about it, Fraser followed Lawrence out the door.

During the silent drive to the hotel, Fraser wondered how conscious Lawrence's effort had been. Had he instinctively phrased his appeal in a way that would actually move Fraser? Or had he calculated it out beforehand? Or had he just assumed that the glow of his celebrity would carry Fraser along no matter what Lawrence said?

When the door to Sykes' room was wrenched open, Fraser was shocked to find a solemn-faced Allen Dulles on the other side.

"Major Fraser," he said. "I hoped you would come, old boy. Sykes declines by the minute." Dulles stepped aside, revealing a classic sickbed tableau. A person leaned over Sykes, probably the hotel doctor or someone from the British medical service. Two others sat on the far side of the bed.

The light was muted, but the first look sank Fraser's spirits, then left him cold inside. The purpling of cyanosis was setting in. Sykes bled from his nose, fought for breath. Fraser had never seen a patient return from that stage. He wheeled on Lawrence, not bothering to conceal his anger. "You should have told me your friend was like this. I can't help him."

"Doctor, after coming all this way, which I appreciate so terribly much, won't you just take a look?"

"I can't work the miracle you want. The war has taught me not to waste time on those I can't help. You must know that, too."

"What am I to do?"

"Let your friend know he's not alone. You can do that. I can't. I can't sit at his bedside through the final minutes. It's a duty that would never end."

Lawrence looked crumpled.

In a gentler tone, Fraser added, "It shouldn't be long. For your friend's sake, I hope not. He may have some moments at the end. He'll be glad to see a friend."

Emerging from the birdcage elevator at the lobby level, Fraser paused to wrap his muffler around his neck and rebutton his coat. He had never taken it off.

"Jamie?"

The voice, tentative but familiar, came from beside him.

He turned. The face had aged. He hadn't seen it for close to twenty years. The remaining hair—not a whole lot of it—was gray. The waistline was thicker. But there was no mistaking him.

"Speed," he cried out. "This is unbelievable."

Cook held out his hand and Fraser grabbed it. Grinning, each used his free hand to grip the other's elbow.

"Unbelievable."

"Hold on, there." Speed nodded at Fraser's military cap. "Maybe I should be saluting?"

Fraser smiled. "That sort of thing was never your strong suit."

They each took a half step back.

"You look good, Speed. Real good."

"Fat and old, but still causing trouble."

"And your family?"

Cook's smile vanished. "Jamie. You got a minute? Maybe a few minutes. We could go in the bar?"

NINE

A t a corner table in the hotel bar, they took a moment to regard each other.

"So," Cook said, "have you been back to Cadiz, or Harrison County, Ohio?"

"Not once."

"Me neither."

"What's it been…eighteen years?"

"At least." Cook waved down a waiter.

Back home, Fraser thought, Cook might set off a stir by sitting in the bar of the Waldorf Astoria and summoning the staff. Yet his old friend didn't seem out of place with the cosmopolitan clientele of the Majestic. Maybe things had changed back home since Fraser left.

When they ordered beer, the waiter offered a trace of a sneer but left without comment. Cook smiled. "Tell me about Miss Eliza and your daughter."

Fraser kept it vanilla, positive, talking mostly about their home in New York, how the big city had made him into a real doctor, or closer to one. He mentioned doing research at Rockefeller Institute. He had never stopped being proud of that. He passed off joining the army as part of his work on infectious diseases.

"Back in Cadiz," Cook said, "folks always thought you were a real doctor."

"Lucky thing, too. But I've learned so much since then. We're learning so much in medicine now."

Cook shrugged. "I'm not sure I've ever become a *real* anything. Just kept bouncing around, since I buried the newspaper, anyways. I came here for this Pan-African Congress that's starting soon over at the Grand Hotel."

"That sounds like a big deal. What's it about?"

The waiter arrived with their beers.

Fraser lifted his. "To old times." After they drank, he understood the waiter's expression when they placed their orders. The beer was a mistake.

Cook leaned forward. "Listen, Jamie. I can't really chitchat now. Don't have the heart for it, or the time." He drank some more beer, evidently indifferent to the taste. "I know we didn't end on such great terms."

"Not that bad."

"Yeah, well, maybe I didn't end on such great terms with you."

Fraser stared at the table, remembering how angry Cook had been. He looked up and said, "Okay."

"I knew I was right and I haven't changed my mind." Speed shrugged. "I know why you did what you did. For love."

Fraser said in a low voice, "Yes, for love. But I stood by that newspaper of yours for three years."

"You did. And I lost your money. Every dime. I know that."

Fraser gave a small smile. "It's only money."

"Look." Cook looked straight into Fraser's blue-gray eyes. "I'm hoping you can put that aside. Maybe you can help me. I didn't come here looking for you. I had no idea you were in France. But then I saw you get off that elevator, and you being an officer, I've got to ask."

"Please. Ask."

The words poured out as Cook launched into the tale of Joshua's nightmare. The decorated hero was facing a twenty-year sentence for desertion. No appeals left. Every American officer who had commanded him, every soldier who'd served with him was dead or on a ship back to the States. Joshua would follow them soon, in chains. Cook kneaded his knobby old catcher's hands so hard that Fraser almost flinched at the sight. Cook had a half-dozen statements plus transcripts from two trials, but the army paid no attention to any of it. He'd gone up the chain of command like you're supposed to, almost to General Pershing himself. He tried civilians, too, even ambushed Colonel House in the lobby of his hotel. No one cared. He got Dr. W.E.B. Du Bois himself to send a letter to Pershing. No luck.

Cook had a new angle, one Du Bois thought up. He was trying to get the Clemenceau to help. Du Bois thought they liked to embarrass America about race. After French officials refused to authorize the Pan-African Congress to be held in Paris, Clemenceau personally approved it. Du Bois figured the French wanted to have colored people around to make the Americans uncomfortable. And that all fit together pretty well, because Joshua served under French command for several months, won a medal from the French. Maybe they'd be willing to do something for him, another way to embarrass the United States.

After finishing in a rush, Cook added, "I'll do anything to get him loose. Someone's got to care about this."

Fraser took a minute before speaking. "That day, back in Cadiz, that Fourth of July. We were down by the stream after the picnic. Was Joshua the little boy you were playing with?"

Cook nodded.

Fraser chewed his lower lip for a moment, then sat forward. "Speed, the only Frenchmen I know are doctors. Not the sort of pooh-bahs you need to get to. I don't see how I can get you to those types."

"Once they get him in some military prison back home," Speed shook his head, "I don't know what hope there'll be."

They were sitting in silence when the waiter came by. They ordered another round but stayed mute. The situation sounded dire, but Fraser had no way to address it. And who were they to each other, after all these years? A movement at the bar caught Fraser's eye. It was Dulles, looking somber.

"There's a funny thing," Fraser said, nodding at the bar. "That fellow there, the young guy with the prissy mustache."

Cook looked over his shoulder.

"His uncle's the Secretary of State."

Cook turned back to Fraser with an eyebrow raised. "Sounds like a place to start."

"He's a surprising young man. Has a knack for turning up next to just about everyone in Paris. You can wait a few minutes?"

"Take all the time you need."

When Fraser approached Dulles, the younger man spoke first. "He was gone in minutes." He took a sizable swallow from a martini. "You were right."

Fraser leaned back on his elbows against the bar, listening.

"I'm not used to this sort of thing. What a business. Sykes was only forty years old. He had six kids and actually claimed to like his wife." Dulles took another swallow. "What a business."

Fraser began to offer his sympathy, but Dulles shrugged. "I'm not sure why it has me so down. I truly didn't know him from Adam. It was Lawrence who was cut up about him. He looked like he was ready to slit his wrists in some excruciating Mohammedan ritual. It's just that Sykes was right in the middle of this situation over the Near East. He was someone who might have mattered."

"It's never easy watching someone die," Fraser said.

Dulles finished his drink. "Join me?"

Fraser agreed, then added, "You know I've been sitting with a most interesting fellow over there." He pointed to Cook. "He played professional baseball with Cap Anson. Actually, he was the last Negro player in the pro leagues. Speed Cook."

Dulles perked up. "Major Fraser, you are far more interesting than I gave you credit for. That might be just the thing to chase away low feelings." After taking a second look at Cook, Dulles added, "It does appear the man's speedy days are behind him, but I'd love to have a chin with him. Lead on."

Dragging a chair over for himself, Dulles shook hands with Cook and demanded, "I understand you played pro ball."

"Nine years." Cook straightened in his chair.

"Well, I must hear your most scandalous stories, especially about John McGraw and Cy Young."

"They were after my time, young man. But I can tell you about Old Hoss Radbourn, won sixty games for Providence in 'eighty-four. Or Cap Anson out in Chicago, maybe the meanest man I ever met. And I met a whole lot of mean ones."

Dulles laughed happily and raised his glass. "I wish to hear America sing of the baseball gods of yore."

Cook complied. He offered tales of base runners sharpening the metal cleats on their shoes until they became slashing weapons. He told about gamblers who provided any sort of pleasure a ballplayer could want in return for a strikeout or an error at the key moment in a game. He talked about the ways pitchers doctored the ball to make it jump unpredictably. Catchers like Cook did it, too. And the ways he had for tricking umpires and opposing players.

Dulles ate it all up, but was especially gripped by stories of the brawls on the field that sometimes brought the fans out of the stands to join in.

After two more rounds of drinks, Dulles asked what brought Cook to France. At the mention of the Pan-African Congress, Dulles waved a dismissive hand. "Just a bunch of over-educated Bolsheviks," he said, "jerking off in their sherry glasses." He wagged a finger at Cook, then at Fraser, then back at Cook. "Now, real Bolsheviks, you know, the Jewish kind, they're a real danger. Here and in America." He enunciated his words with care to give them greater emphasis.

"Is that," Cook asked, "what the United States government thinks?"

"That's what President Wilson thinks. The world is on fire. We're in a race with Bolshevism." Dulles wagged his finger again, a habit Cook already disliked. "Negroes need to be careful about getting too close to the Reds. That won't turn out well."

"Do tell." Cook looked at Fraser, who was glassy-eyed, in no condition to plead Joshua's case. "My family's been in America a long time, maybe longer than most, even if they didn't come voluntarily. My boy, he's been here in France, a sergeant in the army. Won a medal for his service."

Dulles smiled. "Why, you must be very proud."

Cook breathed deeply, then plunged into Joshua's story for the second time that night, maybe the fortieth time that week.

Dulles listened, sipping his drink, making sympathetic sounds. When Cook got to the end, the part about approaching the French government, Dulles traced a fingertip around the rim of his glass. "You want to appeal to the French government," he said slowly, drawing out the moment. "Well, would Premier Clemenceau be high enough for you?

Cook was instantly sober. "You can get to Clemenceau?"

"One can never be sure about these things, of course. But maybe. I'd say a definite maybe."

"You'll try?"

"I wouldn't mention it if I wasn't willing to try."

"Well, I'll definitely owe you for that."

"Yes. Yes, you will." Dulles smiled. "You never know when there might be a time when you could help me out."

Cook couldn't imagine how that might happen, but he assured Dulles that he would be at the younger man's service.

Dulles stood and swayed slightly. "I'll get word to you by tomorrow evening, through Major Fraser here." He smiled down at Fraser, who wore a pleasant expression but seemed to be listening to some internal conversation, not to them. You'd better look after him."

Dulles picked up the check, which was fortunate. Cook couldn't have covered it and Fraser was in no condition to manage the arithmetic.

TEN

O nly two mornings later, as directed by Allen Dulles, Cook and Fraser approached a modest house on Rue Benjamin Franklin, the home of French Premier Georges Clemenceau. The address seemed to promise French benevolence toward American supplicants.

Cook was on edge. He had barely slept, his mind cycling through the different ways to explain Joshua's troubles and ask for Clemenceau's help. A scratchy, anxious feeling was making him irritable. He worried about the words he should use, the best way to start, the expressions he should place on his face. He wore his good black suit and white shirt with a new Parisian necktie. He knew he would have only a couple of minutes with the French leader.

They passed through a small sidewalk crowd that had gathered to watch Clemenceau depart for his day. A tall, bulky army officer answered the door. With a short bow but not a word, he took them straight back to the library, then retreated to a far corner of the room, still silent. Clemenceau sat behind a massive U-shaped desk of gnarled, shiny reddish wood. His sad-looking eyes studied a paper. His white mustache needed trimming.

"Gentlemen." He spoke brusquely, with not much accent. "I have only a few moments. How may I help you?" Engagement washed the sadness from his eyes. He was all business. Cook began in a rush, his overnight planning instantly forgotten.

After no more than three sentences, Clemenceau stood, halting him in mid-sentence. "You see before you on my desk the problems of all France, not to mention those of Africa and Asia and Italy and Greece, of many other nations. Do you really expect me to turn from these matters and kneel to put a bandage on this small problem of a single American when it is your own government you should be speaking with?"

"I have tried speaking to my own government for weeks," Cook said. "And this is my son, who fought with your French soldiers. His life will be ruined."

"Not by France it won't." Clemenceau paused and stared at him. "I cannot weep for your son any more than I can weep for every French son who has died in the last four years. It is terrible to be a father. The worst things in my life have involved my children, things I could not change. I cannot help you." The premier began stuffing papers into a worn leather briefcase.

The large army officer emerged from his corner. Still silent, he gestured the way out.

A cold wind whipped their faces as Fraser and Cook stepped from the house onto the pavement. The citizens waiting for Clemenceau turned away in disappointment. Minutes before, Cook had overflowed with jagged energy. Now it was an effort to follow Fraser's slow sashay down the street, hunched against the wind.

Speed spoke first. "The Congress convenes at ten this morning." He shook his head. "And I couldn't care less about any Pan-African crap right now."

"Speed." Fraser rummaged for something to say.

"This was a long shot. I knew it."

"We'll think of something else. Maybe try Dulles again. Maybe figure something out for when we're back in the States."

"How can you be so dense?" Cook's energy surged. "Colored men in jail don't just mosey on out. They rot in there."

"For Pete's sake, Speed. We got you into that house. We'll just have to try something else."

Cook shook himself against the cold. It hadn't bothered him before. "I should get over to the Congress. Make myself useful to someone."

Fraser watched him stride away. He hadn't been an easy person nineteen years ago, and he wasn't any easier now. Then again, his son was facing the ruin of his life. Fraser didn't know how he would respond if Violet were in a fix like that. Girls didn't get into that sort of trouble, but they had their own sorts. He realized that Cook was walking in the wrong direction to get to the Grand Hotel, where the Pan-African meeting was. After a moment's hesitation, Fraser set off after him.

At the sound of a ragged cheer behind him, Fraser looked back. Clemenceau was climbing into the rear seat of an official-looking car. The driver slammed the door, sat in front, and started off. The waiting men and women called out and waved. The car passed Fraser and turned left at the next corner. Clemenceau was staring straight ahead.

Fraser turned the corner in time to see a man in shabby clothes step into the street behind Clemenceau's car, level a pistol, and begin firing. One. Two. Three. Fraser froze in disbelief. Four. Five. The car swerved to the right. It rammed the curb, ran up on it and fell back. The gunman pivoted. He kept shooting. Six. Seven. Fraser broke out of his trance. He ran toward the car.

Cook got to the gunman first, tackling him from behind. A group of Frenchman leapt into the scrum, scrabbling over each other to get at the shooter. Fraser ran past the pile. He pushed aside several people who surrounded Clemenceau's car, shifting and shoving to get a better look, their voices animated and their words incomprehensible. The motor was still running.

"*Je suis un médicin*," Fraser announced. For once, his Ohio pronunciation did the job. The people made way for him. He pulled open the rear door.

Clemenceau sat upright, staring forward. His face was white. He turned to Fraser. "You?"

Fraser repeated that he was a doctor.

"So am I," the premier said.

"Are you hurt?"

"Yes. Maybe not so bad. They must not see. Jacques!" The driver was slumped over the steering wheel.

The opposite door of the car opened and a gendarme's head appeared. "Monsieur Clemenceau! Are you shot?"

"Yes, but it is nothing. Drive me to my house—"

"You must go to the hospital."

Clemenceau closed his eyes and opened them. "If I am not driven to my house immediately, you will regret it. This man is my physician"—he waved a hand at Fraser—"they are his instructions." Clemenceau closed his eyes again.

The gendarme hesitated.

Without opening his eyes, Clemenceau said, "Now."

Fraser climbed into the back seat while the gendarme pushed aside the driver—who had begun to moan—and took his place. The driver's head had cracked the windshield.

Fraser put his arm around the premier. "The bullets, they entered in the back?"

"Where else does a coward shoot you? Only one, I think." Clemenceau opened his eyes and spoke to the gendarme. "You know the way?"

"Everyone knows where Monsieur Clemenceau lives," the gendarme answered.

"It would seem so."

Friday morning, February 21, 1919

When Fraser opened Clemenceau's front door from the inside, he enjoyed the astonished look on Allen Dulles' face.

"Really, Major," the younger man said, "I shall have to give up being surprised by you." Dulles turned to the older gentleman with him. "Colonel House, allow me to present Major Fraser of the medical corps." While the other two shook hands, Dulles continued. "Does this mean you're responsible for the premier's miraculous recovery?"

"That can be attributed, I believe, to the man himself, who has the hide and disposition of an alligator."

House smiled. "But they call him 'The Tiger.'"

Fraser made way for the two callers. "That will do, too, I suppose. I leave it to the premier to explain the medical situation. He acts as his own physician. I offer suggestions. He rejects any that don't coincide with his."

The visitors kept their coats on as Fraser led them back to the small garden behind the house. Clemenceau was walking slowly around a stone bench in the thin, cold sunshine.

"You are the eighth wonder of the world," Colonel House said as he embraced the premier. "I hope to grow as strong as you when I reach your age." His soft twangy voice suggested quiet toddies on a warm porch at twilight.

Clemenceau smiled. "Not so bad for seventy-eight, eh, Colonel?"

"The newspapers say that the doctors won't take out the bullet."

"They are fine physicians, the newspapers. I find I am sentimental. After all the trouble that demented anarchist went to in order to insert the bullet, it would be ungrateful to remove it."

Dulles shook hands with Clemenceau, adding his wonder that the bullet would not be extracted.

"At my age," Clemenceau shrugged, "it won't trouble me very long."

"And your doctors agree?" House looked back at Fraser as he raised the question.

Clemenceau sat heavily on the stone bench. "What can they do? I am a physician and I am *le premier!* Having Doctor Fraser here with our Parisian doctors allows me to ignore medical advice in two languages."

"But," House added, "such an appalling episode. You have the president's deepest sympathies and fervent wishes for a speedy recovery."

"Yes, it was a shameful episode. A Frenchman stands not ten feet from me and fires seven times. Yet he hits me only once! Who will respect French marksmanship? Our honor is forever stained. It will cause men in Berlin to think about invading France again." Clemenceau sighed. "Of course, men in Berlin need very little encouragement to think such thoughts."

"The president instructed me to urge you to take all the time you need to recuperate. Your able colleagues can assist you with the negotiations. France cannot afford to lose you."

"Pah." Clemenceau moved to stand. He accepted Dulles' steadying hand under his elbow. "My colleagues have the souls of rabbits. And this negotiating, as you know too well, requires little energy." He nodded to House. "I am like the hedgehog." He shrugged. "I yield nothing. The hedgehog does not grow tired. Come, Colonel House, let us walk and talk. If I stop moving, I may not begin again."

House took Clemenceau's arm and they resumed the premier's slow shuffle. The other two men, realizing they had been dismissed, went inside. Seated in the front parlor, Dulles demanded a full account of the shooting.

When he finished the tale, Fraser asked about the assassin.

"He's just some stray anarchist. They grow on trees in this country. Yet more evidence that the disease of revolution is loose in the land. Loose in every land, it seems." Dulles narrowed his eyes. "Major, did you and your baseball-playing friend have any luck with the premier? On that young soldier's problem?"

Fraser shook his head.

"I see. Well, that may be all right. You see, I've just had an idea. Would you deliver a message to him, your speedy Mr. Cook? I have a proposition he might wish to hear."

ELEVEN

Friday afternoon, February 21, 1919

E ntering the elegant lobby of the Grand Hotel, Fraser caught sight
of Cook talking with a small, balding man with a goatee. Holding
a cane with a gloved hand, the smaller man looked at home in the deluxe
setting. Cook—beefier and nowhere near as well-dressed—did not. The
smaller man was doing the talking, gesturing with his cane while Cook
glowered.

Fraser remembered that glower. He decided to wait at the doorway
for the disagreement to run its course.

Cook turned sharply on his heel and came straight at him. Falling
into step with him, Fraser asked, "You all right?"

"Let's go outside." Cook slowed when they hit the cold air. At the
edge of the hotel's awning, the steady rain stopped him altogether. The
moisture gave density to the powerful smells from the carriage horses
drawn up closest to the hotel, and from the motorcars idling in the next
lane over.

Fraser waited without speaking.

"The great Dr. Du Bois"—Cook waved back at the hotel—"chooses not to understand that people don't function like machines, whenever he wants them to, however he wants them to."

Fraser waited.

"All right, all right," Cook finally said. "Sorry. You came here for something, not to watch me throw a tantrum. What's going on?"

"Allen Dulles wants to see you."

"He's got another idea?" Cook looked interested.

"Not one he shared with me. But he wants to meet you tonight at nine." Fraser allowed himself a small smile. "He said the Eiffel Tower, on the second level."

Cook took a moment, then smiled. "You're kidding. The Eiffel Tower? How young is this guy? He's been reading too many John Buchan novels."

"I've never asked about his literary tastes. I figured you'd go to the North Pole to see him."

"Damn right. You coming?"

"Speed, think about it. It's the second level of the Eiffel Tower."

Cook grinned. "Sorry, I wasn't thinking. Still don't like high places?"

"Just the ones that are far off the ground."

"He really said the Eiffel Tower?"

Friday night, February 21, 1919

Sandbags huddled around the base of the tower, protecting the bold steel-work from any devious German assault. A few American soldiers wandered around the tower's base, staring up through the intricate struts and pointing.

Cook's ears popped as the elevator rose to the second level. Four other sightseers, swaddled in scarves and coats, huddled in the elevator with him. When he stepped out onto the tower platform, he quickly pushed up the collar of his pea coat against the wind. He missed his gloves. He forgot them when he changed clothes in the rented garret Du Bois had arranged for him. At least the rain had stopped.

Cook showed no reaction when he spotted Dulles, who was lecturing to a large group of people shifting from foot to foot, trying to keep circulation going in the frigid wind. Faces peered out from wool and fur. Some were flushed, others nearly blue with cold.

Cook walked to the east side of the tower, which had a view across the Seine, then miles of twinkling lights stretching into the inky distance. Without a moon, stars cast diffident light on the mist that clung to the river. The bridges shone through the mist. Past the river, more than a hundred miles away, Joshua sat in the army prison camp. But for how much longer? He could feel it all getting away from him. He had to come up with something.

Joshua had been a gentle boy, fond of every kind of animal. Even squirrels, which Cook considered mostly rat. Little Joshua would spread bread crumbs on the ground and lie down in the grass to wait for the squirrels. They would get closer, run away, get closer, then finally snatch the food and rush off. From a catalog, Aurelia ordered Joshua a book about birds. He learned their names and habits, recited their migration patterns. He never cared much for Speed's baseball stories, but he listened as if bewitched when Aurelia told him about the time the passenger pigeons roosted for three days in her home town. Just a few years ago, when the last one of those stupid birds died, Joshua had mourned them.

Cook worried that Joshua wouldn't be tough enough, even encouraged him to go off to war. As soon as Joshua shipped out for Europe, Cook remembered the story of Abraham and Isaac. He hadn't thought about it for years, but it wouldn't let him go. At least Abraham could say that God made him be willing to sacrifice his own son. Who says no to God? What could Cook say—that vanity made him do it? That he was ready to sacrifice his son in pursuit of a mirage that his race would advance?

He had to look it in the eye. He had been a fool, pure and simple, to push his son to fight.

"Hello." Dulles had left his group, which was clustered around the elevator, stomping and snorting. "You're an easy chap to pick out."

"All over France."

Dulles stood next to him and took in the view. "Sorry for the melo-dramatic setting, but I'm devilishly busy. Since I was deputed to explain Monsieur Eiffel's genius to some of the more provincial members of our delegation, I thought to save time by meeting you at this memorable yet easy-to-find spot." He looked up at that the top of the tower. "It's quite something, you know. This tower caught Mata Hari. Yes, it's true. Those clever French put a radio antenna way up at the top and used it to inter-cept her most secret messages. And then they hanged the poor woman."

Cook was cold and getting colder. "Why are we here?"

"Yes, well." Dulles cleared his throat and resumed his study of the eastern horizon. "I arranged to review the war record of your son, Sergeant Cook. He's been a brave soldier. The French thought the world of him."

Cook nodded but didn't turn. A few boats plowed through the river in both directions. "Can you help?"

"I can't arrange Joshua's release. The only person with the power to do that is President Wilson, and he's not even here in France. He's coming back in a couple weeks, but I just don't see it as a case that would move him right now."

"You mean, Joshua's colored."

"Not solely, but that's part of this picture."

Cook waited. Dulles had to have something on his mind.

"I do have an alternative. I believe I can arrange for Sergeant Cook to be misplaced."

This time Cook turned his head. "Which means?"

"The army will have to move him from his current…location so he can be shipped home. During that process, it might happen that he would be left unsupervised. The army misplaces things constantly. During the fighting, they misplaced entire regiments."

"And?"

"Sergeant Cook need simply absent himself and make his way to a certain address I can provide. It's in the Montmartre district here in Paris. That area has rather a wide variety of residents. He's not likely to stand out there."

"Sounds dangerous. He could get shot as an escaped prisoner."

"I can't entirely rule that out, of course. You may well prefer that he serve his sentence. I believe it was twenty years? You can see him when it's over."

Dulles turned to leave, but Cook grabbed him by the bicep and squeezed hard. "Tell me the truth. Is it dangerous?"

Dulles smiled with an unexpected benevolence. "Life, my dear man, is dangerous. Look at poor Monsieur Clemenceau, who was only leaving for work one morning."

"What happens when Joshua gets to that address?"

"He'll be safe there." Cook let go of his arm. Dulles took from his pocket a folded paper. "For a time. I expect to make use of him, of course. I cannot yet say how. That part of the plan is not yet ripe. But I will. He must be prepared for that. If he is not"—Dulles assumed a facial expression that apparently was meant to be intimidating—"then the army will find him again, with all of the consequences that would flow from that discovery."

"This use you'll make of him. Does it involve anything dangerous?"

"Mr. Cook, I just answered that question. You seem to forget that Sergeant Cook—without any assistance from his father—has charged German trenches. I'm sure he's equal to any challenges he might confront in peacetime Paris."

When Cook accepted the paper, Dulles added, "Get word to me through Dr. Fraser within the next forty-eight hours. He seems a sound fellow. The good doctor can come and go at the Hotel Crillon without drawing the attention that you doubtless would. I can give him the details for the misplacing. Sergeant Cook will be transferred from Chaumont in three days. After that, I can't help you."

Cook watched Dulles cross the platform and press the button to summon the elevator. He hated that young man for his cockiness, his education, his relatives. But he needed him. Lord, Cook thought, Dulles had better know his business.

The younger man grew impatient waiting for the elevator. He walked over to the metal stairs and began trotting down them. After waiting a decent interval, Speed walked over to the stairs and looked down. They zigzagged back and forth and back and forth as far as he could see. Dulles was already a dozen flights down. Cook's knees ached at the thought of using them. He moved in front of the elevator doors and settled in to wait.

TWELVE

F rench farm life, viewed between boxcar slats on a slow-moving train, charmed Joshua. The land looked soggy, weary of winter, yet with patches of snow not yet yielding to spring. The sun cast long shadows as daylight slipped away.

The vertical slices of countryside seemed quaintly luxurious, a world without artillery barrages or bayonets, without bullets or barbed wire. People didn't piss or crap into buckets while others stood nearby, pretending it wasn't happening. Noise, even in a rattling boxcar, knew its place, never presuming to overpower or terrify. The front lines, more than anything else, had been exhausting. Not just the lack of sleep, the constant digging and rebuilding of trenches, the crawling around on patrol, every sense jangling. It was having to do the opposite of what he wanted to do, what he should do, every moment of the day and night. Even when he wasn't thinking about it, or didn't know he was thinking about it, some part of his brain was screaming for him to run away, get away from this insane place and never turn back. Controlling that scream, doing what was plainly stupid, wore a man out.

He thought that was one reason he didn't react right away when he was convicted. Though he hadn't deserted, he'd wanted to. Maybe the army should punish him for that, for thinking wrong the whole time he was at war.

Then again, after the front, prison wasn't so bad. While under arrest, he no longer lived in an ooze that coated everything, crusted on his clothes and his skin, left him smelling of earth, cordite, excrement, and whatever gas either side most recently released. For the first time in months, he had no lice. The earth didn't shudder with detonations. The sky didn't recoil from terrible blasts. He could lie still, feel his muscles and his breathing. During exercise period the sun had warmed his face. Breezes came, even to prison yards. After eighteen months of living with dozens of other soldiers, solitude was a joy. He had seen other prisoners reading. Maybe soon his mind would be quiet enough so he could read. Maybe then he'd be able to think, too.

But when his father visited him, Joshua's façade of resignation and acceptance crumbled. One look at the old man's deeply lined face, at his pain and his anger and his disappointment, told Joshua that he'd been spinning lies for himself. The army was turning his life inside out, punishing him, punishing his family, for something he didn't do. Suddenly, Joshua could feel the hurt because it sat across a wobbly table from him and throbbed. He and his father hadn't said much. They never had. But that fierce old man brought him back.

Squealing train brakes made Joshua wince. They were stopping for the eighth or ninth time. He had lost count. Either the French railways were in tatters or a trainload of American soldiers and prisoners commanded very low priority. Joshua watched an old woman walk alongside a cart pulled by a brown donkey. He couldn't make out the cart's load, but it seemed almost more than the donkey could manage. Perhaps, he wondered, the donkey used the same struggling stride no matter how heavy the load. A play for sympathy. If your job involved hauling a cart all day, that would be a smart move.

The train started up with a lurch that seemed too dramatic for the low speeds the engineer favored. After another ten minutes, they pulled in to Troyes, pulling past the passenger platform in the dim twilight.

The boxcar doors rumbled open, pulled from the outside by two of the three guards responsible for the half-dozen prisoners. They were changing trains, the guards yelled. The prisoners jumped down. The guards lined them up single file and drove them to the train station. Inside the station, Joshua's shoulders relaxed with the smell of coffee and tobacco and the yeasty funk of people sitting in damp clothes. He took the aromas in through his pores, storing up the sensations.

A high wall clock with Roman numerals chimed the quarter hour. The civilians in the station were mostly women draped with the ubiquitous yet stylish head scarves. They paid little attention to the American prisoners, who were mushed out a side door of the station, leaving its warmth to the soldiers who entered behind them.

A guard nudged Joshua and pointed him toward a vile-smelling *pissoir*. Two years before, he would have shied from pissing in semipublic. Another life. The cold air was sharp as it reached his private parts. He relaxed gradually, felt the warm flow. Standing, lost in his own regrets, he finished and closed his pants, then turned. The guard was gone.

In his place stood a tall, fair-haired fellow with a trim mustache, hands in his pockets. He looked to be on his way to a cocktail party. "Sergeant Cook, walk a few steps with me." He nodded away from the train station. When Joshua turned that way, the man added, "Don't run. That would ruin a good deal of very careful planning."

They walked a few hundred feet, side by side, when the man slowed. A squared-off truck stood near the curb. In no hurry, the man opened the rear door and indicated Joshua should climb up.

The truck fell dark when the door closed behind him, Joshua still on his knees on the truck bed. Hands thrust a bundle into his arms. A familiar deep voice told him to be quiet and listen.

What his father related in the darkness, his voice tense and urgent, was more fantastic than any bedtime story.

"You have to make a decision, son, that will define your life. There's only a minute to get you back onto the train, if that's your choice. Then you go back to America like this, go to some military prison. They won't tell me which. If that's your choice, your mother and I'll keep fighting for you, trying to get a pardon or a new trial or anything else that might help. But I've failed at everything so far. I have no idea if there's anything left that would work."

"What's this now?" Joshua held up the bundle in his arms. His eyes were adjusting to the dark. He could make out his father's hunched form.

"That's the uniform of a Senegalese regiment of the French Army. You can put it on and board the next train from Troyes to Paris. There's a ticket in the breast pocket. That young fellow who walked you over here would meet you at the Paris station and take you to a place. It's supposed to be a safe place. I'll be there. We'd wait there, wait for further instructions from that same man."

"Who's he? He's my age."

"Don't be fooled. He's some big shot in the government. Some say he's a spy. He must be to make this happen. If you do this, if you put that uniform on, that man will have complete power over you. He's going to ask you to do something for him. He won't tell me what it is. It has to be dangerous or wrong, or both. Nobody takes a colored soldier out of prison to do something that's on the up-and-up. Doesn't happen. So that's your choice. And your time to decide is pretty much up."

Joshua sat back and started to unbutton his trousers. "Daddy, that's not hardly a decision. Give me some room to get this uniform on." As he struggled in the dark with the buttons of the Senegalese soldier, he finally placed the smells in the truck. It was chocolate. It was a chocolate truck. He started laughing.

———

Fraser leaned over the seated patient and placed the stethoscope against his chest. He didn't usually see patients this late at night.

"Deep breath." He listened. "Again." He pulled the earpieces out and draped the instrument over his shoulders. "You were gassed."

"Just a trace, really. Not like others. I was slow putting the mask on, but those masks were bad. You couldn't see anything."

"I've heard. That shrapnel wound give you trouble? Any infection?" Fraser pointed to the patient's calf.

"No. They sent me right back to the line with it. I think I got six hours off, most of it waiting to see the doc."

"Have you had the flu?"

"Back last spring. Before we went into the line. Wasn't bad. Not like it was later."

"Good. That may give you some immunity. It's come back, here in Paris. Not as bad so far."

"No kidding?"

Fraser looked down at his clipboard. "Do you have the dreams?"

"The dreams?"

"You know what I mean."

Joshua took a breath. "Yeah, some nights."

"Do they keep you from sleeping?"

"Some nights."

Fraser figured that meant most nights. He patted Joshua on the knee. "Considering what you've been through, Sergeant, you're remarkably sound. Please dress and step into the office."

Speed stood by the office window, looking out at another dirty night, sleet making the streets gleam. He looked the question at Fraser.

"He's okay. Breathed some gas somewhere, but the symptoms may subside over time. Otherwise healthy, though not very well nourished."

Cook slapped his own flank. It made a solid thwack. "His father more than makes up for that."

Fraser smiled. "Good to see you joking, but his weight loss also matches him not sleeping so well. It happens with lots of them, but you should keep an eye on it. None of them comes back the way they used to be."

"He's not shell-shocked?"

"No, not like that. But he's not like you and me, either. They've been through hell. Keep an eye on him."

"For what?"

"Hard to be sure. Anything different from before."

Cook was quiet while Fraser tried to organize the chaos on his desk. He made no medical record of his examination of Joshua because, officially, Joshua wasn't there. Finally he sat back. "Seems that Dulles boy can move mountains."

"I can't let myself think about the sort of hold he's got over Joshua. I'm afraid we've exchanged the frying pan for the fire."

"There he is," Fraser said when Joshua walked in. Joshua had ditched the Senegalese uniform for French workman's clothes his father had brought. "Say, young man. I wonder if you remember the last time we met?" When Joshua looked confused, Fraser went on. "It was the picnic on the Fourth of July, our nation's birthday, in 1900. We were next to a stream in Cadiz, Ohio."

"What was I, four years old? I'm supposed to remember?"

The older men laughed. Cook stood. He was surprised how tired he was. "I need to get this young soldier tucked in. Who knows what's next?"

THIRTEEN

Tuesday, March 18, 1919

"Gentlemen, gentlemen." The president glided into Colonel House's large office in the Hotel Crillon. Clemenceau and Lloyd George, seated next to the fire on the chilly mid-March afternoon, rose with wide smiles and open hands. They had not seen each other for a month while Wilson was back in America, while Lloyd George was in London, and while Clemenceau recovered from his bullet wound. The president, half a head taller than both and conspicuously clean-shaven, warmly returned their gay greetings, grasping the hand of each.

As Wilson settled into his seat before the fire, attendants brought them tea and cookies, then retired from the room. Clemenceau assured his colleagues he was fully recovered from the shooting.

"Your health," Wilson said, "is a miracle."

"Ah, no," the Frenchman answered. "A miracle would have been to prevent that madman from shooting at me." He added with a twinkle, "It seems that during our recess, I may have had the best time of the three of us."

The other two offered thin smiles.

"You know how the unions can be," Lloyd George said through his feather-duster mustache. "One must listen sympathetically, care deeply, and get lots of people talking to each other. A few are bound to agree with each other sooner or later, then you're off to the races. Wouldn't you agree, Mr. President?"

Showing his teeth in what might have been a grin, Wilson shook his head. "Being a younger nation, our approach to political disagreements may be a bit more bare-knuckled, but I'll bring them around. I had to lead our people to understand the importance of the war, the need for us to become involved." The others nodded. "Now I have to lead them to understand the importance of this peace. I'll do it. Tell me, gentlemen, all this news of the different revolutions has been worrisome."

The others commiserated over the entrenchment of Bolshevism in Russia, its spread into Hungary, the anarchists and socialists who sometimes commanded the streets of Berlin.

Lloyd George pressed on that last point. "I worry about the Germans. There's revolution all around us. Indeed, even in our midst. Look at the lunatic who shot the premier. But we cannot make peace with a Germany that has no government. We must get on with this conference, work straight through to a treaty, and find someone who will sign for Germany."

Wilson held up a forefinger. "Of course, you are right, Mr. Prime Minister. Certainly about the risk from revolutionaries. But I must insist that the peace be based on our principles. Our principles are what stand between the world and another conflagration like this last one."

Clemenceau's teacup and spoon clattered onto a side table. "Exactly. I agree exactly. I must always insist, though, that one principle comes before all others. Germany must never be able to do this again. Twice I have seen German troops trample the sacred ground of France. Twice I have seen German shells blow up streets in Paris, right here in the beating heart of civilization. Our first principle must be to deny Germany the ability to do this a third time. How can we face the judgment of history if we allow it to happen again? If we do not stop them now, they will do it again. Germany is like the lion that hunts the antelope. The lion has no choice. Hunting the antelope is what he will do. He can do no other. Germany will make war if she can, and it is poor France's misfortune to live next door."

"Surely," Lloyd George broke in, "France is no defenseless antelope."

"Let us move Britain next to Germany," Clemenceau fired back, "and then we'll see whether you feel like an antelope."

Wilson raised a pacifying hand. "We are better than the animals of the jungle. We must create a world where humans no longer act like them. Haven't we had enough of that? It's the human soul and spirit we're talking about here."

Lloyd George sat forward. "I've spent some of the last month thinking about the structure of our talks, as I'm sure you gentlemen have. I wonder that we might be well served to clear out the underbrush a bit before we grapple with these massive issues. If we can resolve the situations of some of the smaller places, then soon enough we'll be much closer to the end. Surely, for example, we can resolve our business in Africa, and in Asia, and even in Arabia. With the earlier agreement between our two countries over the Middle East"—he nodded to Clemenceau— "that can be settled amicably." The British prime minister sat back.

Wilson set his cup and saucer on a side table. "I share your concern that we find a method for advancing our pace, but your example of Arabia is not one I would have chosen. Your two nations have behaved like bullies in the schoolyard, dividing up those lands between yourselves. But who has consulted with the people who live there? What do they want? That is the question we are honor bound to ask now."

Clemenceau slapped his own thigh. "Mr. President, you ask exactly the correct question. Perhaps we could find a way to do so."

"Precisely. We must ask those people who live there," Wilson said.

Lloyd George forced himself to nod as though he agreed with an idea that seemed the very picture of lunacy—seeking the views of a passel of preliterate nomads and rug merchants. Clemenceau, he decided, could not truly agree with such lunacy. He was merely playing along.

"I have thought of a way to accelerate our progress," Wilson began again. "I urge that we conduct more conversations among the three of us, like this. Having additional parties and personalities engaged in our exchanges only produces confusion and complications. Not to mention an endless series of leaks to the newspapers."

The other two nodded firmly, muttering their agreement. The Big Three might squabble, but they were united in their anger over the press —even Clemenceau, who had been a newspaper editor for many years.

Wilson continued. "Over the last month, when we three were not engaged for our own specific reasons, the negotiations made very little progress and the newspapers enjoyed a carnival of unauthorized disclosures. Indeed, much of what progress was made may very well need to be redone."

After a few moments of quiet, Clemenceau said, "Mr. President, to be as clear as may be, you propose that three of us should meet in secret."

Wilson nodded sagely.

Lloyd George shot a glance at the Frenchman. Clemenceau's management of the American president was a thing of beauty.

"An interesting idea," Clemenceau said slowly, "and, if I may say, a very bold one." He looked thoughtfully at the ceiling. "Sir, you have persuaded me." He struck the arm of his chair with the flat of his hand. "I concur entirely. How very wise of you."

Thursday, March 20, 1919

"I must speak with you immediately." Lawrence, who had approached Dulles on the street, kept his eyes fixed to the side of the American's head. Lawrence's anger came through in his clipped speech and rigid posture.

"Of course, Colonel," Dulles answered. "Perhaps we can cross over to the president's residence?"

Upon their return from the United States, the Wilsons had settled in a less baronial home that stood near Lloyd George's lodging, on the happily named Place des Etats Unis. Daisies gaily bobbed their heads in the small square, heralding the loosening of winter's grip on Paris. Having the English-speaking allies so close to each other was undeniably convenient, and no one cared any more if it looked like they were making confidential arrangements with each other. The treaty-makers had long since abandoned any pretense that the Allies were not dictating the peace.

"Now Dulles, can you truly believe that the French mean to send a commission to the Middle East to gauge Arab public opinion? And we're supposed to be so fatuous as to believe that they will then follow whatever policy the Arab people want?"

Dulles chose only to smile and arch an eyebrow, hoping he appeared enigmatic. The peace conference was teaching him not to argue with zealots. Far better to let them blow themselves out.

"My God, man!" Lawrence exploded. "It's the grossest form of insult. The French wipe their asses with Arab public opinion, and that opinion is hardly difficult to divine. The Arabs have ruled themselves for thousands of years and wish to continue to do so. They do not wish to have a bunch of fat-assed French and English siphon off their wealth." Lawrence stopped to face Dulles, forcing the American to turn toward him. "Don't you know that your president has just signed the death warrant for the Arab state?"

Dulles adopted a confused look. "Is that a specific document?"

For once, Lawrence looked at Dulles. "You sport with me. You think it makes me seem ridiculous. But you have a responsibility to history here. You understand that. Of that much I am sure. I am not so sure your uncle or the president understand it. You must make them understand. It's not enough to be well-meaning. One must also not be stupid. History will not be kind to those who are stupid."

Dulles watched Lawrence stalk away, his stiff-legged gait a fair barometer of his fury. As he turned back to the president's residence, Dulles saw his brother standing in front, looking like the Man in the Arrow Collar. The brothers waved to each other and Foster waited. When Allen reached him, Foster asked, "Lawrence knows?"

"Does he ever."

"That man will bear watching. He and his crafty Hebrew friends."

"Speaking of crafty friends, what do we hear from Standard Oil?"

"They are patient. For now. Not forever, I fear. They watch Colonel Lawrence closely."

"Who could look away?"

The president felt wrung out. He sank into the chair in his dressing room. His left eyelid began to twitch. Blasted thing. He held the eyelid steady with a finger. He must be getting old. The evidence was everywhere. He was tired so often. He hated to think this was what the rest of his life would be like.

He had to get through the peace conference. He had been amazed at what a mess Colonel House made of the negotiations while Wilson was back home. If you want something done correctly...He sighed inwardly. It was too delicate a process, even for House. Wilson let his good eye wander the room. At least these quarters were less regal. That Murat Palace had been appalling, suitable for the Sun King, not for the president of a democracy.

"Who are you?" He didn't recognize the valet who entered with his evening clothes. He took his finger off his eyelid.

"John Barnes, sir."

"Where's Jerome?"

"He's come down with the flu. Mr. Hoover has, too. Just today."

"Ike's sick?" Wilson expelled a breath. "Without our chief usher, the wheels will come off for real around here."

The valet faced him from about ten feet away. "I hope not, sir."

"How are they doing, both of them?"

"We've been told they'll recover. That's all I know."

That, Wilson thought, is what was always said. He would have to ask Grayson to get a straight answer. "Where do you hail from, son? I can't quite place your accent."

"Ohio, sir, then New Jersey, then New York. My father always insisted that we not speak with an accent."

Wilson laughed softly. "I suppose that means your father doesn't approve of me."

"Oh, no, sir. We all supported the Wilson ticket. Both times."

"Well, John Barnes, you brim over with correct answers. Tell me, have you ever done any singing? In the church choir perhaps? You have a strong-sounding voice."

"They only let me sing in the pews, sir. I'm loud but not too accurate."

Wilson smiled. "Loud but not too accurate. You have described the Italian negotiating style to a tee. The French, too."

The bar was smoky and noisy, filled with unshaven men in heavy boots and dirty jackets. To Joshua's eye, many of the women sprinkled through the place also could do with a wash and a shave. He had yet to see the flower of French womanhood. Soldiers at the front, on short leave, couldn't afford to be choosy. Neither, to be truthful, were the French women near the front, many of whom casually accepted Negro clientele. As did this bar, where Joshua and his father weren't the only colored people. Nobody paid much attention to them.

At least the singing had finally died down. Not that Joshua didn't enjoy a rousing chorus of "The Internationale," with its thundering demand for justice and revolution. The patrons of Chez Dennis, however, knew all six verses and insisted on singing them all, steadily losing any sense of melody as they trudged manfully through the turgid business. The last stanza sounded like guttural threats from a dazed but dangerous guard dog.

Even with his tie off, Joshua's work clothes set him apart. Chez Dennis was not a haunt for the valets of Paris. In contrast, his father, nursing his second beer of the evening on the other side of the table, looked like he had spent the day with a shovel in his hand—which, actually, he had.

"Can't say I like that man," Joshua said, "but I can't say I hate him, either."

His father looked up.

"He seemed to see me as a man."

Disdain twisted Cook's mouth. "As long as you're in your place, brushing his suits and polishing his shoes."

Joshua shrugged. He didn't need a lecture on class consciousness or race pride.

"I've got to write your mama and sister," his father continued. "Tell them you're alive."

"No, you can't do that. They know who you are, that you're my father and she's my mother. They'll read everything you write, especially this fellow Dulles. When I was in the army, they read everything I wrote."

"It's cruel not to tell them. I feel like a liar every time I write."

"Go on home and tell them yourself. You can't do anything more here. You sprung me out of prison and here I am, drinking bad beer with the revolutionary vanguard of Paris' working class. That's amazing. Thank you, Daddy. I'll never forget it. But you can go home now. It's my problem from here on out."

Cook reached over and squeezed Joshua's forearm. "It is amazing. I can hardly believe it. But I'm not going anywhere until you're back home yourself, and you're Joshua Cook again."

"John! John Barnes!" Allen Dulles beamed down on them.

Joshua straightened in his seat and nodded to an empty chair.

After perfunctory small talk about the weather—it was growing slightly warmer—Dulles asked about Joshua's situation at the president's residence.

"He seemed to accept me. He didn't ask a lot of questions."

"Excellent," Dulles said through a broad grin. "That's just first rate."

"Why am I there?"

Dulles turned up his smile to a higher wattage. "Ah, all will be revealed in the fullness of time. Tell me. Did he talk about today's negotiation?"

Joshua considered his answer. "He seemed real tired. Maybe he's a bit impatient with the Italians and the French. You don't need me in his house to know that."

"Ah, yes, good. You know, he and Clemenceau really went at it today, an old-fashioned shouting match. The premier said that Wilson should be wearing the Kaiser's helmet, which triggered an outburst of steely Presbyterian outrage over the vindictiveness of the French." Dulles allowed himself a soft chortle. "But I wander from the point. You must be patient, Mr. Barnes. He'll get more comfortable with you and speak with you more. He's a sociable man. Tell me, is the president making any plans to go anywhere? Is Mrs. Wilson?"

"I heard some talk, just from other staff you know, that he's going to tour what they call the devastated regions. Which I guess is the part of France where we fought the war. Say, if you ask me, the man should stay home in bed a few days. He looks pale, has that funny twitch in his eye, this one." Joshua pointed to his left eye.

"Did anyone come by to powwow with him on the sly, just tête-a-tête?"

"Nope."

"Not Colonel House?"

"Nope." Joshua thought a second. "There was that little doctor of his, the navy man, Grayson. No one else."

"Only Grayson?" Dulles asked.

Joshua nodded.

"Interesting. One thing I want to remind you, Barnes. You must take special care on the street to attract no attention from French or American authorities, MPs or anything like that. If you're detained in some fashion, there will be distinct limits on what we can do for you." With a nod, Dulles rose and left.

"He's not much of a drinking man," Cook said. He and Joshua drank in silence.

"Can't say I like him much, either," Joshua said, "but he's kept his word so far. Nobody's bothered me, and I do prefer being free."

"It's a kind of freedom, not even living under your own name, but listen to what he said. You can't afford to take any chances out there." The older man cleared his throat and sat straighter.

Joshua could feel the speech coming.

"Your mother and I didn't raise you up all those years, see to your education, send you off to college, just for you to be someone else, someone's lackey. You're made for better things. You can do things in this world that we never could. You owe that—" he stopped, aware that his son wasn't listening. His eyes were darting around the room.

"Joshua!" he said sharply.

Joshua looked at him. "You done?"

"No, I'm not done—"

"Well, I am." The younger man made ready to stand. "Don't ever do that again."

"What? What am I doing?"

"Acting like I'm a four-year-old boy who needs to be schooled. That's over."

"Who got you out of that prison? Who made that happen? I'm not ever going to stop being your father."

"I said thanks. I'll say it again—thanks. This thing with Dulles… maybe it'll work out. Maybe I'll end up back in jail. Maybe it'll get me shot as an actual deserter." Cook sat back as if he'd been slapped.

"But that schooling-the-four-year-old thing? It's over, right now and forever. Or we are." Joshua stood and began fumbling in his pocket.

Cook held up his hand. "Stop it. I'll pay."

Without looking up, Joshua threw some bills on the table. "I got it."

Cook stared at his son's back as he stalked out. The boy was young. He couldn't see how far they had to go. Dulles got him out of jail. That was good. Hell, it was great. But what mattered was how it all ended. How did Joshua get his life back, his life as Joshua Cook, a young man of talent and promise and consequence? That was the problem that was eating at Cook, keeping him awake at night. He had no plan for that.

FOURTEEN

John Barnes sized up the two men arriving for late tea with President Wilson. Each left the impression that he came from another world, but those worlds were very different. The slender Arab prince in sweeping robes wore a mild expression that bordered on the beatific. He seemed to emerge from a time long ago. The Englishman, Lawrence, barely seemed to inhabit his small body, its outsized head, the mismatched Arab headdress and British army uniform. One moment he seemed huge, vibrantly present and magnetic. The next moment, he seemed a refugee from another planet, lost and detached from the here and now.

Barnes had volunteered to assist the maid with the tea service, hoping to overhear something for Dulles. He carried individual cups from the sideboard to each man. When Barnes served Wilson, the president looked surprised, then carried on.

Lawrence, waving the tea away with a single motion, was in the midst of an animated description of a recent airplane flight over Paris. "If only the prince and I had had a few bombs," Lawrence said as Barnes retreated, "we could have taken care of this wretched peace conference

92

once and for all. We were reduced to throwing seat cushions down on an unsuspecting citizenry. Great fun, nevertheless!"

When the three men were alone, Lawrence began to translate for Feisal. "The prince," he began, "wishes to explain to you that the French claims to Syria are absurd to the point of insanity."

Lawrence quickly grew impatient with the role of mere translator. As he leaned forward to speak, Feisal sat back and watched. "The simple truth, Mr. President, is that Clemenceau doesn't really care about Syria and the Lebanon, not at all. He will pretend he has a mission to defend the Christians of Damascus, as the British will pretend they wish to protect the Jews of Palestine, but in both cases it is a thing of the imagination, conjured up for public consumption, perhaps to salve their own consciences, should they ever locate them. The prince and his people bear no ill will to Christians or Jews, so Clemenceau knows he has no reason to oppose us. And the British, well, they have themselves in a pretty cock-up. They promised the prince's father that they would restore Arab control once the Turk was beaten. They cannot betray that solemn commitment for this filthy deal with the French."

Wilson indulged a small smile and sat back in his chair. "The French are so often absurd," he said. "Their absurdity on this question will be revealed when our commission travels to the Middle East to gauge Arab public opinion." He smiled more broadly and gestured with his cup. "And that treaty they signed with Britain over these lands—Sykes-Picot —my heavens, Colonel, it sounds like a type of tea."

"The commission will be a triumph, of course," Lawrence answered, "but there is only one key to this situation. And that key is you." He turned his violent blue eyes on the president. "If America holds firm—if Wilson holds firm—all will be well."

Perhaps he so rarely looks people in the face, Wilson thought, because it's so unnerving when he does.

The prince broke the next silence, restoring Lawrence to the role of translator.

"We have talked to Clemenceau," Lawrence related. "He blusters about the French tradition in the Holy Land back to King Baldwin of

Jerusalem. When he does so, truly, we think he must be joking in that exquisitely sober way of his. There is no such tradition."

Lawrence burst out of his translation again. "You know, Mr. Wilson, that Clemenceau only cares about the Germans, about bringing them to their knees."

Wilson smiled and nodded his agreement.

"And the British are on all sides of the question, so they will join whoever is the strongest. *You* must be the strongest. You can carry the day for an entire people, one that has earned its liberty with blood shed fighting the Turks."

Placing his cup and saucer on the low table before him, Wilson spoke directly to the prince, leaving pauses for Lawrence to translate his words into Arabic. "You may rely on me. And may I compliment you on your alliance with the Jews. I have been spoken to by many, including Brandeis and Baruch, and they have quite persuaded me. It reassures me that despite religious differences, this region can be a model of how different groups may exist peacefully, side by side. It will stand as a lesson in harmony and fellowship for people everywhere."

───────

"You remain a remarkable specimen," Fraser said to Clemenceau while peering at the bullet wound in his back. It had largely healed over, only a puckered dent of flesh still visible. He was in the premier's bedroom, a large though simple room that looked out on the garden. "There can't be five men your age in Europe who could have survived that shooting and be carrying on with the bullet still inside them."

"Ach, it's not such a miracle. It was a small pistol, the bullet goes through the wall of the car first, then the cushion, then it collapses into my back, grateful for the rest."

Fraser couldn't suppress a laugh. "You and your exhausted bullet may put your clothes on."

Clemenceau stood quickly, then staggered to the side.

Fraser steadied him. He guided Clemenceau back to a sitting position. "Perhaps you're pushing too hard?"

Clemenceau shook his head while staring at the floor. "This is not because of my friend the bullet. Since I was a boy, I become dizzy from standing too soon."

"But your strength is not what it was."

"That has been true every day for the last thirty years." He stood more slowly, found himself solid and reached for his shirt. "I must be strong so I can speak sense to your very spiritual president, who believes that the German people are meek as mice. I also must resume my exercise regimen with my gymnastics instructor."

Fraser shrugged his agreement.

Clemenceau laughed in triumph. "This is why one must have many doctors. That fool Reynard forbids it, but you do not. Today, I trust American medicine."

"You trust those who agree with you."

"Who does not? But I am a physician, too, so together, you and I make a majority!" While buttoning his shirt, Clemenceau asked, "You are distracted, doctor?"

"Sorry if I seem so. I just received word that my wife and daughter will soon arrive from New York."

"You are not pleased?"

"It's been a long time. The war, you know."

Clemenceau began stuffing his shirttails into his trousers. "I had an American wife, you know. These American women can be terrible. My wife thought that because husbands have affairs, it is acceptable for wives to do so. It is difficult to understand how a society can survive with women who hold such ideas."

On the first floor of the house, they found the Dulles brothers seated in the parlor.

"You are here," Clemenceau said to them, pausing on his way to his library, "for more talk of Syria."

Foster Dulles stood quickly. "There are some matters we would like to review with you. We won't need much of your time."

"But I have agreed to send your president's commission to Damascus. There, they will discover that all Arabs wish to be Frenchmen. Is it not enough that I agree to such foolishness? Have you Americans thought up something yet more foolish that I must agree to?"

Foster's face moved into an expression that may have been intended as a smile but fell short of the destination. "As the Premier knows well, there are many ways to agree to a course of action. One can agree to an idea—say, the creation of a commission—yet never actually do anything about it."

"But," Allen Dulles broke in, "we don't wish to detain the good Dr. Fraser from his many and vital duties."

When Fraser reached the sidewalk, he felt spring all around him despite the gray sky. He sidled through the small crowd that waited to gawk at the wounded premier and climbed into a French military car for the ride back to the hospital.

The exchange with Clemenceau had been humiliating. He often felt humiliated when Eliza was the topic.

Upon learning that she was crossing the Atlantic to see him, his first thought was that the journey was designed to set Violet loose on Paris society. On reflection, he thought that was unfair to both mother and daughter. Indeed, he could not deny the basic geography. He had left New York. Now Eliza was, in some fashion, coming after him. He felt dread, excitement, a whisper of hope, a presentiment of disaster. Could matters between them be better? Even worse?

The car passed a couple walking down the boulevard. The man pushed a perambulator. The woman held his elbow with one hand. Sadness washed over Fraser.

FIFTEEN

The syncopated stylings of the band at William Nelson Cromwell's mansion weren't pure jazz, but they carried a definite New World bounce. Fraser thought Eliza and Violet would enjoy the Cromwell soiree, though it had been odd to receive the invitation from Allen Dulles, not from the powerful New York lawyer who staged these extravaganzas to extend his influence throughout the peace conference. Fraser didn't know Cromwell, but that didn't restrain the lawyer's enthusiastic greeting in the front hall, nor his proclamation that Fraser was the savior of the French premier. Fraser couldn't help but preen a bit under Cromwell's stroking, watching for its effect on Eliza.

It was Fraser's first time inside Cromwell's preposterously large pile of rococo excess. During wartime, the mansion had been a prized destination for the socially ambitious. Cromwell's serving tables groaned with scarce caviar and champagne at events honoring those caring for war orphans or raising funds to rebuild a giant Braille printing press. Cromwell—with formal manners, ruddy complexion, and anachronistically flowing white hair—carried the romance of daring and not entirely ethical exploits in South America. It was Cromwell, the whispers had it, who engineered the revolution in Panama that cleared the way for the great canal.

Fraser and Eliza sat at a side table, their chairs turned to face the dance floor, their shoulders nearly touching. The evening had been neither as easy as Fraser had hoped nor as difficult as he had feared. Attentive waiters ensured that their champagne glasses never dropped below half-full. Violet's seat had been empty for nearly an hour as a succession of officers and gentlemen insisted on dancing with the golden-haired American with the dimpled smile.

Fifteen months had not dimmed Eliza's looks. Still no gray in her dark hair. Still a fetching smile and figure. The shifting shades of her hazel eyes still could transfix and confuse. Still with the focus and intelligence that allowed her to manage theatrical companies lopsided with exotic personalities. She was easy to fall in love with all over again, but something held him back, anxious about leaving safe ground.

"She's quite the belle," he said, nodding toward Violet. Where had that young girl acquired such self-possession? She plainly knew now how her teal dress flattered her, how her grace drew the eye, how her hair reflected the light. Those were no surprise. She had those gifts in girl-hood. But now there was a compelling poise.

"She has her father's looks." Eliza smiled at him.

He thought it not a bad smile. "Better than his brains."

"Jamie." Her voice was soft. "How are you? Your letters seemed so, so…empty, almost sterile."

He swallowed some champagne, then spoke without thinking. "Like most of the men here, I don't have much idea how I am. I feel like I may never know. The things you see and do, and then see and do again, and over and over. I…well, it's been nothing like the lab back at Rockefeller or my practice in Manhattan. I've been useful here. I'm glad I came. I was proud to be here. But…." He looked over at those ambiguous eyes. What was in there, behind them? He had once lost himself in them. "But I shouldn't simper and whimper. I barely left the hospital, safe and sound here in Paris. I was living the life of Riley compared to the men in the trenches."

"Father." When he looked up, Violet's glow was undeniable.

Fraser stood for his introduction to a lieutenant of fusiliers.

Violet sat as the lieutenant withdrew.

"He looks far too young to go to war," Eliza said.

"Most of them do," Fraser said. "Especially the lieutenants. He was either very lucky or late to the front. Lieutenants didn't last very long."

"Oh, Father, isn't this just heavenly? The music, the chandeliers, the champagne, the beautiful furniture—"

"The young men?"

"Really, Father." She smiled. "Though they are nice. I can't begin to think what they've been through."

"Actually, it was a very different Paris during the war. It could alternate between a somber fear and an almost frenzied merrymaking. The war was so close. The main trenches were barely fifty miles away. Panhandlers and deserters on every corner. Everything felt, I don't know, desperate."

"Father, there's something I want to say. While you've been away, I made a resolve that I will no longer be the giddy, thoughtless creature you have found so tiresome."

"Violet, I never said—"

"No, Father, you didn't have to say it. I knew what you were thinking. Please give me credit for that much intelligence. I'll admit there was a period when I didn't care so much what you thought, but I was young."

Fraser resolved to hold his tongue.

"But do allow me a night in Paris to be totally, blissfully, entirely giddy and thoughtless. It's Paris, with music and champagne, and so many, many officers."

Eliza raised her glass. "Shall we drink to the officers, those here and those no longer here, and especially to our own officer, Major Fraser?"

"Yes, Mother. That's perfect." After the requisite sip, she resumed. "After tonight, I'll want to know all about how you cured Premier Clemenceau and all the poor soldiers, and about the desperate business of making peace. I've been reading the newspaper accounts very faithfully, haven't I, Mother?"

Eliza nodded agreement.

A figure loomed next to their table. Fraser, feeling an agreeable champagne fuzziness, couldn't be sure how long the figure had been there. When he turned, it proved to be, perhaps inevitably, Allen Dulles. After Fraser made the introductions, Dulles and Violet wafted off to the dance floor.

"He seems an impressive young man," Eliza said.

"Rather a dangerous one, to be truthful. He turns up next to very powerful people at the most uncomfortable times. I wouldn't like Violet to find him too interesting."

"Dear, you make him sound positively fascinating. Perhaps I should get to know him." After a moment, she reached over to press his forearm. "That was a joke, Jamie."

"Of course."

"Perhaps not at the best moment."

He gripped her gloved hand and placed his other on top of it. He hated all these feelings inside him, suddenly longed for the emotional anesthesia of the last year.

"They're staying on the floor for the next song," she said, nodding to the dancers.

"Is this one slow enough to shield you from some of my clumsiness?"

She squeezed his hand. "Finally. You do take some warming up, Major Fraser. That much hasn't changed."

As they stood, a young black man arrived. He was dressed in formal clothes.

Startled, Fraser said, "Joshua?"

"John Barnes, sir, from the president's residence. You're Dr. James Fraser?"

Fraser nodded, the champagne fuzz in his head resolving with surprising speed.

"Admiral Grayson, physician to President Wilson, asks that you come with me to the residence as soon as possible."

"Now?

"There's a car outside, sir."

"I hate to do this," Fraser said to Eliza.

"Don't be silly. The president calls. Violet and I will manage perfectly."

"What will we manage, Mother?" Violet asked as she walked up with Dulles.

"I'll explain, dear. Jamie, go! History beckons."

He didn't think she was mocking him. Maybe she was.

In the foyer of the president's residence, Joshua delivered Fraser to a Secret Service agent. After two flights of stairs, the agent knocked on a bedroom door and retreated. Admiral Grayson, looking harried, welcomed Fraser in a low voice. The president's bed was against the far wall, next to an open bathroom with the light on.

Grayson drew Fraser aside. "Sorry to disrupt your evening, Major, but I would value your opinion. The situation is pressing."

"Of course, Admiral."

"Late this afternoon, after a difficult conference session, the president was struck by a shocking fever. It spiked to one hundred three. He experienced a blinding headache, joint pain, stomach distress, weakness, and fatigue. The fever's dropped a bit, but the other symptoms remain. I believe it to be the influenza, but would like you to take a look. I should add"—he looked over his shoulder to ensure no one had approached them—"in recent days the president has been subject to rages that are quite unlike him. It seems that Clemenceau, that filthy Frenchman, goads him mercilessly. That man sounds like an imp from hell."

Mrs. Wilson's solid figure sat next to the president. Her brown curly hair, cut short, reminded Fraser of a protective helmet. Her broad face was severe, thin-lipped. When Fraser approached from the other side of the president's bed, she stood and stepped back.

Wilson wore the vague look of nearsighted person without spectacles. Not a strand of his slate-gray hair was out of place. He tried to raise himself to receive Fraser. His breath came hard. Using Grayson's instruments, Fraser took vital signs, listened to the heart and lungs while automatically interviewing the president. Wilson said he felt weak, couldn't concentrate, was uncomfortable in his "equatorial regions."

With that, the president nodded to the nearby washroom. He pulled the covers aside. Grayson stepped forward and walked Wilson to the toilet. In his blue striped pajamas, very much like the ones Fraser favored, Wilson looked reduced, slender. Then again, no man cuts a noble figure in blue striped pajamas.

Fraser, who stood when the president rose, turned to Mrs. Wilson and asked about the president's appetite.

"A little broth. A nibble or two of bread. He's had very little."

Back in bed, Wilson pulled the covers to his shoulders with both hands and wriggled slightly, then closed his eyes. Mrs. Wilson resumed her seat. She reached into a nearby basin, wrung the water from a terry cloth towel and pressed it to his forehead.

"Shall we confer?" Fraser asked Grayson.

"The president and I would like to hear your views, Doctor," Mrs. Wilson said. "We have a lively interest."

"Of course," Fraser said. "I concur with Admiral Grayson's diagnosis. The president has a rugged case of influenza. I've seen too many cases not to recognize it. Some, uh, recent flashes in temperament is another symptom. In his condition, he can't manage any sort of stress right now. Actually, not for some time to come." Fraser folded his arms. "Mr. Wilson, you may have weathered the worst of it, but it's important not to be deceived into thinking you're well. The influenza is tenacious. It will fool you. You can think you're recovered long before you are. The most important things are rest and drinking a great deal of fluids."

Wilson spoke weakly to his wife. "It seems fitting, doesn't it, dear? That I should have the influenza, since so many of our people have suffered with it. The president should have whatever disease every American has." A shallow cough began but quickly grew into a fit. Wilson turned red from the effort. When it subsided, he sank back into the pillows with a wheeze.

"Everyone here should be wearing cotton masks," Fraser said, "and no one should care for the president who hasn't had the flu."

"Really now, Doctor," Wilson said, recovering from the coughing spell. "That seems foolish. I don't require a mask."

"Sir, you already have the flu. It's the health of the others that concerns me. Many doctors and nurses have died after contracting the disease from their patients." Looking at Mrs. Wilson, Fraser added, "You must keep him quiet and resting for as long as possible."

Wilson smiled slightly. "Who will argue with Clemenceau while I lie here?"

Mrs. Wilson and Grayson walked Fraser to the door, where he wheeled on them. "Now, please remember. Complete rest is essential, no matter the demands of public business. I understand him to be a very hardworking man, but hard work is a luxury he can't afford. You must enforce that limitation. As well as the requirements of masks except for those who have had the flu."

"I'll do my best," Mrs. Wilson said.

Fraser nodded. "Good. By the way, on the way over, I learned that the young man who fetched me has had the influenza, so he also could provide care for the president."

"Surely," Mrs. Wilson replied, "we are not reduced to having pickaninnies care for the president."

Fraser inclined his head toward her slightly. "I mentioned it only because he already is in your house."

SIXTEEN

Friday, April 4, 1919

"This flu can work for us." Foster Dulles was pacing before Lansing's desk in the Secretary of State's office at the Hotel Crillon. He stopped, one hand balled into a fist that he held to his mouth. "With Colonel House taking over the negotiations, we'll finally have someone rational to deal with, someone who understands that the United States has actual interests in the world that deserve to be protected. Not someone who actually has to stop and think whether America should accept a protectorate over fucking Armenia!"

"Foster, my boy, you're kidding yourself," Lansing said, puffing on a very large cigar and rocking back in his desk chair. "Here in Paris, the president's kept Colonel House on a very short leash. Not as short as my leash, to be sure, but very short. House won't be able to do what his own good sense tells him to do, and he'll know it. And then," Lansing held his cigar to the side and studied the ash, "the president will be back in the saddle. More's the pity."

"Maybe not. You must listen to what Allie has to say."

The younger brother was leaning against the fireplace mantel. He held his pipe in a tobacco pouch and absent-mindedly packed the bowl.

"Well?" Lansing asked.

"We now have an unofficial source in the president's residence," Allen said. "It's sort of off the books." Lansing raised an eyebrow but Allen ignored the implied question. "It seems the flu has pushed the president just the tiniest bit off his rocker."

"How can one tell?" Foster asked.

"He's been rampaging through the residence, terrifying the staff. He's accused all the French employees of spying for France."

Lansing smiled. "That's hardly a delusion."

"Yes, yes, but we know about the two who actually are. He's accused all thirty of them, no matter how high, low, or illiterate." Allen pulled his pipe out of the pouch and placed the stem in his mouth, then patted his pockets in search of a match. He took the pipe out. "And there's more. Wilson declared all government cars off-limits to employees, reversing his policy from only a few days before, and for no apparent reason. And, this next one's my favorite."

Allen found matches in a cup on the mantelpiece. He struck one and began to light the tobacco. "He became distraught"—he inhaled sharply to draw the flame into the bowl—"over having furniture of different colors mixed together in his library"—another sharp inhale—"so he had them all sorted by color, every last one of them." He waved out the match and tossed it in the fireplace. "The result of this brilliant bit of leadership is that the red chairs and settees have been dragged into one corner, the gold into another, and so on. Then he went on an absolute tear because one piece was missing, though it turned out it had only been moved."

Lansing studied his cigar ash again and smiled slightly. "Yes, that may be more than his usual. Even that toady Grayson would have to recognize that the president is not fit. Does Colonel House know of the president's...troubles?"

Foster broke in. "Of course he does. He's negotiating with Lloyd George and Clemenceau in the room next to Wilson's bedroom."

"Oh, dear. That means Clemenceau knows, too?"

"Of course he does," Foster said. "His spies are still on staff."

Lansing sighed. "He doubtless can barely contain his glee. He's dealing with an American negotiator who has no idea how much authority he has, whose principal is at least slightly delusional. On top of which, Lloyd George also is sick now. For a man who was recently shot, matters are going extremely well for Monsieur Clemenceau."

A secretary knocked and entered, excusing himself for the intrusion. "The message seemed important," he said as he handed it to Lansing and left.

Reading the paper, Lansing began to scowl. He balled up the paper and threw it at the wastebasket. He missed. "The good doctor Grayson," he said in a low growl, "announces that the president has cabled his ship, the *George Washington*, to be ready to sail to America on extremely short notice."

Silence fell in the room. Foster sat down heavily and began to stroke his chin with his thumb and forefinger. "So, Wilson's going to take his bat and ball and go home? The man is out of control. What will everyone think?"

Lansing stood abruptly. He placed his cigar in a large ashtray and turned to gaze out the window at the Place de la Concorde. "It's one thing," he said over his shoulder, "to have the president on the sidelines with the flu. It's something else entirely to have a deranged man steering the nation."

"Maybe it's a bluff, this threatening to go home," Allen said. "A negotiating ploy."

"A bluff!" Lansing exploded. "For what possible purpose? This is the most misbegotten negotiation I've ever been a part of. We've never even prepared a list of goals that the United States government wishes to achieve in the peace. Wilson's already got his League of Nations. Now what's he bluffing for, Armenia?" Lansing shook his head. "Our poor country."

"Our poor world," Foster put in.

Sunday, April 6, 1919

Her voice startled Fraser, calling his name from far down the long hospital corridor. He never expected to hear that voice here. Equally jarring was Eliza's pale green dress, loosely draped. It probably came from a recent excursion to a fashionable Paris couturier, along with the striking pink and green scarf. She looked wonderful.

"I thought we were all to meet at the restaurant," he said as she neared.

"I wanted to see your hospital, perhaps even steal a few moments with just the two of us. Since you've assumed responsibility for the health of the great men of the world, you're not easy to see. Are your rounds done? This is all right?"

"I've just finished." He took her elbow and steered her into his office. There was no denying how sweet her smile was. Why, he wondered, would he think of denying it?

He sat in the patient's chair next to hers. "So, you've planned another afternoon of instruction at the Louvre for our little girl?"

"Thank the Lord, no. First, we will stand in the endless line to see the gigantic *Pantheon de la Guerre*, so we can find out what all the fuss is about."

"That's the painting?"

"It fills an entire building, they say. The concierge insists that 'eet ees naught to be meesed!'" She smiled. "Then we shall roam Paris while Violet takes artistic photos with that new camera of hers."

"I'd like to try that camera some time. What did it cost? I understand they're pretty steep."

Eliza rolled her eyes. "A gift from her Uncle Wilfred, who insists on spoiling her."

Fraser grimaced to hear the name of Wilfred Clarke. "Does Violet know yet who Wilfred is? His connection to you and...?"

"She knows he's a fine actor I work with and that he's our dear family friend. That's all she needs to know."

"Eliza." Fraser looked away, acutely aware of the dangers in the topic. "She's going to have to know sometime."

"Jamie, it's my family, my story. I'll tell Violet when the time is right and not before. She doesn't need to be weighed down with the sins of the past. I know what that weight feels like."

"She's grown up a lot. I think she's ready, and you don't want her finding out from someone else." Fraser knew plenty about the weight of that secret from living with Eliza. But he didn't expect to persuade her on this subject. He never had. It was her family secret, though maybe not so secret as she might wish.

Eliza smiled and waved the subject away. "Enough of this." She ducked her head conspiratorially and dropped her voice. "I've been dying to hear how the poor president is. I hope it's nothing serious."

He decided to follow her change of subject and mimicked her tone. "You mustn't say a word of this."

Eliza put on a solemn face, then traced a cross on her bodice and lifted her right hand. Theater people knew the right gestures.

"I fear he's really not so well as he thinks. If the newspapers are to be believed, he's returned to work long before he should have."

"Against doctor's orders?"

"Against this doctor's orders, but it turns out that world leaders pick and choose which doctor's orders they follow. Even if I say something quite direct, perhaps bordering on rudeness, Wilson proceeds as though I haven't spoken at all. At least Clemenceau pays me the courtesy of rejecting my advice. The president just ignores it. And I never know what Grayson has been telling him. They seem more like father and son than patient and physician."

"It must be difficult to tell the president he's wrong about anything."

"It is for Grayson. And now"—Fraser pointed to a paper on his desk — "Premier Clemenceau wishes me to consult with him tomorrow morning."

Eliza placed her hand against her cheek and opened her mouth in mock alarm. "I trust you'll bring your pistol."

He smiled. "It's an odd summons, since he seems to have recovered amazingly well. I hope he hasn't had a setback. When the great ones call, we little people answer." Fraser shook his head. "My current patient roster is surprising for a country sawbones from Cadiz, Ohio."

"I fell in love with that country sawbones. He was impressive in a slightly unfinished way."

Fraser sagged back in his chair. "That fellow's long since buried, I fear, by this avalanche of death." He waved vaguely at the office door.

Eliza sat back as well and waited a beat. "You haven't spoken much of it, the soldiers."

"So many suffered, and died. The suffering, it's still going on. And the dying." He fought off the burning in his eyes and tried to command himself. Then he found his voice. "The thing was, they mostly did it quietly, bravely, as though it was all right, as though it wasn't some hideous crime." He swallowed. "They didn't curse me or curse God."

"Did you?"

Fraser looked at her, but he wasn't really seeing her. "No. No, I didn't. What's the use?" He licked his lips. "It was terrible at first. Every patient, every soldier. And then remarkably fast, I just couldn't feel it any more." Fraser waved toward the corridor. "I saw the same thing in the other doctors, the numbness. It's our brand of shell shock. It was a whole lot safer here than in the trenches, but we're all damaged. Somehow." He tried for a smile that came out twisted. "My mother always said that self-pity was my least attractive quality."

"You've been brave, Jamie."

"No, not like them." Now he really did look at her. "And I ran away from you."

She looked frozen, even afraid. He never thought of her as afraid. This was the moment, but not in the hospital, his hospital.

"Is the restaurant close enough to walk?" she asked.

————

The city was creeping out from under the long, cold winter. Though it had snowed a week before, buds were showing on trees. Horses' breath no longer formed fog. Motorists opened their windows. Strollers allowed their coats to fall open. Cafés placed tables and chairs on the sidewalks where hardy souls, warmly bundled, stirred their coffees, shook out their newspapers, and gazed over the streets.

"We've been here five days," Eliza said, "and you haven't asked why we came."

"My first thought was that it was for Violet. And I will say," Fraser ducked his head in tribute, "that you were right about her. I scarcely recognize her, at least when no band is playing nearby."

"I wasn't right about everything. I wasn't right about us."

Fraser looked over. She stared straight ahead.

"It was a relief when you left. I admit it. I thought I would clear my head and would, well, you know, conclude things with Howard. I think you expected me to. Howard certainly did. I think it was when he became a Four-Minute Man, fairly strutted about it, started rehearsing before the mirror."

"What's a Four-Minute Man?"

"They were trained to give four-minute pep talks to the public to make them want to make more bombs and buy more bonds." She looked at Fraser. "It was just too disgusting to compare what you were doing with his empty little cheerleading, with his cutesy jokes and calls to arms —other people's arms. I started being rather short with him, then really quite unpleasant. Then it was such a relief when he went off on tour. My God, what was I thinking? Me, of all people? An actor." She shook her head. "Violet and I started quarreling, every day it seemed. It was months before I realized, before I was willing to admit, that perhaps I missed you."

Fraser locked his face against showing emotion. "There was none of this in your letters."

She took his hand and dropped her gaze. They resumed walking. "No. I couldn't write my feelings any more than you could. The paper always looked so empty, just scratches of ink that couldn't tell you what was inside me, not really. But it was more than that. You had been so angry, so cold. And then your letters were…mechanical, dutiful. It felt like a long time since we were happy. I didn't want to take the chance of writing it wrong. So Violet and I came here."

She stopped to look into his face. Her eyes seemed darker than usual. She spoke quickly. "I realized I didn't know if you preferred to be alone, or at least without me. That there might be someone else. Some French woman." She sighed. "It's a nation of widows, the newspapers say. The morality of wartime, I could quite understand. Who am I to judge? Or maybe I preferred to be alone and I was making up some wonderful vision of the way we used to be that never was and never could be. I couldn't find the words to write all that so I came to Paris to see you and hear you, to find out for myself." She smiled and blinked a couple of times. "Oh, dear. I'm rattling on."

"Eliza," he said in a tight voice. "I don't prefer to be alone. I'm afraid I'm used to it, more used to it than I thought I could be. But I don't prefer it."

She touched his cheek with her gloved fingertips. "I suppose we can work on that. But it must be together."

"Yes, of course. Together."

He knew he should feel relieved and warmed. Part of him did. But he also felt the old wariness. This was too easy. Would the hurt come back? Could he trust her? Or had he become someone who couldn't believe in a good thing?

SEVENTEEN

The door to Clemenceau's house opened. A very large man in a French army uniform—a colonel?—gave a slight bow and took Fraser's hat.

"Ah, Dr. Fraser," Clemenceau called out from his study. "Come in." The premier beamed at him from behind his desk, which was so large it almost swallowed him up, then came around to stand with Fraser. The smile was evident only because Clemenceau's mustache stood nearly parallel to the floor. His long whiskers entirely concealed his lips. "I am told that the car retrieved you from Mrs. Fraser's hotel. I conclude that things are well on the home front."

Fraser felt himself flush. "Very well, sir."

Clemenceau took Fraser's hand in a warm grip. "Oh, my poor friend. I had no idea. You are in love with your wife." He separated from Fraser and took up a raincoat draped on a chair. "These American women. I fear she makes you unhappy, but that is our fate. We all end badly." He shrugged into his coat. "Sadly, I have no time for such important subjects. I must be off. Allow me to present Colonel Boucher." The large man from the door bowed again, even more formally this time. The premier was gone before Fraser could speak.

"Please, let us walk in the garden," Boucher said with a heavy accent, "where I can apologize for this small trick on you. I hope you will agree with me that the trick is a small one."

They walked into a day of half spring. The sun was playing peekaboo, bringing warmth one minute, then fading before a chill breeze, then shining back again. Boucher showed no interest in the weather. He sat heavily on the stone bench and painstakingly opened a packet of cigarettes; Fraser, still standing, declined his offer of a smoke.

The Frenchman lit one and dragged greedily on it, blowing smoke up and away from them. "It is an act of patriots," he said, brandishing the pack, "to smoke the Gaulois, even though they are vile." He stood with a moan. "I am the patriot, always."

He took Fraser's arm and began to walk in a circle around the small garden. "I wish to speak with you concerning the Cooks, the father and the son. You know them, of course."

Colonel Boucher, Fraser thought, must be a spy, but he was all wrong for the job, far too large. Spies should be slender, reedy creatures, cat-quick physically and intellectually, capable of hiding behind pillars and slithering between fence boards. Like Allen Dulles.

Boucher was immense, powerful-looking, ponderous. Far more likely to pound you into submission with his bare hands than to outwit you with a fiendish ploy.

Some weeks before, the colonel was explaining, the French Bureau Deuxième received a routine report that the American Army had lost a prisoner, a Sergeant Joshua Cook. Boucher looked meaningfully at Fraser.

Fraser resolved to hold his tongue until the Frenchman was done. He already had missed his opportunity to deny any knowledge of the Cooks.

"One of my colleges," Boucher continued.

"Colleagues." Fraser immediately regretted making the correction. Put a sock in it, he told himself.

"It is so? Coll-EEGS?"

Fraser nodded in response.

"Yes, of course. Coll-eegs. One of my colleagues observed that a Mr. Speedwell Cook visited the premier on February nineteen, the terrible day when Monsieur Clemenceau was shot. She also noted that Mr. Cook helped subdue the criminal who did this terrible and cowardly thing. All France is grateful to Mr. Cook for this."

Fraser waited.

"An agent then was assigned to...observe Monsieur Cook's hotel, in the Montparnasse. There he found a remarkable thing. Monsieur Cook went to the Eiffel Tower and met with an American spy. Really, only Americans could think of a meeting there, *n'est pas*?"

Fraser cocked his head in mute agreement, his respect for Allen Dulles declining swiftly. Apparently he hadn't known the French spies were watching when he met with Cook. Perhaps he hadn't cared.

"And now this Sergeant Cook, we discover for our surprise, he is working for President Wilson, but he is no longer Sergeant Cook! He is named John Barnes. For a simple Frenchman like me, this becomes confusing. I think you Americans must be very subtle."

"Why talk to me about this?" Fraser asked. "I'm not involved in any of it."

"Ah, yes. Why you? It seems that you have not only cared for Monsieur Clemenceau, also earning the gratefulness of all France—truly, we are very lucky in our American friends, are we not?" When Fraser said nothing, Boucher resumed. "Now, it seems, you also provide the medicine to President Wilson. This is very interesting to us. Very."

Boucher noticed that his cigarette had burned most of the way down. He pinched it out and placed the butt into his jacket pocket, then pulled out the Gauloises pack. The breeze blew out two matches before he had fired up a new cigarette and resumed their circuit.

"Now, this sickness of Mr. Wilson, we are told by your government, it is minor. It is nothing whatever. And yet"—Boucher flung his arm wide to express his astonishment—"because of this *minor* nothing he threatens to return to America on the notice of a moment. We are left to scratch our heads, no? This is more American subtlety. We long for someone with the subtlety of an American to help us understand. And my coll*eague*, the same very one, she says to me, 'Colonel Boucher, why not an actual American?' And I think that is very smart. We know just the person, I think. That person is *you*, already such a friend to France." Boucher paused and turned to Fraser with a half-smile on his face, triumphant at having reached the end of his narrative. The cigarette went to his lips for a deep drag.

"Why would I do such a thing, spy on the president against my own country?"

Boucher's arms spread wide again. "Spy! Spy! You make so much… so much of the drama. We do not ask that you dance the dance of the seven veils or take secret photographs of weapons or maps. We ask only that you talk to us. That is all. We are, as you know, your allies. We are America's truest allies, beginning with your own war for independence, won by French soldiers and French ships."

Fraser shook his head. "You're asking me to tell you what I know about the president. That would require me to betray his trust in me as his physician, which is something I could never do."

Boucher flapped his hands to silence Fraser. "I am not smart how I do this. I have left something important out." He took another drag on the cigarette, then pinched it out and dropped it in his jacket pocket. "Please let me say this. We are allies, America and France. We are friends. So our two countries must cooperate. When a person who has made a crime runs from the control of one of us." He gestured to his left. "To the control of the other of us." He gestured to his right. "The one receiving the criminal must say so, and then must help in the capture and proper penalizing of that person." He clapped his hands together to show the capture of the miscreant. "You know this is so?"

Fraser held his tongue, dreading the direction of Boucher's speech.

"But now," Boucher resumed, "we know of Sergeant Cook, his, what do you say, whereabouts? He has been convicted by our ally, our friend, of committing this crime, a very serious one. The French Army shot many soldiers, for this crime of deserting. We know it is very damaging, this deserting. It loses the morale of an army. Sergeant Cook is not to be shot, but deserting is a crime for American soldiers, too, and he is to receive a very big penalty. A man like that, like Sergeant Cook or Mr. Barnes as he is now called, is exactly the sort of man we have promised the American government that we will tell them about. Should we not say to your government, here is your Sergeant Cook? Should we not help you capture him again?" Boucher paused and stared evenly at Fraser.

Boucher, still waiting for Fraser's response, sat on the stone bench. Fraser found it necessary to wipe off a shoe with his handkerchief, stalling while his mind whirled in circles, searching for the best words. He joined Boucher on the bench.

"Colonel," Fraser began, "you did say that Sergeant Cook is now working for the American government, since he is employed at Mr. Wilson's residence?"

Boucher broke out into a wide grin. He opened his arms wide and rocked back. "You see, this is where we find the confusion."

"Certainly, Colonel, the American government would not allow him to work so close to the president if Sergeant's Cook's legal situation were as dire as you suggest."

"Ah, yes, but here is the American subtlety. He does not work as Sergeant Cook. He works as John Barnes. Who knows that John Barnes is Sergeant Cook? I know. You know. Someone in the American govern-ment may know. But the Army is still looking for Sergeant Cook. We have asked them and they say it is so. He raised his eyebrows. "So, it would seem that *they* don't know. We wonder if President Wilson knows."

Fraser felt cornered. He decided to head for the exit. "Look, Colonel, I'm a doctor. I don't know why you thought I was the person to raise these matters with, but I can assure you that I can't help you in any way with them." He stood.

"Ah, but you are exactly the person who can help us," Boucher began. "I wished to speak with you in this way, not in my office, to ask if you could speak with Sergeant Cook, who is the son of your friend Speedwell Cook. In that speaking, you could explain how Sergeant Cook could help America's ally and friend, France. And in return, France could help Sergeant Cook, perhaps by deciding that it need not describe to the American army where Sergeant Cook is."

"This is blackmail," Fraser said, "and hardly the act of an ally and friend."

"I do not know that word. Black? Mail?"

Fraser, disgusted, jammed his hands in the pockets of his trousers and turned to leave the garden.

Boucher raised a hand halfway and spoke again. "Wait, Major. I ask one more question. It is more American subtlety that I do not understand. Sergeant Cook was a soldier of bravery. We have seen his records. My army has given him a medal for his bravery. Why do Americans treat black men, brave black men, in this way?"

Fraser shook his head. Boucher was playing every card he had.

Fraser stepped to the door and into the house, prompting Boucher to follow. "Ah," Boucher called, "you are right to pay no attention. Because I understand little, I am sometimes rude. And because of that, I will never become general. But you and me and Sergeant Cook, we all can help each other and then we all go on and have happy lives, n'est pas?"

Boucher opened the front door for him. Fraser looked up at the sky that opened above them. When the conversation began, he thought his choice would be between being loyal to his country and being loyal to his friend and his friend's son. The choice no longer seemed so stark. Fraser might be able to apply some American subtlety to it. France, as Boucher said, was an ally. Fraser needn't tell Boucher anything the French shouldn't know, and Joshua didn't have to, either. They could manage this. Probably they could.

He turned back to Boucher. "What do you want to know?"

EIGHTEEN

Tuesday, April 8, 1919

Admiral Grayson, wearing his dress uniform, escorted Clemenceau and Lloyd George into the president's bedroom. He pointed to the two armchairs on one side of the bed, then circled to the other side where a straight-back chair sat near the president's head. Wilson sat upright, his papers stacked in two piles on a short-legged tray that straddled his hips.

Before sitting down, each visitor took Wilson's hand and expressed pleasure at his recovery. The windows stood open, admitting the mingled aromas of spring blossoms and garlic from a nearby kitchen. Clemenceau felt a slight nausea from the smells, along with the constant itch of the eczema on his hands. He put both out of his mind.

Wilson waited for them to settle themselves. "I'm most grateful," he began, "that you're willing to indulge my current indisposition in this way. I assure you I'm feeling remarkably better and am definitely on the mend. But," tilting his head toward Grayson—"my physician insists that we not run too long, so I propose we get right down to it. The current question, I believe, involves the Czechoslovaks?"

Lloyd George spoke. "Colonel House has reviewed with you the positions as they have unfolded in recent days?"

Wilson, who had lifted a paper, returned it to the tray before him. "Gentlemen, I adhere to my former view that we make better progress when the discussion is among those of us who hold positions of ultimate responsibility and are directly responsible to our people. That, it seems to me, is how democracies should make peace. So I propose that we proceed on that basis, without regard to other discussions that may have taken place, with...others."

"As you wish, Mr. President," Clemenceau said. "Under that protocol, I must revert then to the fundamental position of the French nation, that the security of its eastern and northern borders remains paramount. We have seen two wars against the Boche. Germany cannot be allowed to make war on France yet again."

Wilson nodded, keeping a bland smile fixed on his face. "I quite understand your position. I have grown most familiar with it."

After a few moments of silence, Clemenceau spoke again. "Then it is a simple matter, one of justice, to allow France to rebuild those lands devastated by the war. It will take a hundred years to remove the scars that this war has left, but we must begin that work. It is a sacred duty. You have seen them, lands that will never be the same, where gas poisons the soil, where nothing lives, where bombs hide in the ground and will blow up our children and their children? Just before your illness you went there?"

A sober expression replaced the Wilson's bland smile. "I have seen them, Premier. The sight of them would dismay a stone."

"I am not a stone, Mr. President." Clemenceau's eyes were wet. "I am an old man who cannot betray the trust of his neighbors, his friends, his family, all who know that this peace can be a real peace only if we ensure that Germany can never make war again."

"Yes, Premier," Wilson said, "I understand entirely. France must be protected, and America will do so. You have my word."

———

Looking sleek in a vested business suit and a high starched collar, Allen Dulles glided into his uncle's office at the Crillon. He sat at a side table while Lansing finished a telephone conversation about the laundering of shirts, a service which the hotel was not performing at a level expected by civilized society, or at least by Lansing. Dulles concentrated on stuffing his pipe from a roll-pouch of tobacco. The bang of the telephone receiver into its cradle jerked him from his reverie.

"Is this true?" Lansing gestured angrily at the newspaper open before him. "Is our parson-president actually negotiating from his sickbed?"

"I'm afraid so." Dulles pulled the pipe from the pouch and placed the stem in his mouth, but made no move to light it.

"Allie." Lansing paused to restrain his pique. He resumed in a tone still angry but more modulated. "How much longer will I be forced to learn about these developments from the newspapers? It's intolerable. I thought you had a...representative in place who would alert us to such things."

"I can't see him every day." Dulles began to pat his pockets. First his vest, then his jacket, then his trousers.

"My God," Lansing exploded, "why don't you put the matches in the same pocket every time?"

Dulles took the pipe from his mouth and smiled. "That only works if I wear the same suit every day."

Lansing tossed a matchbook to him, but it fell short.

Dulles picked it off the rug. "I'll see him this evening and learn what I can, but we can hardly expect that a president who refuses to disclose his plans to his Secretary of State will unburden himself entirely to his valet, particularly a new one."

Lansing looked stricken. "Dear God, Allie, his valet?" Lansing's voice was a dying swan, then regained strength. "Your agent is his valet?"

After striking a match and taking several puffs to light the pipe, Dulles spoke around the pipe stem. "Technically, I suppose, he is Mr. Wilson's second valet."

Lansing stood and clasped his hands behind his back. He turned to stare out at the plaza. His nephew's insouciance could be grating. More than grating. "Affairs of state in 1919," he said with all the equanimity he muster, "should not resemble eighteenth-century French farce. Tell me about this."

"The principal valet has been down with the flu for several weeks, and we're not hurrying him back into service. He's happy to recuperate at the somewhat glacial pace we prefer. Our representative, as you so delicately describe him, seems a clever chap, certainly for a Negro."

"God deliver us from the clever. The president, you know, is endlessly clever."

"There are worse things."

The desk chair creaked as Lansing dropped into it. "Don't get me started. Wilson's had such a charmed political life that he's afflicted with the optimism of the consistently fortunate. I fear he simply can't appreciate Clemenceau's power."

"Your concern is the old man?"

"It should be yours, too. He can seem an eccentric anachronism with those prissy gloves, the droopy mustache, the way he closes his eyes and seems to drift off during meetings. But he's a tough old bird with a single idea he has held without interruption since 1870. Stop the Boches! Stop the Boches! But he cannot stop history. Germany is richer than France. Germans work harder than the French. There are more of them. And now everything he does to protect his cherished France will sharpen Germany's passion for revenge."

"Surely the president sees this."

"He does, but I fear he cannot resist Clemenceau. Single-mindedness is a great advantage in a negotiation, especially when combined with an unmediated willingness to be rude. Clemenceau cares nothing for courtesy. Cleverness and courtesy are no match for single-minded bad manners."

"Mr. Wilson has been quite single-minded about his League of Nations." Dulles smiled around the pipe stem.

Lansing waved a hand dismissively. "If only it mattered."

Dulles took the pipe from his mouth. "Speaking of which, do you know the joke making the rounds?" He took his uncle's silence as license to continue. "The negotiators are working for a treaty that will ensure the world a 'just and lasting war.'"

"Dear God, Allie. Speak to your second valet. Perhaps he can save us."

NINETEEN

"My daughter says there have been bookstalls here on the riverbank for hundreds of years." Fraser was standing with Joshua before uneven shelves that overflowed with books about French history. "It's wonderful to learn from your own child."

Joshua, an inch taller than Fraser but with the slender build of the young, reached for a volume. He fanned the pages. "They're all in French." He reshelved the book with a smile. "I can parley when I have to, certainly with the mam'selles, but my reading of French is strictly limited to street signs and menus."

As they strolled to the next stall, Fraser said, "Your father's late."

"It's a family joke, that the name Speed was meant for someone else, but Daddy was late being born so he got the name by mistake."

"I never noticed that about him."

Joshua paused at the stone wall separating the street from the drop to the river. He leaned on his elbows to look out. Fraser joined him. The river flowed dark on the overcast day, with green flashes of reflected light.

"The old man says I can trust you. As a rule, he doesn't say that about white folks. But then you don't know he'll be late to his own funeral."

A boat worked its way up the river, its flat deck a nest of ropes and pulleys. The two-man crew made no effort to impose order on the clutter around them, preferring to scan the riverbanks with little apparent interest.

"Okay," Fraser said.

"So, why does he trust you?"

"We have some, I suppose you'd call it some history together." Fraser admired the buildings rising above the far shore, the walled riverbank of Ile Saint-Louis. The stone structures seemed ageless, destined to last far longer than the puny two-legged animals who scurried in and out of them. "A long time ago."

"That history doesn't seem to include being friends."

"Oh, I don't know. Friendly enough." He looked over at Joshua. "It's true we haven't kept up much."

"You're not giving me much to go on."

"I guess I feel like it's your father's story to tell." Fraser straightened and began to move down the walk. Joshua followed.

"But you should know I trust him, too." When Joshua said nothing, Fraser said, "Tell me, how are things with Mr. Wilson?"

"It's indoor work, no heavy lifting."

"No, I meant with the man himself."

"I see more of him than I expected. He and Mrs. Wilson have decided the French staff can't be around him, they can't be trusted, so that just leaves a few of us Americans who can."

"What's he like?"

"We don't exactly pal around together, but not as bad as I expected— you know, for a Southern man." When Fraser turned a questioning eye, Joshua added, "He's the boss, no two ways about that, and he's been pretty patient with my mistakes, since I didn't know the first thing about being a valet. But he's got more personality than I thought he would. You know, he was reciting limericks to me the other day."

"Any good ones?"

Joshua smiled. "God, they were terrible."

"Anything off color?"

"Nah. Probably why they were so bad. But he thought they were great, amused the hell out of himself. It was sort of cute."

Fraser struggled to think of the president as cute, but decided to let it pass. "And young Dulles? How's it going with him?"

Joshua shrugged. "We meet. I tell him what I know, which ain't a lot. Mostly about who comes to the house, how long they stay."

"Does he go away satisfied?"

"Damned if I know. Keeps coming back."

"So what's this I hear?" Speed Cook's deep voice came upon them from behind. They stopped and formed a small knot with the new arrival. Speed glared at Fraser. He lowered his voice but retained its urgency. "Now instead of my boy going to prison for twenty years, you're going to get him shot as a spy for France?"

"Whoa, there," Fraser said, "It's not just Joshua. I'm supposed to be supplying Colonel Boucher with news, too." He stared evenly at Cook. "If I saw a way to say no, I wouldn't have signed either of us up." He waited a beat. "Have you got one?"

"Damn it, Jamie, there are always alternatives," Cook said. "You just got to think of them."

"Fine. Hop on it. I could use some good alternatives."

"Hey," Joshua said. "Is there room for me in this conversation?"

The two older men looked at their shoes.

"Listen, I've got no problem with the French. If I'm working with them, then there's less danger I'll get picked up on these streets, or at least there's one more place I can go for help if I do. The Frenchies have treated me better than the US of A ever did."

"Are you prepared," his father asked, "to become a Frenchman?"

"I don't know. If it means I don't have to be a nigger."

Cook glared at his son. "What's to stop the British from pulling the same stunt, make you report to them? Both of you? And the Germans? How about the Russians and the Poles?" He waved a hand back at the buildings lining the riverside. "There could be five spies watching us all right now."

Joshua turned to Fraser. "What do you think—will the British come around after me, too?"

Cook broke in. "What are you asking him for?"

"You said I could trust him."

"Yeah, I said that, but that doesn't mean he gets a vote," Cook said.

"He and I are the ones doing the spying. We've got the only votes here."

Fraser held his up hands to calm the two men, whose faces had grown hard. "All this talk about spies. Makes me think about going someplace more private."

Cook's hotel room was narrow and chilly. The window looked out on an air shaft. A bare bulb, suspended by a cord in the center of the room, cast a sickly light. He sat in the single hard chair. Fraser and Joshua sat on the edge of the narrow bed.

"Are you changing your hotel every day, like the old days?" Fraser asked him.

"Haven't been," Cook said, "but I'll move after you boys leave today."

Joshua asked, "What's all this about, changing hotels?"

"Ancient history," Cook said, "the only kind two old coots can have. I'll tell you sometime."

"All right, Speed," Fraser said, leaning back against the wall. He looked up at the ceiling and was sorry he had. A squadron of flies circled the light bulb. He looked back at Cook. "Just what are those alternatives that Joshua and I have?"

"Okay, let's try this to get ourselves thinking. Let's try turning it around. Maybe we're worrying too much about what *they* can do to *us,* and not thinking enough about what we can do to them."

"Oh, come on, Daddy," Joshua said. "They're planning to put me in jail for twenty years. What can I do to match that?"

"Wait," Fraser said. "Hear him out."

Cook rubbed his forehead with a gnarled hand. "Let's think about what these people are doing, really doing. That pretty boy Dulles is sending a man to spy on his own president. Since he picked you to do the spying, he's ignoring the verdict of an authorized military court. Near as we know, he can't be sure if Joshua actually deserted or not. Doesn't seem to matter to him." Cook took a moment, gathering his thoughts. "And this Boucher, the Frenchman, he's spying on his own ally. If President Wilson already was thinking about going home early, what might he do if he found out that France was turning his personal staff into their own spies?"

"Hell," Joshua said, "he's got that on the brain already."

"Exactly, Cook said. "Where would that leave Clemenceau, with everything he wants to do to Germany?"

"But it would be just my word against these big shots," Joshua said. "The word of a colored man. A deserter."

"Hold the phone, there," Fraser said. "I'm not colored."

Cook smiled, a smile with an edge. "Yeah? This time, you'll stick with me? All the way?"

"What exactly have I been doing since you tapped me on the shoulder at the Hotel Majestic? Playing checkers?" Fraser took a breath to control his temper. "Listen, I don't think we can afford to rely on Dulles to fix Joshua's situation forever. I don't trust him enough for that."

"Amen," Cook said. "Now you're talking my language."

"I spoke to a lawyer I know over at the judge advocate's office. About a hypothetical situation, I said, just something I was curious about."

"Smart," Cook said. "He'd never see through that."

Fraser ignored him. "He said the president could fix a situation like Joshua's. Wilson could reverse any military sentence, but he'd have to do it within a certain amount of time, which we're already pretty far past."

"Naturally," Joshua said.

"Hang on, hang on. That just means when we get the president's order of reversal, or whatever it's called, we have to get it backdated. That lawyer gave me the form of what the order should look like. The trick will be getting it approved."

"Signed by Wilson?" Cook asked.

Fraser nodded. "And backdated."

A quiet fell over the group.

"Okay," Cook said, his voice a thoughtful rumble. "So, look, this is what we should've been thinking about from the beginning. We've got to give someone in power—American or French, Dulles or Wilson or Boucher or Clemenceau—a powerful reason to give Joshua his life back. So what's that reason? Maybe it could be hard evidence of the dirty business they're making you two do."

"Like what?" Joshua asked.

"Damned if I know for sure. We might have to steal it. We might have to make up some of it. We just need to have something to trade with." He leaned forward with his elbows on his knees. "Let's take them one at a time. What about Boucher? What can we get on him, or from him?"

Fraser shook his head. "I don't know about him. His office must be in a military building somewhere, so there's bound to be guards all around. And we have no connection to the French anyway. My uniform can get me into some places run by the Americans, but it doesn't work so well with French guards."

"Okay, what about Dulles?" Speed asked.

"That's easier," Fraser said. "He's staying in a public hotel, one where my uniform works a whole lot better."

"And I'm at the president's residence," Joshua suggested.

"Wilson won't have anything that shows you're a spy," Speed said. "Dulles is keeping that a secret from him."

Joshua burst out, "Criminy, I'm not stupid, I know that. Maybe I can get a look at something else, something that we still might use to trade with."

The three men grew quiet again.

"If we take something from Dulles or the president," Fraser offered, "they'll come after us to get it back."

Speed sat up. "Why would they think it was us who stole anything? There's got to be hundreds of spies here in Paris right now—French, British, Bolsheviks, Germans—all sneaking around stealing things from each other. It's a regular spy convention."

"Speed," Fraser said, "I've got a thought. My daughter has this new camera. It takes photos in regular light. Why don't we use it? We won't have to actually steal anything. We can just take a photo of it, which will prove it really exists."

"Sure," Joshua said. "Or we could get photos of them actually doing things—like photos of Dulles or Boucher talking to me as John Barnes, tie them directly to me."

Speed offered a thin smile. "Okay, so we've got some ideas, some alternatives. Maybe we start watching Dulles, his habits, the kinds of things he carries around, how he carries them."

The others nodded.

"Joshua, you'll see him at the residence if he turns up there. And I can keep an eye on him at the Crillon."

"I don't know, Speed," Fraser said. "If you hang around there too much, you'll get pretty conspicuous."

Now Cook was grinning. "I'm going to be very conspicuous. It turns out the hotel has been looking for an English-speaking bartender who can mix up some of those fancy new cocktails the Americans like. I wowed them with a drink Johnny Williams has been making up in Harlem. He calls it a sidecar. They're going to feature it, play it up big."

"That's good," Fraser said. "That's very good. Bartenders hear a lot of things."

"It won't hurt to have some work to keep some money coming in, either," Cook said. "My expenses have been outrunning my resources."

Joshua broke in. "I don't mean to rain on this parade, but what makes you think we can do all these things, run around learning secrets, and facing down the US government. I haven't had a whole lot of luck facing down the US government."

"These two devious old minds," Speed answered, nodding at Fraser, "are capable of more than you're giving them credit. Especially when we can call on strong young legs." After a beat, he added, "We need to move fast. This peace conference can't last forever, and God knows where they'll take Joshua after that."

TWENTY

Colonel Boucher, not naturally a cheerful man, smiled during the early morning ride to Clemenceau's house. Paris in mid-April was in full bloom. The magnolia shimmered pink and white in the breeze. Chestnut trees wore delicate blossoms. He had dreamt of seeing this again, a Paris spring without war. Despite four years of man's worst efforts, the world was still alive.

He had much to feel cheerful about. France prevailed in the long war by a hair's breadth, staggering to the armistice on a sea of American soldiers, British grit, and the willingness of more than a million Frenchmen to march to their deaths. Now France was poised to win the peace, as well.

Clemenceau received him in his study. "Forgive me if I don't get up," the premier said. "I have felt some dizziness in these last days."

"Monsieur Premier," Boucher said, "I am dizzy, too—dizzy with your great success! After all of Wilson's fine speeches about justice and benevolence, you have won English and American guarantees—they will defend France against German attack?"

Clemenceau nodded in confirmation. He allowed himself a small smile.

"It's a miracle! That will be the piece de résistance, which makes all of your other successes even greater."

Raising a finger, Clemenceau said, "Never underestimate the hedgehog. But Colonel, you will be my favorite intelligence officer even if you do not flatter me."

Still standing, Boucher answered, "But why should I take such a chance?"

"Very wise, I'm sure." Clemenceau reached for a paper to the side of the desk. "As for business, I think it's time for us to address issues other than Germany. I fear I may have neglected them. We may have missed some, ah, opportunities." He held his hand out for the intelligence officer to sit down, then leaned back and stared at the ceiling. He laced his fingers together over his midriff and began. "Some subjects, of course, we may ignore. Let us pass over the Italians and the Greeks and their demands for lands they last occupied two thousand years ago. Both are preposterous."

"Exactly so." Boucher was searching for papers in his briefcase. He pulled out a handful and sat back. "Our view on both is that their appetites are greater than their digestive powers."

"Boucher, you are disgusting. Military men should leave the metaphors to those with literary sensibilities." Clemenceau looked over his nose at the man. "I am interested in the argument between Japan and China over the Shantung Peninsula. What do you and your wise colleagues make of that?"

"From a military standpoint, we are content to have Japan and China fight. So long as they fight each other, it should make our position in Indochina safer."

Clemenceau gathered his brows in concentration. "Should we not fear Japan? Their fleet grows. Their army expands. They are modern and extremely ambitious."

"We fear everyone," Boucher said, "but China is a very great meal for even the most ambitious nation to swallow—"

Clemenceau held up his hand. "No digestive metaphors, my dear Colonel. I would like to hear more from your men who follow Japan."

"Of course."

Clemenceau's eyes passed over Boucher's head to the wall beyond. "Talk to me of Syria and Lebanon. Many tell me that we must acquire them. In some fashion that Mr. Wilson finds acceptable, of course. But the reasons I am given are nothings. To protect Christians? To restore the glories of the crusader knights? France has been bled white in this war. We have no blood left for such sentimental matters."

"For business, sir."

"For business. I shall tell one million mothers of one million poilus moldering in their graves that their sons died to make Frenchmen more rich. Boucher, it is not only your metaphors that are disgusting." Clemenceau used a forefinger to stroke one side of his exuberant mustache.

Boucher remained silent.

"There is the matter of oil in Mesopotamia. It doesn't go so well. Mr. Lloyd George is impossible. The man will say anything. We have sympathetic talks. He is charming. He is agreeable. But when I return here I realize I have gained nothing. So I stop having sympathetic talks. We argue. We shout. I return here and still, I have gained nothing. Perhaps we must fight a duel."

Boucher smiled at the premier, who had survived perhaps a dozen duels.

Clemenceau made a face. "All right. No duel. Did you bring the map?"

Boucher pulled from his briefcase a map of the now-defunct Turkish Empire. He spread it on the desk before Clemenceau. Both men leaned over the map as Boucher traced the route a pipeline might take between Mosul and Damascus, perhaps five hundred miles long, and then on to the Mediterranean.

"My predecessors were stupid in that agreement with Sykes," Clemenceau said. "We cannot give up Mosul. We must have part of the oil."

The two men straightened up.

"There are advantages," Boucher said, "to pursuing a commercial arrangement for the oil in Mosul, rather than a political one. We tell the English that we will build the pipeline for them and keep it safe across Syria and Lebanon, so long as they give to Frenchmen part of the oil of Mosul. Then we leave to England the pleasures of dealing with that country and its quarrelsome people." He leaned over to point again. "It also allows us to confine ourselves to our historical claim for Syria and Lebanon, where the Christians are most dense. It would have the advantage of being consistent with what France has said before."

Clemenceau's eyes fixed on Boucher without actually seeing him. "I wonder about this Gulbenkian and his Turkish Petroleum Company? We would use him for this?"

Boucher shrugged. "Ah, the Armenian. When one lies down with dogs, one…"

"Yes, yes, but the British have decided that fleas with petroleum are not so bad, and so do I."

Boucher shrugged again.

"So, I shall haggle with this Armenian and Mr. Lloyd George over shares in the Turkish Petroleum Company on behalf of prosperous Frenchmen who despise me."

Boucher nodded.

The premier waved for Boucher to remove the map. "The prince of Arabia was here yesterday. He is most impressive. He could be in the cinema. He spoke of this commission of Wilson's to determine public opinion in Syria and Arabia."

"Yes, sir, the Americans continue to want that."

Clemenceau allowed himself a smile. "I told the prince that France would support a sort of independence for local communities in the area. No matter how that was translated into his language, it will commit us to nothing."

"We should be," Boucher said, "concerned about that Colonel Lawrence. He is always buzzing around the prince. He didn't come here with the prince yesterday?"

Clemenceau shook his head. "We didn't know where he was, which concerns us. Among the British and Americans, no doors are closed to Lawrence. He seems to cast a sort of spell over them."

"And the Jews are also troublesome over these scraps of desert?"

"They, too, find no British or American doors closed to them."

Boucher plunged ahead. "You have not selected any French members for this commission of the Americans?"

"No. I say vague things. I marvel at the weather. The spring is beautiful, no?"

"My office might have some suggestions for proper commissioners."

"That won't be necessary."

"That is well."

"Yes, I shall wait. The president and Mr. Lloyd George, they cannot stay in Paris forever, but we, Colonel Boucher, we live here." Clemenceau smiled. "Only the British could muddle a situation so totally, confusing it with this Armenian and the saintly Colonel Lawrence. But they cannot quarrel with France over this bed of sand." He pulled himself upright. "What do they care of Arabs or Jews? It's sentimental nonsense. France will have Syria, Britain will have Mesopotamia, we will share the petroleum. The Arabs, they will have their cinema star. And the Jews will have the same nothing they've always had."

"What of Mr. Wilson and his Fourteen Points? The promise of self-determination of peoples?"

"Yes, the inscrutable Mr. Wilson. He's like the heavens on a cloudy night. He opposes, he preaches, he opposes, he scolds, he grows ill, he recovers, he grows ill, he still opposes. And then—poof! He agrees." Clemenceau spread his arms in mock wonder. "He is like a storm that moves on the wind. When the storm is done, ah, that is when the hedgehog scurries out and gathers up his berries."

The president stood before the window of his dressing room, feeling snug in his robe of deep blue flannel. Two blackbirds perched on the window sill, pecking at the crumbs of morning toast he had placed there. He thought they were the same two birds every morning.

He smiled, thinking of the day before, how he had surprised the others, perhaps even shocked them. When that Italian popinjay, Signore Orlando, threatened to walk out on the peace talks, Wilson didn't bat an eyelash. With the same frosty look he used while presiding over the university senate at Princeton, he had shrugged. "You must," he had said, "do what you think is best." While the translator rendered his words into Italian, Lloyd George and Clemenceau exchanged one of their meaningful glances, the ones he wasn't supposed to notice. They expected him to implore Orlando to stay. Fiddlesticks on that. Wilson had no obligation to stop a man from playing his hand badly, something the Italians excelled at. So out Orlando stalked. He would be back, sooner than Wilson would prefer. And the other two had been reminded that Woodrow Wilson does no man's bidding.

The president began to hum.

Joshua knocked at the door, then entered with the president's black-button boots, freshly polished. He set them down next to the closet.

Still smiling, Wilson turned and began to sing, keeping time with his hand. "The Son of God," he began in a low voice, "goes forth to war!"

Joshua recognized the martial stride of the hymn. It had stirred him as a boy.

"Barnes," the president cried, "you know it! I see by your expression that you know it. Join in!" Wilson's pure tenor launched into the second verse in a stronger voice. "That martyr first, whose eagle eye, could pierce beyond the grave."

Joshua picked up the tune, but the words were slow to come to his lips, a half beat late if at all.

Wilson conducted the hymn through the third verse.

Joshua remembered the final line of that one. He sang clearly, "They bowed their necks the death to feel, who follows in his train?" Memories of soldiers flooded Joshua's mind. He felt his emotions crowd in.

Wilson began to cough. Soon the cough was a full-fledged fit.

Joshua, pushing back his agitation, stepped over to steady the president. He helped Wilson sit.

When the hacking subsided, the president slowly regained his breath. Smiling, he patted Joshua's arm. "Thank you, Barnes, for the song and the help. It's a splendid tune. Makes the heart leap up."

"Yes, sir. It did start to come back to me. Shall I get Admiral Grayson?"

Wilson stood a bit gingerly. "No, it was nothing. Grayson needn't know everything."

Eliza winced from the sun's glare off the gilt and mirrors of Angelina's Café. After an evening at the opera, it felt very early. Jamie, who had to stay at the hospital most nights, had insisted they meet at 7:30 so he could still make his mid-morning rounds. That meant she had to tiptoe out of the hotel suite while Violet slept.

Eliza couldn't help envying her daughter's talent for sleeping. Eliza woke three or four times most nights. Mornings usually arrived like a distant shore she had been swimming to for hours. She would feel a sort of relief that she didn't have to struggle with sleep any more. An appointment at 7:30 in the morning was completely uncivilized, but Jamie wanted to meet then, and she had come a long way to reconcile. No point arguing over smaller matters. Not now, anyhow.

She had learned—a bit late, to be sure—the dark side of her husband's level disposition. At first, she found his even demeanor irresistible after years of accommodating the extravagant personalities and egos of her own family, not to mention the theater world where she'd worked so long. But equanimity had its own risks. It took her years to figure out that when Jamie talked about something that was very important to him, he looked and sounded very much as he did when saying something he cared little about. Perhaps a shrewder woman could perceive some telltale sign of the different intensity of his feelings, but Eliza still struggled to sort him out. She had misjudged his preferences all too often. It seemed such a basic aptitude, one that should have been natural in any loving marriage, or at least one she should have developed in nearly twenty years with the same man. Yet she had not. She found him as inscrutable now as in their first year of marriage.

Through her recent lonely days in New York, she had resolved to address the problem directly. She would simply humor him when at all possible, whether his preference turned out to be based on whimsy or passion. She applied that resolve to this request to see her at 7:30. A man could do worse things than insist on seeing her.

Listening to Eliza's clumsy French, the hostess looked severe. She swiftly walked to a table in the rear of the café, where Fraser rose to greet Eliza. She was glad he wore the dark blue double-breasted with the gray stripe. It made him look like a distinguished Englishman, not another stodgy American with a vest straining to cover an ample middle. Because he'd lost weight in France, the suit fit well.

After ordering the obligatory hot chocolate and croissants—Angelina's specialties—Eliza described the Verdi opera of the night before. Jamie started to speak, then stopped. She offered an opinion on the soprano, who Violet had much admired. Jamie started to speak again. He stopped again. She decided against filling the silence.

He cleared his throat, an almost comic rendition of a man with some heavy burden to disclose. "Eliza, you remember Speed Cook? From many years ago?"

"How could I forget him? That man nearly ruined our life together before it started. The lies he printed! Thank God no one believed him."

"I never supported what he wrote, you know that. But neither were they lies."

Eliza took a breath. She wasn't prepared for this. "Jamie, why must we go over this? Do you enjoy punishing me?"

"No, no, that's not what this is about. Let me start again. Speed's here in Paris."

She sat back. "Ah, he wants money again. He can hardly think we'll pay him off again so many years later."

"Eliza, that's hardly fair. He's never asked me for a dime."

"Might I remind you of your investment in that terrible newspaper of his. You don't owe him anything. Nothing at all."

"That's not true. You know it's not true."

The waitress arrived with their order. With a sure feel for the moods of her customers, she set the items down as though mines lay beneath the table's surface. The interruption helped reduce the tension.

"So," Eliza began again, taking a croissant from wicker basket, "what does he want?"

The pastry was warm. It smelled of butter as she pulled it apart.

Fraser took his time with the story, explaining Joshua's military record, his acquittal, the inexplicable reversal by the commanding general. He floundered over the right description of how Allen Dulles arranged for the army to misplace Joshua, and then Joshua's current situation. "You see," he finished, "the situation is quite desperate. I must help them."

Eliza took her time responding. The world wouldn't come to an end, she decided, if she had another croissant. "This has to have been going on with you and the Cooks for, what, a month?" She looked up from her roll.

He nodded over his own pastry.

"When were you going to tell me about it?"

He made a small face. "I thought the subject might be uncomfortable for you. Both because of the past, and because…well, I didn't know how things were going to go when you arrived."

She sharpened her look. "Does this, you telling me now, does it mean it's gone well or badly since I arrived?"

"It's been splendid. You've been splendid." He assumed the earnest look she could remember from their first days together. "I want there to be no secrets between us."

Eliza lifted her cup of chocolate and held it with both hands. "How can you trust someone so…different from us?"

"You mean because he's a Negro?"

"Not only that. Everything about him. What do you really know about him?"

"I know him. Oh, I haven't spent so much time with him, and not for a long time, but in the days like the ones we shared, you get to know someone, what's inside them. Our worlds haven't been so very different.

He grew up in the next town over from Cadiz." He pursed his lips. "Sometimes you just know."

She put the cup down. "So, it doesn't matter what I say. You're going to risk a great deal for this man and his son."

"Eliza." He put his hand on hers. "He's not 'this man.' He saved my life."

"My question was, are you going to be taking more risks?"

"I expect so. But I'll be sure that nothing touches you or Violet, of course."

Eliza broke in briskly, shifting her silverware to avoid looking at him. "Stop it, Jamie. Just stop it." She gave him a stern look. "Anything that involves you involves Violet and me. I won't have it any other way. Don't you know that's why I'm here?"

His face wore a mooncalf look that no man his age should have.

She found it silly, though. Almost disarming. "Do you have more to tell me?"

"No, that's it."

"No paramour squirreled away in some remote arrondissement, pining for the return of her American lover? No godmother serving you fine pastries and all the comforts of home? You never answered that the other night."

He shook his head. "No." He smiled slightly. "I suppose I lack the imagination for such things."

"That's not terribly flattering, Major Fraser," she snapped.

His smile dissolved into confusion.

She liked having him a bit confused, but this was too easy. It always had been. She took a moment. Impatience, she reminded herself, is not a virtue. "I suppose I've allowed you to feel that way." She sighed. "This Speed Cook, it's odd how we seem wrapped up with him."

"He was there when we first met, that time at Creston Clarke's."

Eliza smiled. "You two were quite preposterous, pretending to be theatrical agents." She reached for Fraser's hand and squeezed it. "Have you missed him all these years? Have I kept you two apart?"

"So much kept us apart. Black and white. The business about your family. Then his newspaper went bust, which it had to. But I'm glad to know him again."

"I suppose I can try to like him, Jamie. I can't do more." She placed her napkin on the table. "Violet may wake up any time. She'll wonder where I am."

Waiting for the check after Eliza left, Fraser looked away from his reflection in the mirror. He didn't need to be reminded of his own aging and decay. Yet behind that receding hairline, beyond the pouches under his eyes and the deep lines carved on either side of his mouth, his spirit still could frisk like a six-year-old, then career like a sixteen-year-old, then sag like the man of sixty he would become all too soon.

Eliza had said she'd try to like Speed. Maybe she would try. Maybe she wouldn't. Married so long and he couldn't be sure. How could his feelings be so scrambled? He smiled at the waitress and nodded for the check. She ignored him.

Catching a glimpse of that smile in the mirror, he resolved to stop his endless woolgathering about Eliza. He was growing tired of himself. That was part of why he was glad to be working with Speed again. Speed didn't think himself into knots. He didn't wring those big, twisted hands in indecision. No, Speed got angry. Then he'd do something, say something, make something happen.

And so would Fraser.

TWENTY-ONE

C ook had known a few saloons in ten years as an itinerant baseball player and another two decades banging around the world. He had certain expectations about them, including that Monday nights were slow.

But that rule didn't apply to the Hotel Crillon bar during the peace conference that seemed destined never to end, like some song where the composer couldn't figure out the final chord so just kept chasing the notes around the page. Indeed, the peace conference reminded him of something from a class he took in college, one of the few where he didn't daydream about baseball or girls. Some philosopher came up with this idea that if you travel half the distance to your destination, then half the remaining distance, then another half, you'll never actually reach it. It was a paradox, that's what they called it. It seemed to describe the peace conference, daily halving the distance to its target of a final treaty, yet never actually reaching it. Day after day, as the negotiators met in secret, the Crillon filled with ever more feverish journalists and expert advisers, supplicants and hustlers, and dubious-looking hangers-on who fell into no obvious category other than that of men who looked dubious. Happily for the Crillon's owners, they were all thirsty.

Behind the bar, Cook never hurried. Haste would set the wrong tone. With its dark wood and low light, this bar was a deluxe joint, not for the shot-and-a-beer crowd. Its leather chairs could accommodate drinkers of the most generous pretensions. When Fraser walked in and took a position at the near end of the bar, Cook didn't speed up. Fraser had nearly emptied the nut dish before Cook came by.

"Say, barkeep," Fraser said with a smile, "I hear you've got a new cocktail here, called a boxcar?"

Cook's face showed no expression. "Do you mean the sidecar, sir?"

"Perhaps I do." They shook hands. While Cook mixed the drink, Fraser eyed the three brazil nuts left in the dish. They looked like rocks. He decided against them. A group of three next to him spoke intensely in what sounded like Spanish. He tried to eavesdrop, but could make no sense of their talk.

"Don't even try," Cook said has he slid the drink in front of Fraser. "It's Portuguese. Can't make hide nor hair of it. I think they're planning to buy Rio de Janeiro when they go home, after they peddle some bogus Brazilian bonds to a lot of French suckers." He picked up the bills Fraser had left on the bar, then handed his change back to him. Fraser dropped the coins on the bar as a tip. The room key, which Cook had slipped to him with the coins, went into his trousers pocket.

"Lively night?" Fraser said.

"They all come here." Cook started rinsing glasses in a sink under the bar. He had a good view of the lobby from that spot. He added, his voice covered by the enthusiastic Brazilians, "The Dulles boys went up an hour ago. Haven't seen them since. Could be anywhere in the building."

"Well, I can't hang around tonight. I've got six a.m. rounds at the hospital."

"You heard about Thursday?"

Fraser shook his head.

"May Day. Lots of chatter about it. The unions, the Bolsheviks, the anarchists, they're all planning some big whoop-de-do. You know, they couldn't raise hell during the war without getting shot, so they're itching to do it now. I hear it may get rough."

"Sounds like that would be a good time for my project." Cook nodded. "Maybe Joshua could arrange to make some report to Dulles the day before, make sure I find something good in Dulles' papers? Or maybe he could give Dulles something that he shouldn't have, then I find that."

"I'll mention it to him." Cook looked over Fraser's shoulder. "Or you can tell him yourself."

Joshua approached them, still in his valet suit. "Another rush, Major Fraser. Admiral Grayson again, at the residence."

"What is it?"

"Don't exactly know, but there's some grim faces back there."

Standing to leave, Fraser said to Cook, "Let me know anything you hear about Thursday. I'll shoot for it."

Grayson met Fraser in the third-floor corridor. He looked tense and tired. "I suspect," he began, "it's some recurrence of the flu."

Fraser adopted a stern look. "From what I've read in the newspapers, the president hasn't even begun to take the sort of rest that I prescribed, the sort of rest that's crucial for recovery."

"Look here, Fraser," Grayson snapped, "Woodrow Wilson is not some infantryman from Des Moines who can go off and rest in a hospital for weeks on end. Need I remind you who he is and what he's trying to achieve right now?"

Fraser choked back a retort about how dead men can't achieve anything at all. Grayson spun and led him into the president's room.

A nurse rose from the president's bedside, making room for Fraser. Mrs. Wilson remained in her chair on the other side of the bed. Wilson was propped half-upright on a stack of pillows. His skin was gray, his breathing labored, his eyes closed behind his glasses.

Taking his pulse, Fraser asked, "Can you tell me, sir, what happened?"

Wilson opened his eyes. "Ah, Doctor. You will form the impression that I'm frail."

"The strongest fall sick, sir. Did this spell come upon you as it did last time?"

"No, not at all." Wilson's voice was hoarse. He struggled to clear it. "I couldn't hold my pen. My hand, you know. It's happened before, years ago. I can write with either hand, well enough, anyway. It's sort of a parlor trick."

Fraser concentrated on his patient's voice and appearance.

"This time, I lost some vision."

"Which eye?"

"The left." He pointed with his right hand.

"How is it now, the vision?"

"The same. I can see you, and of course my sweet Edith." He smiled slightly.

"And you could walk? No limping?"

Wilson took a breath. "Yes, though I was awfully tired. Really too tired to walk."

Fraser completed the examination with one-word instructions to the patient. His concern deepened and his anger with Grayson mounted.

When he stood up and exhaled noisily, Wilson asked, "Your verdict is?"

Fraser was forming a sentence in his mind when Grayson spoke. "Please, Mr. President. Allow me to consult with Dr. Fraser. We'll be back in a moment."

Following Grayson out of the room, Fraser thought the top of his head might blow off. When Grayson closed the door behind them, he burst out. "If that's the flu, I'm the queen of Sheba. You must know the last wave of flu has subsided throughout the city. And you also must know that the president has suffered a stroke, very likely not his first. From all appearances, this may be a damaging one." When Grayson said nothing, he added, "He's very sick."

For a moment, Grayson avoided Fraser's eyes. He looked alarmed. Then he drew himself up. He clasped his hands behind his back and looked Fraser in the face. "You don't know Mr. Wilson's constitution as I do. I've treated him for many years. He's not showing symptoms of a stroke, but rather a recurrence of flu. I'm shocked, and not a little disappointed, that you don't see it."

"Good God, Grayson, a medical student would recognize this as a stroke. You must tell the patient the truth. He needs rest, a great deal of it, and we have no idea the effect this episode will have on his faculties. His judgment, his personality, they could be altered. If they are, heaven help us and the nation."

"You misunderstand, Major Fraser, the role of being physician to the president."

Fraser could think of nothing to say that he hadn't already said. Hitting Grayson probably wouldn't help the president.

"Barnes!" Grayson called to Joshua, who was standing at the head of the staircase, awaiting any assignment. "Please arrange a car to deliver Dr. Fraser wherever he needs to be next." With a sharp nod at Fraser, Grayson stepped back into Wilson's room and closed the door behind him.

Fraser considered following him into the room and speaking directly to Wilson, but decided against it. He had been summoned to consult with Grayson, not to take charge of the president's care. And the president must be able to tell that this bout was nothing like the flu he had suffered weeks before. And even if he was too sick to realize that, then certainly Mrs. Wilson must. Very likely Grayson's misdiagnosis was exactly what the Wilsons wanted. Well, Fraser would be no part of it.

Frustrated, Fraser began to walk toward Joshua. As he reached the end of the corridor, the younger man unexpectedly lifted a tray holding a pitcher, then turned quickly and collided with Fraser, spilling water over both of them.

"Son of a bitch!" Fraser exploded.

Joshua grabbed a towel from a nearby table and began to dab at Fraser's suit. He insisted that they step into a side room where he could dry Fraser's jacket and trousers.

Behind the closed door, Fraser continued to sputter. "For Christ's sake, Joshua, there had to be another way to pull me aside. I'm drenched." He wrenched the towel from Joshua's hand so he could use it himself.

"Sorry. This is what came to mind."

"So you heard?"

"I figure they could hear you out on the street."

"And you understood."

"Not real complicated, is it?"

Fraser gave the towel back. "Use it on yourself. You're as wet as I am."

"The thing is, do I tell this to Dulles? To Boucher? I'm supposed to see both of them tonight, and this is real dynamite."

Fraser took a breath. "I don't know." He tried to think. "Oh, hell, no, you can't tell them, certainly not Boucher." He drew his lips into a tight line. His trousers felt clammy against his skin. "Based on what Grayson says, I suppose we have to assume that the president wants to conceal his true condition. And you"—he pointed his finger at Joshua—"work for the president."

"I work for a lot of people. And even if I work for him, is he in his right mind? Should his instructions be followed?"

"Right." Fraser leaned back against the door frame. "Right. I'm sorry. I don't know how I can help you with that."

"How about you -- what are you going to say to Boucher? You work for the president, too, as a soldier."

Fraser pulled his trousers away from his skin. "Damned if I know." He made a quick face. "Oh, I suppose I do know. I certainly won't bring it up."

"And if Boucher does?"

"I suppose I'll lie. It's quite the fashion right now."

Two men began to rise from a table of four in the dining room of the Hotel Majestic, where the British delegation was headquartered. One turned to the smaller of two men who remained seated. Holding out his hand, he said, "I'm afraid my conversation didn't interest you much."

Colonel Lawrence ignored the outstretched hand and replied in a low voice. "It didn't interest me at all."

The other seated man, solidly built and jowly, tried to cover the moment by bidding a matey farewell to those departing. When they were gone, he finished the champagne in his glass and nodded to a nearby waiter for more. He turned a bemused look on Lawrence. "Throwing over that career in diplomacy, are we?"

Lawrence leaned forward on his elbows. "Mr. Churchill, nothing good will come of this diplomacy here in Paris. Not for Palestine or for Arabia or for Britain."

"How can you be so certain? Most of the known universe is here in Paris, all expecting great things of this conference."

"President Wilson, I'm afraid, is like an amiable host, endlessly prattling on about the League of Nations while the guests pilfer the silver. And the PM, well, he's simply unable to focus on anything beyond the next edition of the *Times*."

"You're most unfair," Winston Churchill said. "Mr. Lloyd George often plans his strategies so they anticipate several consecutive editions of the newspapers."

Lawrence leaned even further forward. "You must understand. Clemenceau is irresistible, a force of nature. Bullets in flight turn away from him in terror."

Churchill took a moment to light a long, fat cigar, then spoke again. "What do you wish me to do? Mr. Lloyd George is my leader. I am but a modest Minister of War for a nation no longer at war."

Lawrence hated the cigar smoke. He tried to ignore it. "Get him to stall. He must delay. He's very good at that. He can stop and tie his shoelaces, go out for a drink of water, or call in sick with indigestion. Mark my words, Churchill. No wise agreements will be reached here. Arabs, Jews, British, all will be better served by agreements reached somewhere else. Anywhere else. We must cut our losses."

Churchill held his cigar out and stared out into the dining room. "The game, Colonel, is over Mosul and its oil fields. The Royal Navy must have them. It would be frightful to watch them fall into French hands."

"To block the French, we can use the Americans."

"Ah, the Americans," Churchill said. "My mother's people." He puffed on his cigar, then picked a piece of tobacco off his tongue. "They can seem innocent at first blush, but it's a tiresome ruse. They know rather too well what to do with oil fields."

Lawrence shrugged. "But don't you see, the Americans' interest would be strictly commercial—they wouldn't disturb us politically, nor get in Prince Faisal's way."

"If you're serious about this, Lawrence, you must be able to solve this equation. How can we help the Americans just enough in this business to make it worth their while to stand with us, while setting up Feisal and our Jewish friends?" He placed the cigar back in his mouth and waved for the bill. "That's what you must identify. The PM has been extremely good on this issue. He grasps that we must have those oilfields. And you may be assured that I will be watching very closely to make sure that the British position doesn't weaken."

TWENTY-TWO

W ith the Metro closed for the May Day demonstrations, Fraser hired a taxi to take him to the Crillon. The taxi's progress stalled more than a mile from the hotel, the streets choked with excited people eager to make their voices heard after four years of compelled patriotism. Fraser paid the driver and set off on foot.

For the first several blocks, the demonstrators seemed cheerful, more like springtime revelers heading to a maypole dance than proletarians seething with resentment over the class struggle. He passed a group of smiling men who were pinning flowers on each other's lapels. The spirit rivaled that of the day in December, four months before, when Paris greeted President Wilson.

The mood began to shift as Fraser neared the Place de la Concorde. There were fewer women and no children at all. The faces looked harder. Strides seemed more determined. Some men carried wooden clubs poorly concealed in sleeves or inside waistbands. Fraser wondered what other weapons nestled under jackets and coats, or chafed legs inside boots. He shifted his leather attaché case, which he had slung over his shoulder, so it rested against the front of his body. Then he casually

149

draped his arm across it, hoping to frustrate anyone thinking to pluck it off his shoulder.

Flags, large ones, waved above the sea of heads. Black for anarchism. Red for socialism. A few French tricolors. The flagstaffs would be good weapons in brawls like the ones that were flaring in Germany and so many other countries. Voices shouted out slogans that sank, indistinct, into the crowd's rising roar. Gendarmes stood anxiously in pairs at every corner.

Looking down cross streets, Fraser could see companies of soldiers formed in ranks. At other streets, nervous cavalry horses stood in ragged lines, stamping and snorting, their muscles twitching.

He now had to weave around groups that listened to angry soapbox speakers. Chants welled up, staking out martial rhythms. Fraser realized his uniform would provide little protection when a melee broke out. A uniform might even attract violence from these demonstrators.

A chant began to dominate the crowd, one he could make out. "Down with the government! Down with the government." Just two blocks ahead, the street spilled into the plaza. He brushed against shoulders as he squeezed through the crowd, nodding and keeping a mild expression on his face. With a last lunge, turning sideways, he made it to the Crillon's side entrance. He tried the handle, but it was locked. He shook the handle. That didn't help. He pounded on the door. There must be someone on the other side. No response.

The crowd was a solid mass between him and the plaza. There was nothing to do but push. Muttering "Pardon" and "*excusez-moi*" as an incantation, he started the effort. His progress was slow. At the corner of the hotel, he could see that the demonstrators had surged around the captured German howitzers that stood in phalanx on the immense square. The chant had died out, overcome by a deep, angry din. Individual cries bounced over it all. The roar washed over him then receded, like the ocean beating against a shore. Even voices close to him dissolved in the welter of sound. Cavalry was massing at the plaza's western end, to the left of the Crillon, at the Champs-Élysées. Those horses were restless, too. Their helmeted riders, headgear molded into a forward-leaning crest, kept their eyes forward, their faces blank.

Fraser's heart began to pound. Then his ears did. He couldn't look away.

A cry cut through the uproar, clear and ringing, though individual words flew by. The troopers drew their sabers. They shouldered the weapons. Fraser turned. With new urgency, he pushed toward the hotel's front. Demonstrators flowed past him in the other direction, away from the cavalry. He snatched a glance. The line of horses was advancing. With a final heave, he reached the Crillon entrance, which was ringed by uniformed bellmen. Here, his American army uniform worked. Two bellmen made room for him to pass. He hurried up the steps into the lobby.

The eerie quiet inside was unsettling. He straightened his uniform and checked that Violet's camera was intact. Cook was leaning in the doorway to the bar, which was empty behind him. He gave a slight shrug in Fraser's direction. Fraser strode briskly past him, heading for the rear of the hotel where the public restrooms were. He planned to take the rear stairs to Dulles' room on the fourth floor.

Lansing and his nephews each stood before a different window that overlooked the Place de la Concorde.

"My God, Foster," Allen called to his brother. "Look at those splendid fellows. It's rather like watching the Princeton line as it marches down the field against Yale."

"Yes, but Princeton doesn't use swords."

"More's the pity. Then again, Yale doesn't use clubs and rocks, though they doubtless would if they could get away with it."

Lansing cleared his throat but kept his eyes on the spectacle below. The troopers were swinging their heavy sabers, crashing them down on the demonstrators. For the most part, they used the flats of the swords against heads. The demonstrators had retreated fifty yards or so. Now they were so compressed they had nowhere to go.

"If you boys would abandon your schoolboy comparisons," Lansing said, "you might take note of the immense historical moment before you.

There"—he held his arms out, his voice sinking to a sepulchral level —"writhes the animal that threatens civilization, this beast of revolution, long-toothed and bloody." He shook his head. "It has fed on the credulous and the feebleminded in Russia and Hungary. In the streets of Germany, in Egypt. Even in China. Everywhere, fools are on fire with this hateful philosophy of overturning the world, putting those on the bottom on the top. It's a form of madness."

"Uncle," Allen said with a wry smile, "aren't you being a bit melodramatic? This is France. Every time they have a war with Germany they finish it off with a dust-up among themselves."

"Wait until this beast slinks into New York and St. Louis. You may no longer find me melodramatic."

"Look!" Foster pointed down at the plaza.

The cavalry's advance had stalled. Some horses shied and reared. The troopers, many shouting at once, withdrew. They reformed their line. They started again at a brisker pace, swinging their sabers in a more determined manner, crashing against the wall of bodies. Many demonstrators turned and tried to flee, only to find themselves trapped. Some fell and slipped from sight, pinned to the unforgiving stones. Others fought back, swinging clubs and heavy tools against the troopers, grabbing at their legs to drag them down. Those who fell disappeared under the many-limbed creature writhing on the plaza. Riderless horses, eyes wild, screamed and sprinted toward the Champs-Élysées.

When shots rang out, the crowd roar grew, fueled with fear and rage. The cavalry reformed its line, advanced again.

Allen, transfixed by the struggle, pulled out his pipe and tobacco pouch. "Rats." He gave the pouch an irritated glance. Empty. He walked to the door to the corridor. "Be back in a jiff," he called over his shoulder. "Just getting tobacco."

"For heaven's sake, Allie," Lansing said without taking his eyes from the plaza. "Have a cigar if you must smoke. This is history unfolding before us."

"I've been watching history unfold for the last four months, and a depressing spectacle it is. Won't be a moment."

TWENTY-THREE

F raser stopped to catch his breath at the fourth floor landing. The stress and long hours at the hospital had taken some pounds off his middle, but they hadn't done much for his stamina. Or his nerves.

When his chest stopped heaving, he peered into the hotel corridor. Cook had sketched a layout of the hotel for him. Dulles' room, Number 471, was on the back side, around the corner from the stairwell. A suitably inconspicuous location for a spy, an apparently junior functionary like Dulles. The corridor seemed deserted. With the demonstration lapping the sides of the building, most of the American staffers should have sought quieter quarters for the day. He was definitely hoping Allen Dulles had. To get to Number 471, he would have to turn one corner from the stairwell, a total distance of maybe forty feet. Thirteen strides? He took a breath and fingered the room key in his pocket. He stole another look into the corridor, checking both directions. He stepped out.

As Fraser rounded the corner, the door to Number 471 swung open. Dulles emerged from the room, then reached back to check the lock behind him. A startle reflex caused a hitch in Fraser's stride. Then he picked up again. Dulles looked up as Fraser approached. The younger man smiled.

"Major Fraser, you're on the wrong side of the building if you want to see the excitement."

Fraser stopped, straining to keep the panic in his mind from contorting his face or clotting his voice. He tried for a befuddled look. "Ah, Mr. Dulles." He looked up and down the corridor. "Say, I was looking for Major Barrett. We were to meet here in the Crillon, but he wasn't downstairs. And with the staff out defending against the unwashed hordes, I can't find anyone who knows his room number."

"Barrett? Barrett?" Dulles cocked a hip and looked off reflectively. "Can't place him."

"He's a gray-headed fellow, an old duffer like me. He's been detailed from the medical corps to Mr. Hoover's program, the food relief."

"Hoover, yes, good man, doing the Lord's work. Although those surly louts out on the plaza could make a fellow swear off feeding the hungry for the foreseeable future." Dulles looked curious. "You were meeting today? Surely you knew that this was the day for Mother France to eat her young."

Fraser was growing comfortable with his lie. He decided to be garrulous, a harmless doctor beyond his best years. "That was certainly foolish. May Day isn't such a commotion back home. I need his advice on the medical corps demobilization, you know, how do we all get home when the peace is signed—bringing the Army of Occupation back from the Rhine? I guess he's been diverted by the crowds."

Dulles grinned. "You've got ample time for your planning, as I'm beginning to wonder whether the treaty will be signed in my lifetime. Why don't you come watch the festivities with us? Uncle Bert has a front-row pew, and you don't want to be out on the plaza just now."

Seeing little alternative, Fraser agreed. Why the devil, he wondered, had Speed shrugged when Fraser passed through the lobby? If Cook knew Dulles was in the building, a shrug sure didn't get that message across.

Moments after Fraser and Dulles strode down the hall together, a small figure in British khaki emerged from a room across from No. 471.

He moved quickly and resolutely. With a room key, he let himself into Dulles' room and quietly closed the door behind him. Once inside, his bright blue eyes lit on the papers strewn on the desk. He began to sift through them, sorting them into piles. The pile closest to him held papers dealing with Syria, Palestine, and the petroleum of Mesopotamia. There were more than he had dared to hope.

The arrival of Fraser and Allen Dulles drew little attention in the office of the Secretary of State, as all eyes were trained on the violence on the plaza. Fraser and Allen stood before the room's third window.

"The shooting's stopped," Lansing said. He pointed to his left. "You can see there, the army seems to have matters in hand."

For more than a minute, the four men watched without remark. The struggle was now at the plaza's eastern end. Horses and sabers, wielded with a furious discipline, were driving the demonstrators back into the streets of the city. Fraser couldn't make out individuals in the writhing mass that retreated from the Crillon. Troop trucks idled before the hotel, loading up with arrested demonstrators who shouted defiance despite bound hands and bleeding skulls. A few scrambled over the German howitzers, leaping from one to the other in a perilous fashion that no sane person would try. Some figures, in random groups around the plaza, crouched over bodies on the ground. Not far from the hotel, two bodies lay unattended.

Fraser had seen street violence, once a race riot nearly twenty years before. At least this clash grew out of political disagreements over principles and values, not raw prejudice and hatred. The result, though, was depressingly similar. Broken heads. Broken bodies.

"Gentlemen," Fraser said suddenly, "I'm a physician. I must go down and offer whatever aid I can provide."

Allen Dulles looked up. "Of course you must," he said, then gave a small smile. "Please give my regards to your charming daughter. And when you get out there on the plaza, do see to the injured troopers first. They are, after all, playing for our side."

Mumbling insincere apologies for his abrupt departure, Fraser left. Once free of the Dulles clan, he dove into a stairwell. He reclimbed two flights of stairs, then again paused to gather his breath and wits.

At No. 471, he used the key to let himself in and began to pull Violet's camera from his case. Then he froze.

"For heaven's sake," said the small man standing at the desk, glancing over his shoulder. "Close the door behind you or we'll have the whole city in here."

Fraser did as instructed.

As the man returned his attention to the papers on the desk, he said, "Clever, you. You must have ditched Dulles and doubled back. As you see," he airily waved with one hand, "I caught a ride on your coattails. I am shocked, though, at this hotel's inability to protect its room keys. I wonder who else has one."

Fraser still couldn't move. "Colonel Lawrence?"

This caused Lawrence to twist toward Fraser. "Do I know you?" He squinted. "I have no memory for faces. You will have to tell me who you are, though I would understand if you would prefer not to, in view of the…situation." The airy wave again. He returned to the papers on the desk.

"I'm Major James Fraser, a doctor. I looked at your friend, Sykes, some weeks ago, when he was ill."

Lawrence didn't look up. "Unspeakable, that." He continued to sift papers. "Let's not speak of it." He turned back to Fraser. "Please don't just stand there gawking. We're both here on secret missions. Bloody awkward, eh?"

Fraser remained silent.

"I suggest cooperation, or at least mutual discretion."

Fraser nodded.

"Fine. You look at that lot." Lawrence pointed to a pile of papers on a divan across from the bed. "I'll finish with these." His attention back on his work, he continued. "I'm looking for connections between England's petroleum lords and the American government…or the English government, or the French government, for that matter. Anything concerned with American attitudes toward an independent Arab nation."

Fraser, beginning to move toward the divan, said nothing. He thought he had planned this excursion carefully, but this was the second unexpected development. He never imagined encountering a fellow intruder, far less one willing to make common cause. Nothing to do about it now. He couldn't allow himself to think about the risks he was taking, how inexplicable the current situation was. Just do what he came for and leave.

"Excellent," Lawrence said. "I infer from your silence that you're bored by the subjects of interest to me. And what do you seek?"

Fraser didn't feel ready to answer that question.

Lawrence continued. "I'm willing to keep an eye out for what you need, get us both out of here more quickly, which would be to the advantage of us both."

Fraser made up his mind as he picked up the papers on the divan. "Dulles may have an agent on the staff of the president's residence, though that may be hard to credit—"

"You mean the black boy? I saw something about it in that pile." He gestured at another group of papers in the desk chair. "Slightly surprising, that."

Fraser moved to that pile and looked desperately for any reference to Sergeant Joshua Cook. He found a memorandum to the file that mentioned neither Joshua nor John Barnes, but did refer to him by position and description. He positioned the paper on a window sill, then turned on a lamp. He pulled the camera out.

Lawrence had finished the papers on the desk. "What a very wise precaution. I feel rather stupid not to have thought of it. This is not my ordinary run of business. Perhaps you would return the favor by taking photos of the pages I need?" When Fraser hesitated, Lawrence added, "Major, we can cause each other great misery or not. I suggest not."

Fraser examined the camera and tried to recall Violet's instructions on how to operate it. "Of course, Colonel. Just bring them over here to the light."

TWENTY-FOUR

F raser was accustomed to seeing soldiers in Paris. They came from Britain and Australia and America and France, from Africa and Asia. Soldiers on leave, still wearing helmets and muddy boots, tended to approach the city with a mixture of awe and anticipation. Moving in small groups or alone, most had read or heard about Paris but never expected to see it. After a quick look at the Eiffel Tower, most went in search of something to take their minds off the dangers they soon would return to. Staff officers, assigned to Paris for the duration, tended to be conspicuous for their self-importance. Occasionally Fraser saw a full unit on the march or a cavalry contingent mounted and spurred, or even a convoy of trucks or a few of the new tanks that looked so terrifying but too often broke down.

With the war over, the soldiers on the streets were all French. From the back seat of a taxi, he saw full infantry units installed deep into neighborhoods, lined up for evening meals at street-corner field kitchens. This was an occupying army. It spoke the same tongue as those it occupied. It shared the history of the people who hurried past them nervously. But it still was an occupying army.

He had been lucky to find a taxi so soon after the fighting, though once more he had to walk the last mile to his destination, a café in Montmartre. The fighting never reached the volatile neighborhood. Rather, Montmartre had carried the political struggle to the rest of the city. Local residents faced careful scrutiny and close questioning at a police checkpoint, but Fraser, on foot, was waved through, his uniform working its magic. A group of sullen young men sat on a curb, watched by several soldiers who looked tense.

For Speed, who sought anonymity, Montmartre had been a natural perch. The neighborhood had long been a magnet for the discontented of Paris, of France, of the world. Rents were low. People came and went at irregular times. Neighbors, assuming checkered pasts, asked few questions. The residents mistrusted, misled, and sometimes actively resisted any government agent. Over almost four months—ever since Joshua escaped from the army—Cook had lived at seven different addresses in the neighborhood, moving when faces seemed too familiar, when vacant nods of greeting threatened to evolve into words.

Fraser found Speed and Joshua in a scruffy café several doors down from the Place Pigalle. Their table, with a jug of red wine and three glasses, was an island of calm amid shouts and arguments. Some faces displayed fresh bruises and cuts, presumably earned during the unpleasantness at the Place de la Concorde. The Cooks seemed to be virtually the only quiet occupants of the room. Father and son were angled so they didn't look at each other. Neither looked happy to be there.

Cook poured Fraser a glass of wine. They toasted the evening, though Joshua lifted his glass halfheartedly. Fraser asked if Cook had developed the photos of Dulles' documents.

"Sure did," Cook said. "I could've used one of those gas masks in that dark room at the *pharmacie*." He wrinkled his nose. "Those chemicals are something."

"Gas masks," Joshua muttered. "You've got no idea what you're talking about."

"Maybe not," Fraser said to Joshua with a smile, "none of us old folks does. But we're lucky that your father's many talents include developing photographs."

Cook waved aside the praise. "I never could afford to put many photos in that newspaper. Couldn't get out to take that many, anyway. That damned rag was pretty much a one-man band, you know. But photos sure did liven it up." He drank some wine and gazed at Fraser. "So I'm hoping there was a good reason for me to eat those fumes developing pictures of documents about oil in Mosul, wherever the Sam Hill that is."

Fraser smiled and poured himself a second glass of wine. He began to relax. The noise of the café reassured him, covering their conversation so it couldn't be heard even a foot away. He sat back and told the story of his burglary, abetted by Lawrence of Arabia. "And if Dulles truly didn't suspect anything funny was going on, our nation's spy business is in very shaky hands indeed."

Cook began to laugh. Even Joshua cracked a smile.

His father raised his glass again. "To shaky hands and honor among thieves!"

They drained their glasses. Cook waggled two fingers at a barmaid, ordering another jug.

"That Lawrence," Joshua said, "he sounds cool as a cucumber. Like his reputation."

"Don't I get any credit?" Fraser demanded.

"For what?" Cook laughed. "For doing what he told you?"

"What else was I supposed to do?"

Cook kept right on laughing. Joshua shook his head in bemusement at his aged companions.

"And why the hell didn't you let me know they were all still up there? What was with that shrug of the shoulders I got in the hotel lobby?"

"Now, hang on," Cook protested. "A shrug's a shrug, am I right? It means I don't the hell know. I'd been all over that hotel locking stuff down for the demonstration and I didn't know where anyone was. You're the one was so steamed up you thought my shrug meant the coast was clear." He smiled. "I'm glad you did. Turned out all right."

Fraser decided not to quibble. He wanted to talk about something else. "There's something on my mind about all this," he said. "I wonder if we might've just acquired a new partner, our British pal. What's to keep him from trying to use Joshua for his own purposes, now that he knows about him?"

His question vanquished the pleasant feelings around the table. Each man stared at his wine glass, feeling the beginnings of headaches.

"That Lawrence," Cook said softly. "He's a man gets talked about. Around the Crillon, I mean. I heard he isn't really part of the British delegation any more. Something about how they stripped him of his credentials and he's here in Paris on his own dime now."

Fraser made a face. "So why's he still here? He told me he's looking for connections between the oil business and the British government. But he's wearing the uniform of the British government. Spying on his own government? For the Arabs? For himself?"

"Might even remind a body," Cook said, "of Dulles sending Joshua to spy on his own president."

The three men lapsed back into rumination. Cook spoke again. "One thing I noticed in those photos I just did for him—couldn't help but read them—there's something going on with the Germans. Seems that Germany owned part of this Turkish Petroleum Company, which the British control now, though maybe there's still some Germans in it."

"Enemies on the battlefield and partners in business?" Fraser asked.

"Wouldn't be the first time, would it?"

Fraser frowned. "But where does Dulles fit in? They're his papers, even though he's not being all that careful with them. Does he want the US in on this oil deal or is he trying to stop it? Or squeeze in for his own slice?"

Joshua snorted. "You folks need to stop worrying about the wrong things. This is all swell about the Germans and the Turks and the British and the goddamned Hottentots, but how's this all going to end for me? I'm still reporting every couple of days to Dulles and to Colonel Boucher, and maybe now to this Lawrence, if he decides he wants to track me down."

"Actually," Fraser said, "Boucher hasn't been after me for a few days. It's been nice not to deal with him. What's he asking you?"

"How the president's doing, mostly—his health, you know, which is still touch and go. Boucher's not as interested in who's coming to the residence, not like Dulles is. I suppose Boucher knows that, anyway. He's got plenty of eyes watching the front door—from both sides of it."

"How much did you tell him about that business between me and Wilson and Grayson the other night?"

"Just that Wilson took sick again, which is the official statement anyway. The president's still going to those meetings with the other leaders, so they can see for themselves how sick he is."

Speed sat up a bit. "What business the other night?" After Joshua filled him in, he asked, "So how sick is the man?"

"He seems to bounce back pretty good, you know," Joshua said. "It's pretty surprising. One day he looks half dead. Next morning he's up singing hymns."

Fraser shook his head. "He's very sick, and the worst thing is, I don't think he appreciates how sick he is. That fool Grayson certainly isn't telling him."

Cook tapped his chin with a forefinger. "Does it affect his mind?"

"Sure could," Fraser said. "It's making me wonder about a lot of things. You see in the papers about China, where they're letting Japan keep this province the Germans bullied the Chinese out of a while back? They're giving this piece of China—no argument about it, it's part of China—to Japan. How could Wilson possibly think that was self-determination for the Chinese? It's straight-up land-grabbing, yet there's Wilson agreeing to it. He did something like that for the Italians, too, some piece of Serbia or something like that. Seems like he's junking every principle he sent us off to war to defend. Things like that make me worried."

Cook kept tapping his chin. "That's dynamite you're sitting on, Dr. Fraser. You're saying the American president doesn't have all his marbles. Imagine if the world knew about it."

Fraser shook his head. "I don't really know it, not for sure, and I can't tell the world what I suspect, even if I knew it for sure. He's my patient. I can't issue a public statement that any patient—much less the president of the United States—isn't in his right mind."

"Well," Cook cocked his head, "it's worth spending some thinking time on. We're looking to find something that Dulles wants to hush up, that he'll pay a price to hush up. You may be sitting on just that thing." He reached down to a bag under his chair, pulled a large envelope out, and tossed it on the table. "Those are for Lawrence. He doesn't get the one about Joshua. You look 'em over. See if you get any idea about something we can use for ourselves." He held up a second envelope. "I'll hang onto our set."

"You're keeping copies of Lawrence's photos?"

"Sure am. Right now we've got no idea what might work in this crazy business."

Wednesday morning, May 7, 1919

Wilson was standing at his usual window when Joshua brought his polished shoes into the dressing room. It was early but the blackbirds were there, right where they should be. He missed the cardinals of Washington. Such vivid colors, such noble heads. The blackbirds of Paris were dreary by comparison, but they didn't know that so they sang just the same. He missed Washington's redbud trees, too, their delicate lavender a soothing sign of soft weather ahead. Paris had magnolias to greet spring, but he always found their blossoms a bit excessive. He would be glad to get back home, back to afternoon drives in the country again. Grayson insisted the drives were essential for his health, but they had been quite impossible during the peace conference.

The president was traveling to Versailles that morning. They were to present the final version of the treaty to German diplomats who had been waiting impatiently to see the treaty's terms. His tail coat hung from the valet stand, under his white waistcoat.

Joshua thought that Wilson, standing in his shirtsleeves and cravat, looked gray, a bit thin, distracted. His eye twitch raced. It had been strong for several days. After placing the shoes next to the table, Joshua stood straight. "Beautiful day, sir. Can I get anything else for you?"

Wilson was slightly surprised to hear the voice, but didn't turn to it. "Barnes?"

"Yes, sir."

"Oh. No. Nothing now. Except maybe a good old Presbyterian sermon."

"Sir?"

"My father, you know, was a great man. A great man." Wilson looked back at Joshua, his expression wistful. "I'd give a good deal to hear him again, perhaps talking about the burdens of the civilized races. He was wonderful on that subject. He really felt that burden." The president walked to the table. He sat to put his shoes on. "Do you speak with your father, Barnes? Perhaps what I mean to ask is do you listen to him?"

Before Joshua could answer, Wilson said, "Of course you don't. I'm being foolish. Your father's back in New York. You told me that. When you next see him, when we get back to Washington, remember my advice. Listen to your father."

"Sir, does that mean you intend for me to return to Washington with you?"

"Of course. Even Mrs. Wilson agrees. We all think you've done fine." Wilson groaned slightly as he leaned to pick up his shoes. "Today's a very big day." He smiled at Joshua. "I will meet the dreaded Germans. And about bloody time, as Mr. Lloyd George would say."

After Wilson had stared into space for a time, Joshua said, "Can I give you a hand with those shoes?"

Wilson looked down at the shoe in his hand. "No. Thank you, Barnes."

Joshua left the room for the valet's station, an alcove off the rear corridor of the third floor. He needed to see to the president's laundry, then prepare his suit for the next day's events. Most of all he needed a cigarette. He opened the window along the corridor and lit up, holding the cigarette outside while leaning against the frame. After months of smoking them, he still didn't care much for a Gaulois, but he could afford them.

He was feeling jittery. They were delivering the peace treaty to the Germans, so the peace conference was starting its last lap. This arrangement with Wilson, one way or another, was going to end. That was all right with him. He no longer gloried in the constricted freedom he enjoyed as John Barnes. It wouldn't do. He recently remembered what

Frederick Douglass said about the life of a slave—that if he had a bad master, he wished only for a good one, but that if he had a good master, he wished for his freedom. In twentieth-century terms, Joshua had moved from Douglass' first category to the second one. He was out of prison. He had a good master, but he hadn't yet won his life back. Not even if he went back to America with Wilson, working as John Barnes, valet. He ached for that third category, freedom, but he still had no idea how to get there, or whether he'd end up back in the first category.

The old man had been right. Life as John Barnes wasn't good enough. The old man was right more than Joshua probably gave him credit for. Being Speed Cook's son had never been easy. The man was so big, so tough, so smart. So angry. How could his son not be a disappointment?

He thought about the time back in Steubenville when he and his friend Morris—cursed by his moon face to be called Lunchpail—were playing Custer and Indians. They couldn't have been more than eight years old.

Two older white boys came by and said they couldn't play that game, that Custer was white and had no nigger troops. Joshua had heard his father talk about the Negro soldiers out West, so he answered that there were lots of colored troops.

"Yeah," Lunchpail chimed in, "and they were too smart to get massacred like Custer."

They took the beating. Lunchpail went down easy and Joshua decided that was the better choice. They got off with a fat lip for Joshua and no visible marks on his friend, but the episode left them with an overpowering shame. Joshua didn't want to face his father. He said they should camp out near Echo Cave, a couple miles downriver.

It got so cold that night. When Lunchpail kept crying, they started to walk back through the moonless night. Soon Lunchpail turned his ankle. They slept in a pile of leaves, huddled together for warmth.

The walking was easier after the sun came up. In an hour, they hobbled into the yard of the hardscrabble Cook Hotel that rarely had guests.

Joshua's mother came tearing down the stairs. She screamed Joshua's name. She slapped him. Then she hugged him hard, spitting out scalding words through tears. Joshua blubbered the story out. He couldn't stop talking.

His father came home an hour later. He hadn't slept, looking for Joshua all night. His face was like a stone. Carrying an axe, he took Joshua into the woods behind the hotel. The man could split wood one-handed, five bulging fingers gripping the axe near the end. He handled it like a hatchet.

They stopped at a tree that was about forty feet high. His father said Joshua had to chop it down and make it fall north, safely away from their shed and chicken yard.

Joshua had split wood before, but he had never taken down a tree. He was eight. That first day, he chopped until a blister popped on each hand. Afraid to come home, he sat out next to the tree until it got dark, then slunk into the house.

His mother washed his hands. "Boy's hands are hurt," she said to his father.

In silent reply, his father lifted his two hands with their twisted and swollen fingers. His face was still stone.

His mother wrapped Joshua's hands in cloth for the second day. He chopped for another two hours, each swing getting more feeble. He had no idea how to make the tree fall in the right direction. When his father came by to watch him, Joshua asked how he could do it.

"You need to figure that out," his father said.

When Joshua went out to the tree on the third day, he could hear his parents arguing, which was something they didn't do. His father wasn't a man you argued with. You could work around him, but arguing didn't work.

A few minutes after the voices ended, his father arrived and took the axe. With what seemed like a single swing, he dropped the tree exactly where it was supposed to fall, then sat on the trunk. Suddenly his father's face was full of feeling.

Joshua was afraid.

In a low voice, his father said, "You listen to me now, son. You listen and remember."

Joshua nodded.

"You made some terrible decisions out there with your friend. One bad choice after another."

Joshua nodded.

"You can't do that."

Joshua nodded again.

"Colored people can't make bad decisions, not ever, not without paying a price." His father looked savage enough to tear up the forest with his bare hands. "Every decision you make, every one, it has to be a good one. D'you understand?"

Joshua nodded again, terrified by his father's urgency.

"That's how you're going to be better than your old man." His father's eyes bore into him. "You've got to be. I won't allow you not to be."

Joshua started bawling.

His father reached out and pulled him against his rough shirt. The shirt smelled of tobacco smoke from the crap game that went all night in the hotel's back room, of the horse that the Cooks used to pull their wagon, of his father's sweat.

Shaking his head, Joshua took a last drag on the Gaulois. He had to get the president's clothes in order. He and his father and Fraser, they'd been stumbling around in the dark for months, trying to make the right decisions. Through it all, Joshua had known that he was lucky, lucky that the old man was still big and tough and smart, and angry enough to take months out of his life to save his son. It was time for Joshua to take care of himself.

He stubbed out the cigarette on the window sill. It left a smudge. He'd have to get something to wash that off.

TWENTY-FIVE

Thursday, May 15, 1919

W ithout waiting for an answer to his knock, Allen Dulles entered the president's library with a bulky package under his arm. Lloyd George and Clemenceau stood near an open window. A warm breeze riffled the heavy, cream-colored curtains. Wilson sat near the window, his legs extended and crossed at the ankles. He was launching into a story, so Dulles waited near the door.

"So there's this colored fellow," the president said, "and he's found a gun and tried to pawn it as his own. The pawnbroker gets suspicious. He sneaks out of the back of the store and finds a policeman who arrests the man.

"The Negro's then hauled before the judge, who takes one look at him and asks, 'Don't you know that it's against the law to carry a gun in New York?'

"'Yassuh,' the darky says. 'I just found that out.'

"The judge then asks, 'And don't you know that it's also against the law to pawn an article that doesn't belong to you, something you just found?'

"'Yassuh,' comes again from the darky. 'I just found that out, too.'

"'So,' the judge asks, wagging his finger, 'what will you do if you ever find a gun like this in the future?'

"The darky thinks for a minute and says, 'I's be sure to pawn it in New Jersey, suh!'" Wilson showed his big teeth when he laughed.

The others smiled politely. Dulles stepped forward into the lull.

"Ah, Mr. Dulles," the president said. "Do pull the chairs back and place the map there on the floor. And please stay to make a record of our decisions."

Sinking to his knees on the carpet, Dulles took the package from under his arm and unfolded it carefully. He smoothed its folds so it lay flat.

The multicolor map of Europe and the Middle East, produced by the British Army's cartography office, measured about eight feet wide by six feet. For today's discussion, Dulles had used different colored inks to outline alternative borders for Yugoslavia, Poland, Hungary, and Austria. The yellow lines were the borders before the war began; red lines marked borders when the fighting stopped, as best anyone could figure out; the blue ones were the British proposal for a settlement; the brown lines sketched the French counterproposal. Labels pasted onto the map marked existing countries or nations that proposed to be born.

Dulles had mastered the rationale for each alternative settlement, though some could be explained only by the naked self-interest of one Big Power or by a small community's fear of being subject to stronger neighbors. Preparing the materials had meant a very late night, not to mention missing another soiree at Cromwell's chateau. He hated missing the party. Like the peace conference, Cromwell's revels could not go on forever.

"Mr. Dulles," Lloyd George exclaimed. His voice contained the rhythm of Welsh lyricism yet only a trace of that accent. "This looks like another baffling exercise in geographic nuance. I trust you are prepared to guide us."

Clemenceau pulled a chair over to the bottom edge of the map. "Perhaps," he said, "we might attempt something more intelligent than restoring colonies that were lost two thousand years ago, as we did for the Greeks."

Lloyd George tut-tutted in a way that no American could. "Did you see that Greece landed troops in Smyrna."

"Yes," Clemenceau answered, "but there is no report yet of where they left the wooden horse. Very cunning of them to conceal it." He tugged on the yellow gloves he used to protect the skin of his hands. "Really, Mr. Prime Minister," he scolded while peering down at the map. Gravity tugged his features and his mustache earthward. His somber expression was that of a schoolmaster reminding a bright pupil of something he should know. "This British preference for ancient claims is nothing but whimsy. The Jews must have Palestine. The Greeks acquire Smyrna. Yet you begrudge France its rights in the Lebanon and Syria, presumably because we have been there for the last fifty years and are actually there now. Our claim is far too strong to satisfy your scholars."

Dulles had pulled two chairs over to flank Clemenceau's. He walked to the top side of the map and knelt so he could point out landmarks, cities, and natural features for the decisions of the day.

"Monsieur Premier," Lloyd George said as he sat, "you have assured us that so far as France is concerned, all depends on the German borders, payments from Germany, and the disarmament of Germany. Having accommodated you on each of these points, even at the risk of sowing the seeds of a bitter German resentment, we discover that France's appetite for distant lands revives, more ravenous than ever. It is both shocking and disappointing, sir. Most disappointing."

Clemenceau turned his head to the British leader without changing his expression. "How can a man be shocked who has promised the same territory in the Near East to France, to Prince Feisal and his Arabs, to your Hebrew friends, to your own petroleum industry and Royal Navy, and to how many others? You will end up disappointing a great many people. But France will not be among the disappointed."

Wilson approached the map. "Gentlemen, gentlemen, perhaps we should get down to today's business. I believe we are back in the Carpathian Mountains, this time with Silesia." He knelt next to Dulles, grunting slightly as ligaments popped in both knees. "Mr. Dulles, would you be so good as to point out the choices before us?"

Friday Morning, May 16, 1919

Fraser knocked on the door of a nondescript office in a nondescript building in an anonymous neighborhood. In response to a shout from within, he entered. Colonel Boucher of the Deuxième Bureau sat at the far side of a nearly pristine desk. The Frenchman's bulk made the desk look like a toy. Leaning forward on his elbows, Boucher's arms seemed to reach across the entire desk. This was the first time Fraser had met him in an official setting.

"Ah, Major Fraser. Thank you for coming. Please sit."

Fraser selected the only empty chair in the room, a spindly straight-backed affair that would never support Boucher's bulk. He sat tentatively.

"You are enjoying our Paris springtime?"

"Thank you very much. Most of all, I'm enjoying a dwindling case-load at our hospital."

"Your patients recover? That is *formidable!*"

"Some recover, those who can. The others…"

"Ah, yes, *la guerre*. Generals should visit hospitals on the day before battle, rather than the day after. Perhaps then we might have less battles."

"Why did you ask me to come?"

"These reports we receive from you and your friend, Monsieur… Barnes, is it?"

Fraser nodded.

"We wish to end this arrangement. It is no longer necessary."

Fraser raised his eyebrows.

"The information, it was not so good. The peace conference, it begins to be finished. Monsieur Barnes, he may return to his life with no further concern for this office."

Fraser straightened. "Colonel, you can't do that. That's completely unfair."

"Ah, do you mean that you and Monsieur Barnes wish to continue reporting to the Deuxième Bureau?"

"That's not what I mean at all. As you well know, the one thing Monsieur Barnes cannot do is to return to his life. He's not John Barnes, but Sergeant Joshua Cook of the American Expeditionary Force. At considerable risk, he's been assisting you and your colleagues in order to gain French assistance in removing an unjust conviction against him. At considerable risk, I also have been meeting with you. The price for this assistance from both of us was clear from the start—that the French government would intercede with the United States to rehabilitate Sergeant Cook. You must do so now."

Boucher clucked. "Must? I *must* do it? I think that is not the way to say that. I *must* do what my superiors direct. Yes, those are things I must do. And that, Major Fraser, is what I am doing now. Monsieur Barnes and you helped us a little, yes. And we helped Monsieur Barnes very much. We did not reveal him to the American authorities so he has not been in the prison. That has been very good for him, has it not? And if Monsieur Barnes wishes to leave our country, we will cause him no problem. I make that pledge to you. Also very good for Monsieur Barnes. The Deuxième Bureau is not his enemy. It is not his friend. This is not what I would call a bad deal for Monsieur Barnes."

"I would call it a very bad deal. You know the risks he's taken to assist France. Right under the president's very nose. You owe him your help. That was your promise."

Boucher dropped his eyes to the single piece of paper on his desk. "By all means, Major Fraser, please tell Mr. Barnes to stop taking those risks, *tout de suite,* at least to stop taking them for France. And of course, we say *merci beaucoup* to a friend. We also say *bon chance.* That is what we say, and it is all we will say."

"This is outrageous." Fraser stood, heat rising from his face and neck. "You realize that Sergeant Cook and I are in a position to reveal how you have undermined the security of the American president, how you have betrayed the ally who saved France against the Germans. What do you think the response will be when that becomes public knowledge?"

Boucher stared at Fraser, then allowed a trace of a smile to show. "I think a few more newspapers may be sold. I think some speeches may be made. The dogs will bark, the caravan will move on." The colonel sat back reflectively. "I also think a few Frenchmen may wonder how this Boucher at the Deuxième Bureau was so clever that he placed an agent so close to the American president. No, he placed *two* agents so close to the American president. Perhaps they will think this Boucher should no longer be a mere colonel, but should be a general. It could be. Stranger things have happened." The Frenchman nodded toward the door. "Au revoir, Major Fraser."

"I shall take this to the premier."

"Bon chance, Major."

TWENTY-SIX

C ook's fist crashed down on the desk in Fraser's hospital office.
    Fraser didn't worry about the noise. It was late. Most of the offices were vacant, their occupants already demobilized and sent back home, a few sent to the Rhine Valley to care for the Army of Occupation. Every day patients left, one way or the other. Only three of the ten wards were still in use. In a few weeks, the U.S. Army would relinquish the hospital to the Paris authorities. Empty crates stood in the corner, waiting for him to start filling them with personal items for shipment home. Since he didn't really have any personal items, the crates stood neglected. If all went well, Fraser himself would soon board a ship across the ocean.

"These are some rotten bastards," Cook fumed.

"Yup."

"What about Clemenceau?"

"I've gone by his house the last two mornings, but he won't see me. I even tried to slip in with his gymnastics trainer. No soap. As far as Clemenceau's concerned, as far as the whole French government's concerned, we don't exist anymore."

"So much for America's first ally, Cook said. "So, it's down to Dulles, getting him to do something to get Joshua's conviction reversed."

"Not necessarily. Someone once told me there are always alternatives. You just have to think of them."

Cook sat back and waited.

"We could leave Joshua on the president's staff, let him go back to Washington with Wilson, then look for an opening there."

"Oh, come on, Jamie." Cook stood and began to pace. "That doesn't work. Who knows if Wilson even remembers saying Joshua can go back home with him, or if the butler or whoever's in charge back in Washington would accept him? And who knows if he could even get in with his phony identity. He doesn't have a passport or anything else that identifies him as John Barnes. He has no history as John Barnes. Dulles is the one who would control all that.

Even if we get over all those hurdles, all we've done is make him John Barnes, servant." He stopped at the window and looked out at the dark street. "Aurelia and I didn't raise that boy to be a servant. He's got a college degree. He's smart, people like him. He's got so much going for him. He can be somebody, somebody who matters in this world. One thing he's not going to do is shine white people's shoes all his life. There's nothing I won't do to stop that."

Fraser kneaded his temples with one hand and grimaced. "Okay, that makes it harder, but okay." He looked at Cook. "Let's think about what we have on Dulles. We've got that memo I took from his room. The more I think about it, the less I feel good about it. Dulles could say a million things to explain it away. He could claim he was just using Joshua to watch out for other spies breaking into Wilson's residence, that it was a countermeasure. Or that Joshua lied and fooled him about who he really was. Then, like Boucher, Dulles takes a bow for his splendid work in unearthing this dangerous escapee and wishes us good-bye and good luck."

Cook started to pace again. "Even if Dulles would be worried about the memo," he said, "why do we think a puppy like him can actually arrange to get Joshua's conviction reversed?" He stopped still and spoke to the wall in front of him. "Listen, Jamie, I can't get it out of my mind. What about the health information?"

"About Wilson? About him being sick?" Fraser made another face and shook his head. "If I do that, reveal a patient's private information, it means throwing in the towel as a doctor. It would be a total violation of the president's trust."

Cook leaned over the desk on his fists. "Joshua's looking at prison for years and years."

Fraser looked away, then back. "What about Lawrence?"

Cook snorted. He started pacing again.

"Think about what Lawrence was doing in Dulles' room," Fraser said. "He claimed he was looking for ties between the oil industry and his own government. The documents he photographed bear that out. But isn't he a wild card here? He certainly isn't acting for the British government. Maybe he's working for Prince Faisal, maybe just for himself."

"So? Where are you going with this?"

"Maybe we can throw in with him. Maybe together we can get more from Dulles."

"What does he care about Joshua? The black boy, he called him." Cook spat out the last sentence.

"Why did he help out the Arabs during the war? Why's he still helping out the Arabs, instead of his own people? The man likes underdogs. Or he doesn't like overdogs, which is close to the same thing."

"Okay, assume we persuade him that he should help us, or that we can help each other. How?"

"Out of this whole lousy war, name three heroes."

"Come on."

"You come on."

"Sergeant York. Maybe Eddie Rickenbacker. There's Henry Johnson, but he was just a black boy, so no one remembers him. Okay, fine. Lawrence is a big hero."

"Right," Fraser said. "The press, the reporters, the politicians, the whole world loves him. If he accuses the American government of doing something stupid, something wrong, the whole world will notice."

"Sounds pretty far-fetched." Cook sat down. His shoulders slumped. "Is that how desperate we are?"

The silence grew between them.

Finally, Fraser said, "We'll come up with something, Speed."

Cook sighed. "We sure don't have it yet. I keep feeling like there's something right in front of us, something a blind man could see, but we can't." He looked across the desk at Fraser. "This place seems empty. Everyone's going home. Your family still here?"

"They went up to Brussels on a tour to see the devastated regions. You know, everyone has to see just how awful it was."

"Sure. If we all see the ruins, then none of it will ever happen again."

"It can't hurt for people to understand what really happened."

Cook shook his head once. "It doesn't matter. The evil's inside us. Sometimes it comes out."

TWENTY-SEVEN

Monday morning, May 19, 1919

"It's a profoundly bad outcome for the Arabs." Lawrence barely moved his lips as he spoke, his voice low yet audible. His face showed no expression. "Clemenceau has absolutely hung Lloyd George out to dry. Just what you would expect. Do you know that that filthy frog actually changed some of the terms of the German treaty while it was being printed, without telling any of his so-called allies? There's nothing he won't do."

He and Fraser strolled among early morning bargain hunters at Les Halles, the fresh food market sometimes called the stomach of Paris. The stalls bristled with yellow and green asparagus stalks, carrots and potatoes still dusted with the soil that nurtured them, cheerfully leafy spinach, turnips with their glowering purple sheen. Fraser's eye snagged on the early strawberries, which made his mouth water, and the chard leaves with bright veins of yellow, pink, and purple. A jumble of races and ages, bags looped over their arms, poked and prodded the goods under the baleful glare of vendors still resentful about rising in the middle of the night to bring their produce to market.

Joshua and his father were in the next aisle over, pretending to examine vegetables while keeping an eye on Fraser and Lawrence. Without his Arab headdress and army uniform, Lawrence looked ordinary, though oddly proportioned. Fraser had slid into a tall man's slouch to avoid looming over the Englishman, who seemed as indifferent to his surroundings as he always did.

"How is it so bad, this deal?" Fraser asked.

Lawrence's reply was crisp. "Under the deal, France would grab Lebanon and Syria, with Damascus. France also grabs one-fourth of the Turkish Petroleum Company. France also builds the pipeline that gives it control over the marketing of all production of Turkish Petroleum. There's no point to having oil if you can't get it to market. Prince Faisal and his Arabs? They get precisely nothing."

"Nothing?"

Lawrence stopped to peer dubiously at an immense bin of mushrooms. It rose to a pinnacle of fungi that plainly made the Englishman uncomfortable. He resumed his stroll without comment. "No Arab nation. No Arab control over the oil. No oil money for Arabs. It's shameful. No deal at all would be acres better than this deal. Clemenceau can't last forever. He may be too tough to kill, but he's bound to be driven from office fairly soon. The French are fickle, and he's always been rather good at making himself unpopular."

"So you want the Americans to blow up this deal for you?"

"Ah, you've been reading those documents I photographed."

"Well, the United States seems like the only Great Power not to get anything out of the deal."

"True enough. One of the few matters on which Lloyd George and Clemenceau see eye to eye is that the less President Wilson knows about this arrangement, the better."

"So we both want the president to do something. I want him to reverse Joshua's conviction. You want him to blow up this deal. You must have some idea how to make such a thing happen."

They rounded the end of the aisle and began down the next one, passing by Joshua and Cook without acknowledging them.

"There is something I recently heard about," Lawrence said, "which you might want to look into. There's supposedly an American official here who's talking to the Germans."

"The Germans," Fraser said, unable to keep his surprise out of his voice. "About what?"

"War. Peace. Profits. The things statesmen amuse themselves with. Perhaps your black boy"—Fraser stiffened, but Lawrence didn't notice —"could find out something about that."

"Which Germans?"

"Ah, Major Fraser, you've driven to the heart of the matter. The Socialists control the German government, at least they do today, which means that they have to make a decision about the treaty, which makes them frightfully uncomfortable. Very little is as unpleasant to a politician as signing a treaty of surrender. Never good for the career. 'Vote for Bob Jones: he surrendered to our enemies!' In this case, the circumstances are even less appealing. It's half a year since the fighting stopped, the Allied armies never crossed the German border during the war, and many Germans don't feel particularly defeated." Lawrence stopped to study a stand that featured onions of several sizes, shapes, and hues. The Englisman said, "Distinctly unappetizing to see them that way, don't you think?"

"Oh, I don't know. There's a sense of bounty." The keeper of the onion stall walked behind them, mutely encouraging them to make a purchase or make room for someone who would.

"The socialists in Germany?" Fraser offered.

They began to amble again.

"Yes, well, some have no problem with the treaty, but some are saying that they'll never sign it. Should they stick to that position, it could get a bit dicey. It seems rather important to get the war ended. Have it down on paper, you know."

"Surely they'll sign. They can't go back to war."

"That's what sensible people would think. But the German soldier is a special breed, all that Prussian righteousness. For our purposes, it becomes a nice question whether the Americans have concluded that it would be best to have another government arise in Germany, one that would be better disposed to signing the treaty. The British government, I hear, is hoping for exactly that to happen."

"Are you suggesting that President Wilson would try to manipulate who's in control of a foreign country? But that would be completely contrary to his Fourteen Points."

"A charitable view would be that Mr. Wilson has no knowledge of such efforts in Germany. After all, no leader of a major government knows everything that's done in his name. Sometimes that's for the best. But you may be right. Perhaps the American conversations with the Germans are about strudel exports." Lawrence took a few more strides and finally looked at Fraser. "Look here, Major, I don't presume to know your business, but your young friend presents a profoundly unsympathetic situation. In order to solve the problem of this supposedly unjust conviction for deserting his post during battle, he has used false pretenses to enter the direct service of the president. There's nothing particularly honorable in any of it."

Fraser felt his stomach churn. This was not a fair description of Joshua's predicament. Then again, it did account for the basic facts. "What's the way out?"

"I don't know and I don't care. I would say that there's no more important question right now than war or peace with Germany. If you wish to gain the attention of any of these leaders, you might look for a way to intrude yourself on that question. Perhaps to facilitate the peace or even to provoke renewed war. You may choose."

"So it must be the Germans."

"Ah. You've been listening."

Trailing about twenty feet behind them, Cook stopped to investigate some carrots. "See those three soldiers back there?" he muttered to Joshua. "I think they're following us."

When Joshua sneaked a rearward glance, a hand gripped Cook's shoulder from the other direction. Two gendarmes stood on that side of them. One barked an order. Cook wasn't sure what he said but responded by barking his own demand, in English, for an explanation of this outrageous conduct. The three soldiers started to close in from the other direction.

Cook said to Joshua, "Run."

Wrenching free of the hand on his shoulder, Cook threw himself into the approaching soldiers. He barreled into the one closest to him, trying to use that one to knock down the others. He dragged two of the soldiers down in a tangle, rifles clattering on the ground. A rifle jammed into his side. Ignoring the pain, he spread his arms and legs to pin the Frenchmen to the ground.

Fraser turned at the noise and began toward it, darting around shoppers who had stopped to gawk. The two gendarmes were trying to get clear of the scrum in order to pursue Joshua while the third soldier positioned himself to deliver a kick to Cook's torso with a heavy boot. Fraser tried to jump on that one's back, but the lack of spring in his legs meant that he mostly fell on the man. Still, his greater height and weight prevailed. Gravity did the rest. They both collapsed on top of the three already down.

The five men writhed on the ground for more than a minute, each struggling for enough purchase to land a punch or a kick. Fraser and Cook played for time, trying to extend the scrimmage as long as possible.

Morning shoppers shouted encouragement to the combatants. A bunch of asparagus landed in Cook's face, stalks first—he had been pushed over onto his side by the soldiers below him—but he didn't know if the vegetables had been aimed at him. Within the battle, grunts and gasps competed with curses in two languages. Fraser lost his focus after a rifle butt collided violently with his skull.

The return of the two gendarmes ended the fracas. With numbers sharply against them, Fraser and Cook soon were face down on the cold cement floor, handcuffed and puffing.

With a bruised eye already getting puffy, Cook turned to Fraser. "Joshua?"

Fraser's shoulder throbbed where he fell on it. Blood trickled down his forehead. His mind was still far from crisp. "Long gone," he managed.

Lawrence wasn't anywhere, either.

Monday evening, May 19, 1919

Colonel Siegel had little experience retrieving staff doctors from police stations. After Eliza Fraser called him about Jamie's arrest, Siegel had spent hours telephoning American and French officials to plead for Fraser's freedom. The arrest, he insisted, was a misunderstanding. In any event, the American army desperately needed Major Fraser's services. The effort taxed Siegel's patience and his French, but he thought he was at the end of it when he picked up Mrs. Fraser and her daughter for the journey to the police station. He had received assurances that Fraser would be released and would face no charges.

The police building was stout and built of large stones. Its interior was suitably gloomy. The three men on duty affected the bored aspect of police officers everywhere, passing the time in the mechanical stroking of lush mustaches. Siegel's uniform faded before the brilliant silver buttons that festooned the gendarmes' jackets, but he still commanded the attention of one officer who wearily heard him out, then withdrew to the rear of the building. To Siegel's pleasure, he returned with the dangerous American desperado, Major James Fraser.

A knot near the top of Fraser's forehead glowed yellow and purple, but a happy smile creased his face. He waved to his team of saviors, turned to the gendarme escorting him, and promptly refused to accept his freedom unless another man named Cook also was released.

When Colonel Siegel understood what Fraser was doing, he called over in alarm, "What are you thinking? Getting you out was difficult enough."

Fraser shook his head. "I can't leave without Cook."

With an imploring look, Siegel won the senior policeman's permission to speak with Fraser privately. The gendarme left the handcuffs on the prisoner.

"Have you lost your mind?" Siegel demanded. "They're not going to let that man out. It's his son they were after in the first place, and *he's* apparently some sort of deserter. This fellow has no visa, no entry papers of any sort, so he's here illegally. For all I know, they're planning to send both of them to Devil's Island. I can't have anything to do with getting this Cook released. He has nothing to do with the army."

Fraser gave a small grin. "Colonel, take a look at these cops." He stepped aside to allow a full viewing. "They don't care about Cook. We're a nuisance between them and their evening meal."

"Somebody cares a good deal. Someone who sent them after this man's son."

"Believe me. We can make this whole thing blow over. There are people close to the president who will make that happen. But I need to be sure that Cook gets released. It's vital. I'm grateful for all you've done, Colonel, but we just need to do a little more."

Siegel could not hold his tongue. "Fraser, you're a damned fool. I need you at the hospital. We've received orders to prepare to advance into Germany, of all the stupid things." He turned in exasperation to Mrs. Fraser and her daughter, who had floated over to listen to the exchange. In the car, they had seemed reasonable women. Then again, until today he would have described Fraser as reasonable. "Can't you reason with this madman?" he asked Mrs. Fraser. "What he asks is quite impossible."

Eliza shook her head with apparent regret. "Reason is a poor tool with him. I'm afraid he's loyal to a fault." She directed her next comment to Fraser, asking, "Dear, if you're staying, shall I send Violet for fresh clothes?"

"No need," he answered. "I might as well smell as bad as Cook does."

"Fraser," Siegel said, "I've half a mind to leave you here to rot."

"If you kick up a fuss for Cook, I'm sure they'll let him go. Less work for them, quicker to the evening jug. They'll be glad of it. They just have to put up a bit of a show. You'll see. Give it a try."

Fraser began to plead with the gendarmes. The senior Frenchman answered vigorously, gesturing to different parts of his body, pointing out injuries inflicted on his brother gendarmes during the ruckus at Les Halles. Fraser responded with a good-humored enactment of his own bruises and injuries.

Eliza dug a 500-franc note out of her purse and pressed it into

Violet's hand. "There's a wine shop next door," she said quietly. "Buy the finest cognac you can find. Spend it all."

The other gendarmes joined the argument with Fraser. Siegel, very near to sputtering, roused himself, advising the policemen of a possible advance of Allied troops into Germany. Major Fraser, he insisted, was essential to the invasion. The gendarmes brightened at the suggestion of new fighting with Germany but saw no reason why that would require the release of Cook. They would do their bit for the invasion by releasing Fraser.

Violet returned clutching two bottles of Courvoisier, which she handed to her mother. "These cost four hundred francs!" she whispered.

With a wide smile, Eliza approached the men, holding up one of the bottles. Did they have glasses, she asked.

Two of the gendarmes looked at the third, who shrugged. Mismatched glasses appeared on a desk.

Eliza poured the liquor and tried not to take any for herself. The gendarmes insisted, though, as did Fraser.

"You clever girl," he said softly. "I'll buy you a case. You can bathe in it." He offered a toast to Lafayette, to Marshall Foch the commanding general, and to the great Clemenceau. The glasses were soon empty. Each gendarme ran his tongue ran around his lips, savoring the rich drink. The senior man offered to pour another round, but the Americans declined.

Fraser pointed to the back of the station house and raised his eyebrows. He said only, *"S'il vous plâit."*

The man reflected for a moment, then adopted an attitude of cosmic indifference. He called Siegel to one side while dispatching a colleague to fetch the remaining prisoner. Cook arrived with his head held high, his mouth resolutely shut. The Americans left. The cognac stayed.

Out on the sidewalk, Siegel handed Cook a paper the gendarme had given him. "This says you must leave the country within five days. After that, you're subject to arrest and imprisonment." He directed his attention to Fraser. "And, you, Major Fraser, can hardly afford to be brawling in the public markets of Paris like some hick private on his first leave. I can't believe you and I are engaged in this nonsense at such a critical time."

"What's this about invading Germany?" Fraser asked. "When did this come up?"

"It's not certain, of course, but the order came through this afternoon. We're to be ready if the Germans don't sign the treaty. Apparently the idea is that we'll all just roll off to war, lickety-split."

"General, you know that can't happen. It's been seven months. The Germans have to sign. They don't even have a functioning government, and we're not exactly battle-ready."

"Based on the orders issued to me, General Pershing doesn't share your strategic analysis. I expect you to be at the hospital in an hour, ready to plan our advance into the Rhineland in support of the army." Siegel made a point of shaking hands with Mrs. Fraser and her daughter as he departed. He simply nodded at the men.

"Well," Eliza said to the newly freed, "aren't you boys a little old for this sort of thing?"

Cook and Fraser dutifully moaned their agreement, but she didn't fall for it. "You seem remarkably chipper for two—what's the best way to say it?—two men of distinguished years, who have been jailed after a street fight."

"May I say, light of my life," Fraser said, "that you should've seen the other guys?" With a chuckle under his breath, Fraser ventured off the curb in search of a taxi.

Cook, remaining with the women, shifted his feet. "Well, Mrs. Fraser," he said, "I thank you for springing me." He held his hand out. "It's nice to see you again after all these years."

Eliza took the hand coolly. "Mr. Cook." She nodded to Violet, "this is our daughter, Violet."

Violet shook his hand more readily. "Mr. Cook, how is your eye?" Violet said. "Do you need to go to the hospital?"

"No thank you, miss. I received medical care from my fellow prisoner." He smiled. "You never know who you'll meet jail."

"I suppose not," Eliza said.

"Mrs. Fraser, I don't want you to get the wrong impression of me, what with this arrest, being ordered out of the country and all."

"I'm not sure it's a wrong impression."

"Mother!" Violet scolded.

Cook shrugged. "I prefer it when people speak their mind. But this is all about my boy, my son Joshua."

"Jamie has told me the story." Eliza's tone was warmer. "I'm sorry for your trouble. For his trouble."

"What story?" Violet said.

"Later, dear."

"When it comes to Joshua," Cook said, "there's nothing I won't do for him. Nothing. And if your husband's willing to help us, and he has been, then I'm just grateful." He looked down. "That's all I wanted to say."

Fraser had snared a cab, which was idling at the curb. "So, you'll stay at the same hotel?" he said to Cook.

"I hate to, but it's the only place Joshua knows to find me."

"He knows how to find me, right at the hospital."

"I'll risk another night at the hotel."

"So," Eliza said, "I assume you boys have hatched a plan?"

Fraser smiled back. "Haven't we, though. There's even parts for you ladies, if you're game."

TWENTY-EIGHT

Saturday evening, May 31, 1919

"Oh, Allen," Violet gushed, "don't you love the whole idea of the Paris ballet?" The lobby of the Palais Garnier shimmered with light from massive chandeliers that dangled forty feet above them, a Damoclean nightmare for any anxious soul inclined to imagine disaster. The Dulles brothers, with Violet and her mother, stood with the shiny crowd. The vast lobby swallowed conversation in a din that rose like a cloud to the distant ceiling. Ordinarily discreet people had to raise their voices to be heard.

"The concierge at our hotel says they've been performing for two hundred and fifty years," Violet continued, turning toward Foster, who was immaculate in evening clothes. "Why, it's older than our entire country!" Her high spirits brought only a chilly smile from the elder Dulles.

"My dear Violet," Allen said, leaning over to be heard, "you must recall that Foster's idea of fun is curling up with a debenture agreement that includes an especially ingenious reordering of priorities in bankruptcy."

"Really, now," Eliza took Foster's arm and drew him toward the stairs to the performance hall. "We're fortunate to have such dashing escorts when Violet's father couldn't be spared from the hospital." She rolled her eyes and gave a small smile. "He said something about invading Germany."

The younger Dulles extended his arm to Violet. "The good fortune is all ours."

Eliza didn't care much for his grin, which seemed distinctly wolfish. Still, the younger brother seemed more of a person than the one she was walking with. At least the younger one could counterfeit being a person. According to Jamie, Allen had agreed to induce the French authorities to abandon any efforts to arrest Joshua Cook. Allen claimed it must have been a misunderstanding.

Jamie wasn't so sure. He insisted that he didn't trust Allen Dulles. Eliza thought that she might.

Opening the door to the service entrance of the Crillon, Fraser shifted his hips in a vain attempt to reorient a trouser seam that was binding a sensitive part of his anatomy. He wanted to reach down and shift the hotel worker's uniform that Cook had pilfered for him, but such a rude gesture would draw attention from the actual hotel workers who lounged at the entrance. Cook had pilfered the uniform for Lawrence to use, so it was far too small for Fraser. When the Englishman landed in an Italian hospital following an airplane crash in Rome, he became unavailable for this particular gambit. Fraser agreed to be the last-minute substitute. Despite the sharp discomfort of the garment, he strode firmly through the hotel's back corridors. He needed to reach his destination quickly.

He lifted a wrench from an open toolbox at the side of the corridor. Even in ill-fitting pants, a man with a wrench fades into the woodwork.

Through a chain of reasoning that was not entirely airtight, Speed, Fraser, and Lawrence had decided that Foster Dulles was the American official most likely to be in contact with the Germans. He seemed the one most engaged with German issues at the conference. His law firm—the Cromwell law firm—had extensive dealings with Germany before the war and shrewd Mr. Cromwell would not miss the opportunity to rekindle those. Dulles' uncle was the Secretary of State and his brother was a spy with a finger in every pie in Paris. So Foster Dulles' room was the evening's target.

Of course, if their chain of inferences was wrong, they were taking a lot of chances for nothing. They took some solace, though, from Lawrence's endorsement of their reasoning in typically Delphic terms. That had been enough to persuade Fraser to agree to the plan, but not enough to feel confident in it. They were deep into a double and triple game, working Allen Dulles for favors while burglarizing his brother's hotel room. It was better when Fraser didn't chew over just how many things could go wrong.

When he reached the stairwell, Fraser seized the moment of privacy to adjust his wardrobe. It didn't really help, particularly when he started to climb the five flights to the roof. Each step wrought new damage. After only a flight, he heard someone enter the stairwell above him and begin to descend. Should he duck into the regular corridor? Or simply carry on, relying on his uniform and wrench as insignia of his insignificance?

He decided that French workmen would never take the stairs in an elevator building, so he stepped out onto the second floor. Two Americans—their nationality obvious from ruddy complexions and brisk steps —passed him without a moment's pause. God bless that wrench. He stepped resolutely in the other direction, ignoring the pain. Reaching the end of the corridor, he pantomimed a man who had forgotten something, acting the part for himself if for no one else. Back to the stairwell, where he could hear the footsteps now below him. He resumed his ascent, pausing at the top to catch his breath. No reason to give Cook an opening to remark on his sorry physical condition.

When Fraser opened the door to the roof, Cook stood ten feet away, a rope coiled at his feet. The glow of Paris outlined his figure. The night air felt fresh and warm. A nearby ventilation outlet released a soapy wetness from the laundry; another produced a yeasty kitchen scent with the tang of crusted animal fat.

Fraser moved awkwardly to ease the pressure of the trouser seam. "These pants are agony."

"Take 'em off," Cook said. "No one here to see you."

After looking around, Fraser agreed. The relief was exquisite. Not wearing pants would be easier to explain than what they were doing on the roof in the first place.

"I sure preferred letting myself into the hotel room with the key," Fraser said.

"Amen." Cook had tried to lift a key to Foster Dulles' room, but the hotel had increased its security measures in response to the threat, however remote, that the Germans wouldn't sign the treaty and war would resume. "They think some nuts might target the people in the hotel." He shrugged. "Nuts like us."

"Seriously, though, who would want to block peace? And why would doing something at the Crillon have that effect?"

"Damned if I know. Bolsheviks, Germans, Italians, take your pick." Cook was laying the rope between a thick ventilation pipe and the rear of the hotel. "Lots of crazy people out there who'd love to throw a spanner into the works, whether it made any difference or not."

"I still don't get it."

"You know," Cook suddenly sounded short. "I wouldn't have believed it after all these years, but you still do it."

"Do what?"

He stopped his task and looked at Fraser. "That white man thing. You figure nothing bad's gonna happen, because nothing bad's ever happened to you."

"Get off it." Anger flashed through Fraser, his hands clenched. "You're not the only person on earth who's had troubles, who's felt pain. How many wives have you buried? How many of your babies? Come to think of it, how many white men have you taken this kind of risk for, the way I am for you and Joshua?"

"On that last question, one." Cook pointed a finger at Fraser. "Exactly one." Their glares were reciprocal. After a moment, Cook dropped his arm, then his head. "It's nerves, Jamie. Pregame nerves. Both of us." He returned his attention to the rope. "Come on. We're up here. You're looking fashionable. Might as well do this thing."

Fraser, still simmering, gave him an appraising look. "What're you up to now, 240? 250? I liked this idea a lot better when it was Lawrence going over the side."

"Hey, I'll be glad to hold the end of the rope if you want to go down there."

Fraser, his blood still warm, stalked to the stone barrier at the building's edge. He looked down. His head swam and his vision clouded.

Cook grabbed him by the shoulders and pulled him back. "Whoa, Nellie," Cook said. "The plan says we keep you up here, right? Let's stick to the plan."

Rubbing the back of his neck, Fraser nodded.

Cook, who had learned a few knots during his seaman days, tied the rope around a sturdy-looking ventilation pipe that rose from the roof. He wrapped the other end around his waist and cinched it, but not with a knot. He wanted to descend gradually. He pulled on his gloves and tossed another pair to Fraser, who dropped one. Cook draped the strap of Violet's camera over his neck and one arm.

Fraser put on the gloves. He picked up the slack of the rope and looped it once around his waist.

"No more looking down," Cook said. "Just hang on. It's not that far to the balcony. Maybe twenty feet. You got the pipe there backing you up. Don't be afraid to rely on it."

Fraser nodded and gripped the rope, testing the best angles for his hands. He looked up. "Let's make this the last time for this kind of stuff, okay?"

"As long as I find that connection with the Germans that Lawrence was talking about." Cook didn't speak his greater fear: that finding a connection between Dulles and the Germans would prove useless because it was thoroughly authorized by the president. Or that Foster Dulles wouldn't mind having those connections disclosed. Cook clenched his jaw. "If I had a better idea, that's what we'd be doing right now."

He pulled the rope tight while Fraser braced himself, leaning back against a rooftop shed, then dropped the end of the rope to Foster Dulles' balcony. It reached. Good start. Cook put one foot up on the stone barrier at the edge of the roof. He looked back and nodded, then swung up, pivoted, and stepped off.

Even braced, Fraser wasn't ready for Cook's weight. Fraser's boots slipped on the roof's pebbly surface. He staggered forward a jerky step, then another, but steadied himself. He leaned back and looked out at the rooftops of Paris, heart racing.

Cook had intended to let himself down hand over hand, but the lurch of the rope startled him. His grip slid. The gloves didn't hold. He jabbed his foot against the wall to slow himself. After another few feet, his toe caught in a space between stones. His hands kept sliding, forcing his upper body away from the wall. Realizing he could flip upside down, he pushed his foot off from the wall and slid the rest of the way down. He landed hard, his feet on a planter. The impact crushed whatever had been growing there. He stood for a moment, gathering his breath and his balance. And feeling lucky.

His palms throbbed from the friction. His shoulders ached. His hip felt like it had been yanked from its socket. Not any worse, he told himself, than catching a Saturday doubleheader.

The French window leading into Foster's room wasn't latched. He was on a streak. He yanked three times on the rope.

Fraser hauled it back up to the roof.

It was after midnight when Eliza and Violet entered their suite, having consented to a post-opera drink with the brothers Dulles. Fraser was in an armchair, in his own clothes. The marital reunion had progressed to the point where he had his own key to the suite.

"Did anyone get arrested this time?" Eliza demanded.

"Nope," Fraser said. "A few bumps and bruises, but your favorite second-story men have cheated French justice one more time. How was the show?"

She walked over and kissed him on the forehead. He reached up and guided her face down for a real kiss.

She straightened up and began to remove her gloves. "I declare,

Violet," she said over her shoulder, "have you ever seen your father as happy as when he's rushing around Paris doing disreputable things with that mangy, broken-down ex-ballplayer."

"Mother, he's not at all mangy," Violet protested.

"And if you saw him shimmy down the side of the Hotel de Crillon this evening, you wouldn't call him broken down," Fraser said. "By the way, I thought you preferred me disreputable."

Eliza stepped to the mirror to remove her hat. "So, did you ne'er-do-wells get what you were looking for?"

"Sadly, no."

Eliza turned around with the hat in her hands. "Do you mean it was for nothing that I sat through that long evening with the Messrs. Dulles. As aptly named a pair as I have met."

"I think Allen is rather nice," Violet objected, dropping into a chair facing her father.

"Well," her mother answered, "I had the duller Dulles."

"He may be the duller one," Fraser said, "but he's intelligent enough not to leave sensitive papers in his hotel room."

Eliza said to Violet, "You get ready for bed now."

"I'm not a child, Mother. I think I played my part tonight rather well."

"Yes, dear, you did. But sometimes old married people need to speak to each other." Following Violet's self-consciously dignified departure, Eliza asked, "So what do we do now?"

"I had no idea you two would make such bully conspirators."

Eliza sat on the couch and reached for Fraser's hand. "There's a good deal to be said for being in these things together, however odd it may be." She squeezed his hand. "Jamie, I'm afraid I can't bring myself to like your Mr. Cook very much, but if Violet were in trouble, I hope I'd break as many laws to protect her as he's willing to break for his son."

"What a splendid sentiment. Because we have further need of you and your charming daughter."

Eliza smiled and sat back. "Women of intrigue, at your service."

"Without a document connecting Foster Dulles to the Germans, we're going to have to keep him under some sort of watch and hope to track him to an actual meeting with them. There's only a week until the deadline to sign the treaty."

"He wouldn't meet them at the Crillon, would he?"

"I thought we agreed that he's dull, not stupid. So we have to keep an eye on him, which is a bit tricky. Speed's hotel job puts him in a good place to do that while he's working, but when he's off shift, we'll have to share watching the hotel. Take turns."

Eliza grimaced. "That deadline for the treaty could be delayed again, couldn't it? It seems they've been making this peace for years."

"We might have to keep up our vigil for as long as a couple of weeks."

Eliza's face filled with dismay. "This suite could get a bit pricey."

"How long were you planning to stay?"

"Of course, I didn't know. We'll just find someplace less posh."

"I didn't say it was a good plan."

"Tell me, Daddy," Violet said as she entered the room in her bathrobe, brushing her hair. "Will I have to spend more time with Allen Dulles?" She struck a theatrical pose, the back of one wrist pressed to her forehead. "Yet another sacrifice by the fair maiden!"

TWENTY-NINE

Friday morning, June 6, 1919

The train from Paris to Frankfurt covered only 350 miles, but it carried Allen Dulles through several different civilizations. It sped from the glitter of revived Paris through patches of clover and wide fields of yellow blooms. It ground to a crawl through the brutalized landscape of the late war. Soldiers in khaki, in olive, and in blue trudged on roads that passed blasted trees and orphaned chimneys charred by fire. Dulles' train was shunted onto side tracks while troop trains hauled men and munitions east toward Germany. Empty trains passed the other way.

On the far side of what had been the front, Dulles and his fellow passengers switched trains. Gaining speed, they pounded through Luxemburg, then the Rhineland, which bore some traces of the Allied occupation. Narrow country lanes housed neat stockpiles of German arms, organized either by the departed troops of the Kaiser or the arriving Allied soldiers. The German countryside, untouched by the war, looked orderly, trim, admirable. Dulles thought he could be crossing farmlands of central New Jersey or eastern Pennsylvania.

Frankfurt dashed any illusion of German prosperity, or at least of German comfort. When the train slowed on the outskirts of town, he watched hunched-over figures scouring trash heaps. They looked gray and pinched, their clothes worn. Though it was early June, men wore short-brimmed caps and women covered their heads with bonnets and scarves.

On the short walk from Frankfurt's massive train station, Dulles felt conspicuous in his freshly pressed suit. The people on the street took no notice of him. Gaunt faces always seem sad, he thought. He searched the eyes of those he passed, hunting for a spark, a fire. Most seemed involved in some internal conversation, devoting little attention to the world around them. He stepped around a man in an army uniform who sat on the walk, leaning back against a building, an Iron Cross at his throat. A crutch lay next to the empty trouser leg. His military cap was upside down to receive coins. Dulles couldn't imagine such ghostly figures resuming the war against the Allies.

The meeting place, Schlueter's Beer Garden, was a mile from the station, wedged into a narrow lot. It held a dozen steel tables sunk into gravel, each surrounded by rickety wooden chairs. Small firs reached hopefully for sunlight between two buildings. Patrons wore coats and jackets. Some rubbed their hands together for warmth. In the back rank of tables, an American army officer sat alone, his cap on the table next to a large ceramic stein. He was blond, with ruddy cheeks and a mustache so pale as to be an illusion. They nodded to each other as Dulles approached.

"Colonel Conger?" Dulles asked.

"Excellent guess. Was it the uniform?"

"I'm Dulles."

The officer's face betrayed no emotion. "Surely they meant to send your father."

Dulles sat, then looked for a waiter. His wave seemed to snag a short, dark-haired man with an apron doubled over his middle.

"The beer is rat piss," Conger said, "thereby eliminating the one remaining reason to visit this bedraggled place."

Dulles ordered beer anyway.

Conger raised an eyebrow. "You speak Swiss German? And not too shabby Swiss German."

"I was posted in Bern. During the war."

"That wasn't your father in Bern?"

Dulles smiled. "Colonel, perhaps we should get to business. I have only two hours here."

"Yes, business." Conger cleared his throat and sat straighter. He nodded to a table on their right. "The man in the unfortunate plaid suit."

Dulles was surprised. "That's the first well-fed German I've seen. So many look like a puff of wind would sweep them away."

Conger allowed himself a small smile. "Ah, you see before you the benefits of public service. The people who were running things had to look after themselves. And don't be fooled by the hungry people. The Germans starved the home folks to feed the troops. That's why it's a mistake to think we'll just brush the German army aside if the treaty isn't signed. These people, they're lousy at giving up."

"That man isn't your contact in the government?"

"No," Conger drank some beer and grimaced. "My contact is just that, *my* contact. I don't want you or anyone else fucking that up."

"So, this man is?"

"He's the cutout. Highly trusted and all that. The name's Heinzelmann."

The waiter brought Dulles' beer. He saluted his companion with it and took a swallow. "Wow."

Conger grinned nastily. "You won't get used to it. But at least the Germans aren't making it illegal to have a beer, even a bad beer. I'll give them that." With a determined expression, Conger drank again.

"Yes, Prohibition takes effect in January."

"It's enough to make a man wonder what he was fighting for. The Europeans may slaughter each other, but at least they'll let you take a drink."

"How do we proceed?"

"Patience, Mr. Dulles. Herr Heinzelmann will join us when he feels like it."

Feeling no inclination to flog the conversation with the loutish Colonel Conger, Dulles sat back. A light breeze brought a chill as the sun slipped behind slate-colored buildings. The beer garden's clientele was young. They were neat and clean. They didn't have the near-ghostly detachment Dulles saw on the street. These people talked quietly. Some smiled. A few laughed. Maybe Germans were always detached on the street. Spirits here, to be sure, were not hilarious. No one was singing any of the jolly or sentimental drinking songs that he had heard in Switzerland. It was still afternoon.

"Do you have a light?"

Heinzelmann approached their table with a cigarette poised between two fingers.

While Dulles fumbled for his matches, Conger tossed a box of them on the table. Heinzelmann took a seat with a grunt and set to work lighting his Lucky Strike, cupping his hands around the flame. Upon closer inspection, the green plaid of his suit was even more appalling. Spectacles made his round face seem perfectly circular. A bushy mustache tilted up at either end.

Dulles hadn't seen waxed mustache tips since he left Bern.

"Thank you, Colonel," the German said.

"My pleasure." Conger cocked his head at Dulles. "He's the money man." After a brief pause, the American officer continued. "I, too, wish he were older, but we must use those tools that come to hand."

With a smile, Heinzelmann nodded at Dulles. "I have grown used to the colonel's bad manners, Herr Dulles. Imagine what he would be like if America had lost the war."

Dulles grinned. "A terrifying prospect."

Heinzelmann spoke to Dulles. "We must make our arrangements."

"Yes. I understand we're talking about a million marks."

Heinzelmann chuckled softly. "That should satisfy you, Colonel," he said to Conger. "Herr Dulles may be young, but he is a Yankee trader like all Americans."

Conger smiled but said nothing.

Heinzelmann sat back. "The price, my young sir, is *three* million marks. Compared to the cost of a renewed war, it is a trifle."

Dulles put a concerned look on his face. "That can't be right. That's not the figure mentioned in my briefing. And, as you say, we Yanks're pretty careful about numbers."

"The quality of your briefing is not my affair," Heinzelmann said, waving his cigarette, "nor is your attempt to win some praise for reducing the price. The price is three million marks. Our marks, you see, they shift in value every day, never to the good. So there must be many."

"So it will take three million marks," Dulles said, "to persuade the German government that it must perform the most basic duty it owes to its citizens, to end the war it has long since lost."

"Ah," Heinzelmann sat forward, "you are young. You wish to talk philosophy, but that would be a mistake, Herr Dulles. We Germans may lose a war, but never a philosophical discussion." He flicked the ash off the end of his cigarette. It blew back onto his sleeve. "The marks you provide will not teach my colleagues anything. They know full well how the war ended. The money will give them courage to sign the treaty. They need courage. Signing the treaty, it will not be a popular thing."

"Courage to do what they know they must do anyway," Dulles said.

Heinzelmann shrugged. "It is one of the puzzles of life—it so often feels foolish to do something merely because it's right." He held up a finger. "But, Herr Dulles, if there is also profit in it, if there is advantage to one's family, then a thing becomes so much more attractive. It becomes even the honorable thing to do." He took a drag on his cigarette, then stubbed it out in an ashtray. "Three million marks."

Dulles looked away while the German used Conger's matches to light another cigarette. He wondered how much of the money would go straight into Heinzelmann's pocket, never getting anywhere near the senior politicians who were the target of the operation. It didn't much matter. Avoiding a resumption of war was worth ten times three million marks, but he knew he had to haggle over the price. It was manly.

They swiftly settled on a price of two million marks.

"We must," Dulles said, "have a protocol for contacting each other."

Conger roused himself. "No official channels," he said. "As far as the U.S. State Department is concerned, this isn't happening."

"But Herr Dulles is part of the American government," Heinzelmann said agreeably.

Conger snorted. Dulles said nothing.

Heinzelmann turned suddenly cold eyes on Dulles. "There is not much time," he said, puffing on his cigarette. "You must get the money to Weimar soon."

"It's not so simple. The arrangements must be made carefully. The deadline for signing the treaty is bound to be delayed, anyway. We will deliver the money in Paris, not Weimar."

Heinzelmann shifted his gaze between Dulles and Conger. Then he shrugged. "All right, Paris. But in ten days. After that, it may be too late."

"We'll try," Dulles said. He leaned forward. "If you provide me with a means to contact you...."

"Yes, of course." He handed Dulles a small piece of paper that included two names, each with a Berlin address and telephone number. "Look at it carefully. Then hand it back to me."

Dulles did as told.

Heinzelmann stood and walked away. His stocky form and short-legged walk called to Dulles' mind a penguin, one with a bad tailor.

"There," Conger intoned, "waddles Europe's last, best hope for peace." He waved to the waiter for the check without smiling. "I'll maintain contact with the cabinet minister."

"Do let me know of any developments."

"You and your fancy-ass friends need to know only one thing. You can't afford to fuck this up."

THIRTY

Sunday morning, June 15, 1919

General Tasker Bliss, facing the Secretary of State in his office overlooking the Place de la Concorde, arched his eyebrows. The gesture drew attention to the general's poorly-focused eyes. Bliss once again had forsaken the spectacles he so plainly needed.

That act of vanity baffled Lansing. Perhaps Bliss thought that if he pretended his vision was acute, others would think his mind was.

No one above the age of six, however, could make that mistake. Indeed, Bliss's hesitancy without his spectacles reinforced the impression that most aspects of the peace conference were well beyond his depth. Bliss' pliability, of course, was the quality that earned him the job of Pershing's chief of staff, and then commended him to the president as a peace conference delegate.

Failing upward, that's how Lansing thought of him.

Despite Bliss' limitations, or perhaps because of them, Lansing found the general a useful source of information. Lansing's exile from Wilson's inner circle was nearly complete. Though excluded from almost every important decision, he still hankered to exercise some influence, somehow to win a seat at the table, or even a view of the table.

"I spoke with General Pershing last evening," Bliss began. "He insists that the Allies can resume the fighting, no matter what those fool French generals say."

"I see."

Bliss would not allow the Secretary of State's reserve to deflect him from delivering his full remarks. "Between you and me, Lansing, invading Germany now, why, it's preposterous. It's really quite a large country. We have insufficient troops, ordnance, supplies, transport. And what I really fear"—he nodded to underscore an insight that Lansing fully expected to be worthy of an eight-year-old—"are the political repercussions. A resumption of the war would trigger revolution in half the Allied nations. It would be a bonanza for the Bolsheviks. After four years of bloody fighting and an armistice, the great powers go back to war."

"You make an excellent point," Lansing said, happy to applaud another mundane thrust by the general. "The socialists in Berlin are demonstrating the total unfitness of their breed to hold power. They're driving the world right back to the brink of catastrophe. Quite frankly, I believe their game is to drive us all over that brink."

"What can they possibly be thinking? Most of them opposed the war in the first place. Many of them refused to fight."

"Ah, General Bliss, we must remember our Emerson. 'A foolish consistency is the hobgobblin' and all that. The Socialists know that the German people don't feel like they've been beaten, and yet we dictate the peace, demanding that they accept the blame for starting the war and that they pay us billions. We behave as though our army currently occupied Berlin, and didn't sit five hundred miles away, steadily dwindling with demobilizations. Any German politician who signs the treaty signs his political death warrant."

"But the Germans can't fight a war now any more than we can. Even less." The general rubbed an eye, no doubt feeling the strain caused by the absence of corrective lenses.

"Is there any sign the president is weakening on the terms of the German treaty?"

"Good heavens, no. Lloyd George, apparently, has become the

cowardly character in the room. I heard the president mutter that nothing short of a thrashing might work with the PM."

"You could sell tickets to that," Lansing observed with a smile, "but is that really a wise position for Mr. Wilson? Wasn't it Lincoln who said that after you've beaten a man, you should let him back up easy? Mr. Lloyd George might be on to something."

"As near as I can tell, the president's completely dug in now. We won't give an inch to the Germans. If they try to negotiate any of these terms, they'll be shown the door. Strictly take it or leave it."

"Interesting, General. I must confess that I've long since given up predicting the president's course. I find him stoutly defending provisions now that he attacked a month ago."

"Politics. It's a damnable business."

"Yes, so it is," Lansing agreed, again happy to do so.

After the general left, Lansing lit a cigar and gazed out at the plaza and the river beyond. The French had finally removed the captured howitzers. Traffic lurched through the huge space, occasional horse-drawn carts bedeviling the motorcar drivers who longed to demonstrate the power of their vehicles. In his splendid isolation, Lansing was accomplishing nothing, but at least he had a wonderful office in which to be useless. It was a solace, a small yet profound one, that Colonel House simmered in comparable impotent isolation in his corner suite, also far from the center of the conference.

Lansing sat with a sigh. Even from his exile, he was doing what he could. The thing was to scrounge up a few presentable Germans to sign the treaty. Renewing the war was unthinkable, no matter what that lunkhead Pershing thought. Lansing had put Foster and Allen in touch with that American colonel in the Berlin embassy. The colonel had developed an excellent contact in the German government, a realistic man—not a socialist—who had recently entered the cabinet. At least he was in the cabinet this week. It was a start.

Money certainly was no object. Lansing and Cromwell had seen to that. He hoped his nephews knew what they were about. This sort of thing was never easy.

THIRTY-ONE

Wednesday morning, June 18, 1919

F raser joined his wife and daughter at an outdoor table on Rue Royale, the entrance to the Crillon visible from their seats, but not from his. The breeze ruffled the umbrella that shaded the ladies from the bright morning light.

"Jamie," Eliza said, "You look terrible."

"I've completed Colonel Siegel's plan for the invasion. It pretends that we can provide first-class medical care for the American Expeditionary Force as it fights its way into the heart of Germany. However fantastic the exercise is, Siegel was delighted to receive it." He wiped his hands across each other. "So now I'm done with that foolishness."

"Daddy, not another war."

Fraser tried to attract a waiter who resolutely failed to see him. "I've never been much of a praying man, but I pray it will never happen." Another waiter approached their table from another direction. Feeling silly, Fraser gestured to the women. "Yum-yums, ladies?"

"I can't pass up a croissant," Eliza said, "though I have had more than my share over the last couple of weeks. They're good here."

Violet also chose the croissant, but Fraser was hungrier than that. He ordered an omelet and sausage with his.

"The newspapers," Violet said, "say the deadline for the Germans to sign the treaty won't be extended anymore. Father, I hope that's true. This is getting dull."

"Really, dear," Eliza added, "we are becoming honorary members of the staff of the café and the hotel, though our French is getting better."

"I've lost track," Fraser said. "When is the current deadline? It's been extended so many times."

"Only three days away, Father."

The waiter brought their coffee, which Fraser fell upon greedily, then sat back and looked across the street at the hotel. "If anything's going to happen with those Dulles boys, it'll be soon." He asked Eliza, "Any sign of them this morning?"

"Not yet. Though I could recite to you this fascinating item on page four of the newspaper about sewer repairs in the twelfth arrondissement. I've read it at least ten times."

"After we've eaten, you two should take off. Come back for a late lunch. Say, at two?"

"Yes. Violet and I can search for something on the menu here that we haven't ordered yet. That will be great fun, won't it Violet?"

"All right, all right." Fraser said. "Just a few more days. Say, where's the camera?"

"In the bag." Violet pointed to a black canvas carryall that sat in the fourth chair at their table. "Really, Daddy, how likely is it that our friends will meet some German scoundrels in broad daylight, then stand for a well-framed photograph? Isn't that the sort of meeting that happens at night, in dark and obscure corners? We can hardly show up and ignite flash powder in a deserted alley."

Fraser finished his coffee and poured more from a pot left by the waiter. He was feeling more human. "Of course, you're right, my dear. That's why we respectable people are here. So if we see something— even at night—we can attest to those events and perhaps even be believed. As opposed to our friends the Cooks, *pere et fils.*"

"Really, Daddy? They wouldn't be believed just because they're

Negroes?"

Fraser took a moment. "I wish I could say otherwise."

"I am curious about this Sergeant Cook," she continued. "What a terrible time he's been through. It's quite tragic. I don't know how he holds up."

Wednesday afternoon, June 18, 1919

Slicing limes and lemons for the evening trade, Cook was at his favored spot behind the bar, the one with the best view of the Crillon's lobby. The bar still had no slow nights. Every night brought a ménage of national leaders and the men who whispered in their ears, plus the lawyers and investors, the businessmen hawking goods, and revolutionaries lusting after power. All leavened with a sprinkling of spies, impostors, and swindlers.

When Fraser arrived in a civilian suit and tie, he leaned on an elbow and ordered a boxcar.

Cook finished the lime he was cutting, wiped his hands on a towel, and stepped down the bar to make the drink. When he delivered the cocktail, he said, "Jokes don't ever grow old for you."

"Neither do you or I."

Cook said he should look at a man at a corner table, the only customer drinking alone.

Fraser turned sideways so he could see the lobby while he sipped his drink. The angle allowed him to take in the corner.

The man was wiry, his ascetic appearance accentuated by his almost shaved head and pince-nez glasses. The corners of his mouth pointed downward in a scowl etched deep into his face.

The sight called to Fraser's mind his mother's warning that if he kept making grotesque expressions, his face might freeze in one of them. This man's mother should have passed him the word.

"Third day I've seen him in here," Cook said. "He's looking for someone."

"With some hair, he could pass for a Dulles. What do you think,

German?"

Cook nodded. "When he paid, I saw deutschmarks in his wallet."

"Maybe we're on to something." Fraser tossed down the remains of his drink. "The ladies are off duty. I'll be around, inconspicuous as ever."

Allen Dulles smoothly fell into step beside his brother in the grand terminal of the Gare Montparnasse. The station's double-level windows admitted streams of the final light of the day. Sweat drops beaded on Foster's face. His posture canted to the left as he struggled with a plainly weighty grip.

"Sir," Allen said with a smile, "have you considered a redcap?"

Foster veered to elude a workman in a snap-brim cap, a maneuver that threatened his balance. With a grunt, he stopped and set the grip on the floor, keeping it between his foot and the wall of the tabac stand. "Really, Allie, don't be juvenile. I'm hardly going to hand this parcel to a redcap."

The younger brother kept his smile in place. "Just a professional note, Foster. On jobs like this, the idea is to not attract attention, so it's better not to look as though you had spent the morning drowning puppies. One should appear relaxed, even bored."

"When I wish your professional advice, I'll request it." Foster mopped his forehead with a handkerchief. "I will admit, however, that this is not my usual line of work."

"I did offer to manage this business for you."

"The gentlemen at Turkish Petroleum insisted on turning over such treasure to a familiar face, and Mr. Cromwell agreed. As you know, Mr. Cromwell insists that accidents don't happen, but are permitted to happen by people who fail to prepare properly. I cannot afford to have an accident happen with this."

"We're rather running this down to the wire. Our German friends grow impatient."

Foster didn't respond.

"So where is Mr. Cromwell now?"

Foster ignored that question, too.

Allen held the door for his brother as they left the station, then hurried ahead to open the car door. Foster grunted when he swung the bag into the car. It landed with a thud. He clambered into the rear seat and sank back with a sigh. Allen entered from the other side and told the driver to take them to the Hotel de Crillon.

"I look forward," Foster said to his brother in a low voice, "to turning this great bundle over to you. My back and I wish you had completed the deal at the original price."

"That load does make one more conspicuous. The whole beast-of-burden appearance."

Foster made a face. "I'll feel a great deal easier when it's on its way to Weimar. Herr Heinzelmann says he has matters arranged, but it's difficult to trust a man in such terrible clothes. You must be sure that the money is paid as agreed. One-third rewards the resignations of those socialists who won't sign the treaty, and the rest goes to salve the consciences of those who will. Neither group must know that the other is being paid, or the whole thing will fall apart."

"It's quite the jumble, isn't it," Allen said, "keeping all those different Socialists straight?" When Foster's only response was a grunt, his younger brother continued. "I'm sorry to pass on the news that Heinzelmann has changed the plan. The bundle is to leave from the airfield at Le Bourget. He thinks the trains aren't safe from any of the socialists."

"Yes, well, I acquired the funds. You must see to their delivery. This must be successful, or heaven knows what will come next."

"Of course."

"When does Heinzelmann propose to take off?"

"Early in the morning."

Foster frowned. "Which morning?"

"The one coming up."

"So in twelve hours," Foster asked, "this wretched affair will be done?"

"Perhaps a bit longer. We do need to get the right vote out of Weimar."

THIRTY-TWO

The moon set by four that morning, plunging the city of lights into deeper darkness. The Place de la Concorde was eerily quiet. Fraser, slumped in the shadow of a doorway a block down from the Crillon, could make out only a few parked cars and the plaza's monuments. The last hotel guests had toddled into the building more than an hour before. A truck rumbled past. Somnolent street sweepers, homeward bound, swayed and bounced in the open truck bed.

A soldier and a gendarme stood at each of the hotel entrances. Their postures said that they were fighting sleep, too. Two taxi drivers had parked on his block. Their foreheads rested against the steering wheels. Last time Fraser checked, Joshua was in the same posture on Rue Royale in a Ford Model T he borrowed from the president's residence. Fraser figured at least Speed was awake at his post watching the back of the hotel. He knew he could count on Speed.

Fraser felt like this was the night. When Speed came off his shift at 1:00 am, he delivered news that jarred Fraser into sharp attention. The Dulles boys had gone through the lobby early that evening. The one who looked like his stomach hurt was lugging a heavy bag.

A pre-war Peugeot entered the plaza from the Rue Royale and pulled up before the hotel. Fraser stepped out to get a better look. A horse-drawn milk wagon blocked his view. He drifted into the street for a better look. His line of sight cleared just in time to see Foster Dulles hustling into the car, carrying a valise that he had trouble managing.

Fraser strolled toward the hotel. Dulles hauled the bag up to his lap and clutched its handle with both hands.

Fraser turned up Rue Royale. As soon as the Peugeot pulled out, he began to run.

"Let's go, let's go," he called to Joshua, banging on the Model T's roof.

Joshua came to full alertness. With Fraser handling the crank, they got the engine started and pulled out in pursuit.

They spotted Dulles' Peugeot halfway down the Champs-Élysées, moving at a stately pace. With little traffic on the streets, they could stay a distance behind Dulles without even turning on the Model T's running lights. The Peugeot's noise must be drowning out the Ford's repertoire of rattles and chugs. The Peugeot began a series of turns through side streets, taking a circuitous route that moved generally east. Every time Joshua turned a corner, anxious they had lost the trail, the Peugeot was in sight, slogging along its stodgy way. The eastern sky showed no hint of dawn.

"What d'you think he's got in that bag," Joshua called over the engine noise.

"Something he shouldn't have, I hope."

Joshua hit the steering wheel with the flat of his hand and grimaced. "I never let myself think you guys might be right about this. It's too crazy. I've been afraid to believe it. But, son of a bitch, maybe you were right." He looked over at Fraser. "It'd be something, getting my life back."

Fraser nodded. He couldn't afford to get distracted by hope. Lots could go wrong. He twisted round in his seat, looking behind them, then shouted, "Where's your father? He was supposed to follow."

Joshua stole a glance over his shoulder. "He must've heard us, with the racket this bucket makes."

"Damn."

After another five minutes, Fraser called out, "They're just wandering around. It's almost like they don't need to get anywhere in particular."

"What's over in this part of Paris?" Joshua asked.

"There's a train station. Gare de l'Est, I think. That must be where they're going. It's over there." Fraser pointed across Joshua to the left side of the car.

The Peugeot's driver seemed to gain focus. The powerful car ceased its exploration of the Parisian traffic grid and moved straight in the direction Fraser had pointed. It stopped near the station entrance on Boulevard de Strasbourg. A broad plaza stretched in front of the station.

Joshua pulled over a hundred feet behind the Peugeot.

Dulles stepped out of his car, not carrying the bag. He walked back toward the Model T.

"What do we do? What do we say?" Joshua said.

"Damned if I know."

When Dulles reached them, he leaned down to peer inside the car. He looked startled. "Who are you?" he said.

Fraser answered, "Friends of your brother."

"Oh, Lord," Dulles said in a low tone and hurried back to his car. Once he was aboard, it jumped from the curb and began to show what that Peugeot engine could do.

"Follow him," Fraser called.

Joshua already had the Model T rolling. "He must've been the decoy. He doesn't have a damn thing."

"Christ," Fraser shouted. "Decoy for who? And where the hell is your father?"

———

Moisture in the predawn air formed a yellow halo around the shed's single light. Several biplanes, already sold off by a military that was preparing for peacetime, sat to the side of and beyond the shed. The driver of a milk wagon pulled hard on the reins to stop his horse a few yards from the structure.

Two short men stepped from the shed, rubbing their hands in the morning cool. One was fat and wore a heavy brown business suit. The other appeared younger and more athletic; he wore the peaked cap and snug-fitting jacket of a pilot.

Allen Dulles emerged from among the large milk jugs on the wagon's flatbed. He jumped down nimbly. "Herr Heinzelmann," he said with a warm smile.

The fat man said something to the pilot, who turned toward the parked planes, then stopped. Four men, three of them holding pistols, were emerging from behind the planes. The unarmed one, with a nearly shaved head, shouted in German.

Dulles understood him perfectly. Nothing about this was part of his plan.

The pilot, closest to the gunmen, froze. He held up his hands. As they advanced, he bolted behind the shed. Two gunmen fired but he kept running, then disappeared into the darkness.

The fat man waited too long to break in the same direction. Also, he was slow. The third shot brought him down. He grabbed at the back of his leg with a shout.

Dulles vaulted back up on the wagon. He shouted to the wagon driver to go, to go like lightning.

Instead, the bastard jumped down and ran away into the night.

THIRTY-THREE

Friday Morning, June 20, 1919

F oster Dulles' car slammed to a stop a half mile from the airfield. The sound of gunfire had carried clearly. Driver and passenger fell into a heated conversation.

Joshua, following closely, pulled the Model T around next to Dulles. "What's going on?" he shouted.

"Who the devil are you?" Dulles answered, his voice tight with anxiety.

Fraser leaned forward and called over, "We've been working with your brother. Who's shooting?"

"I don't know. Probably Bolsheviks. Probably German ones." Foster held up his empty hands. "We have no weapons."

In a low voice, Fraser said to Joshua, "We don't, either."

"My father does. He always does." Joshua slammed the car into gear. "He just needs to show up." Gunning the engine and turning on their headlights, he pulled in front of the other car and mashed the gas pedal down.

"What do we do when we get there?" Fraser shouted over the engine noise. "Help Dulles?"

"I suppose so."

"How?"

"Don't know."

About 500 yards from the airstrip, Fraser shouted, "Seems a dubious battle for us."

"They all are." Joshua's jaw was set.

"OK, but which side are we on?"

"The one that can keep me out of prison."

All right, Fraser thought. We help Dulles. His heart was speeding like a freight train as he squinted into the wind that rushed through the side window. His mouth was dry. This seemed like a very bad idea.

As they neared the shed, more gunshots sounded. The windshield shattered. Joshua swerved to the right, stopping the car. He dove out through the passenger side, landing partly on top of Fraser, who had attempted a similar though less elegant plunge to the ground.

Using his elbows to pull and his feet to push, staying as flat as possible, Joshua crawled away as fast as he could. On patrol, you got good at moving like that or you got dead. When he was past range of the light, he rose to a half crouch and ran deeper into the night. Two more shots made Fraser flinch. He mashed his face into the dirt underneath him, wishing he could climb below it.

"*Raus, Raus.*" A harsh voice on his left.

Reluctantly lifting his head, Fraser saw a man aiming a pistol at him. He could barely make out the man holding it. He stood slowly, his hands raised in a submissive posture. He wouldn't give the man any reason to shoot him. No additional reason, anyway. Across the open space, one of the gunmen turned from the scene, jammed his pistol into his waistband, and trotted toward the parked planes.

Staying low, Joshua circled the milk wagon and moved toward the airfield. He had to get to the choke point, the place the other guys wanted to get to. It was easy to figure that out here. It was the planes. His eyes were adjusting to the dark. He moved faster, still staying low.

He hadn't been on patrol for six months, but the feeling and memory came back right away. Focus. Open every sense. Control your breathing. Let the situation come to you. The other guy is scared too, maybe more scared than you. Think about nothing but what's in front of you, behind you, on either side. Stay low. Stay quiet. Trust nothing. Don't think, react. Be fast.

He veered right toward a low glint on the ground, near the first plane. He had to reach with his hand to be sure. A toolbox. He felt for a likely weapon. His fingers closed around the handle of a wrench. It had a solid heft. He felt to be sure nothing was on top of it. No clanks against the toolbox. He lifted it slowly.

It felt good to have something in his hand.

The man holding a gun on Fraser gestured for him to move around the car. Fraser walked to the front of it. The gunman wasn't large, but he seemed comfortable with the pistol. He had done this sort of thing before.

The man with the nearly shaved head—the one from the Crillon bar —stood at the end of the milk wagon. He was shouting into it. Allen Dulles emerged for a second time from between two large milk jugs. Though the nearly bald man wasn't armed, Dulles raised his hands in surrender. After Dulles jumped down, with the remaining gunman watching him, the man from the Crillon climbed up on the wagon, over the large jugs. He rapped on the floor a few times. He was looking for something. He found it at the front of the wagon. He lifted a burlap sack tied with a plain rope and peered inside. Then he cinched the rope and heaved the bag over the side.

"Herr Keller," Dulles said. His voice was surprisingly relaxed. "I had hoped to meet you in quieter circumstances. We really should talk this over one more time. There may be a way that we can make this work out for both of us, for both our countries. That's always the best course, don't you think?"

Dulles' ease was impressive. Fraser wasn't sure he could speak at all

—either form a sentence in his mind or make his voice work. His mind seemed to be vibrating. He should look for an opening to work with Dulles. That's what Dulles was doing, looking for an opening.

And Joshua. Where the hell was Joshua? And Speed?

The German shook his head. He allowed himself a smile. "No need for more talk. All is quite good." He looked quickly at the airfield as a motor roared to life. "It is time to go. Karl," he called to the man nearest Fraser, then pointed to the bag.

Karl tucked his weapon into his jacket pocket and hurried to the wagon. The bag was ungainly, apparently heavy. He used both arms to lift it, then staggered toward the airplane noise.

"Keller," Dulles tried again, his tone still pleasant. "You're going to kill yourself trying to take off in the dark. You should wait a while." His concern for Herr Keller's safety shone through his warm tone.

Keller smirked. "The sun, it rises now. Just as we planned. Most clever of us, no?"

The light was gaining against the night.

Fraser decided he had to do something. He stepped forward.

"Halt," Keller ordered.

"I'm a doctor." Fraser gestured toward the fat man on the ground, who was moaning, his hand squeezing his injured leg. "That man is hurt."

Keller didn't answer because the airplane engine suddenly cut out. He called back over his shoulder. "Franz! Franz!" No answer came.

Fraser started toward the man on the ground.

Joshua could tell the pilot would be easy pickings. Once the airplane engine started, he knew where the man was—in the cockpit. Joshua stole up from behind, the man bent forward, awash in engine noise, listening to the engine, concentrating on whatever pilots thought about before takeoff.

Crouching, Joshua approached the plane from its dark side. In one motion, he stepped on a wing and grabbed the edge of the cockpit with his free hand. He swung the wrench with the other. The tool thudded into the base of the pilot's neck.

As the pilot slumped forward, his weight pushed the plane's throttle and revved the engine higher. Dropping the wrench, Joshua reached into the pilot's flight jacket. There it was. A Mauser. The long barrel snagged on the pilot's pocket lining, then came free. It felt even better in his hand than the wrench had.

A shape loomed over the opposite edge of the cockpit. Joshua swung the barrel up, ready to fire. The man, wearing a peaked pilot's cap, put an index finger to his lips.

Was he a friend?

Joshua made the visceral decision that this second pilot was on his side. The other man made no hostile move toward Joshua. Instead, he pointed to the back of the plane, then began wrestling the pilot's body away from the controls. Joshua understood. He dropped back to the ground as the engine cut out, then began to circle the plane's tail.

There he was, one of the men opposing Dulles. He was struggling to haul a heavy load to the airplane. More easy pickings. Joshua sprang from behind the tail of the plane and jammed the Mauser in the man's face.

Wide-eyed, the man dropped his load, a burlap sack.

Joshua took a gun from the man's waistband and pushed him to the ground. When the second pilot arrived from his work in the cockpit, Joshua gave him the second pistol. He held it against the head of the man on the ground as Joshua turned to the standoff in front of the shed.

THIRTY-FOUR

Friday morning, June 20, 1919

S peed was pushing the dinky motorcycle engine as hard as he could, but it still wheezed like a TB patient. This Triumph was built for midget limeys, not for full-grown men like him. Give him a good American Indian or Harley-Davidson. He could cover some ground on those.

The last thirty minutes had been a nightmare. He'd been watching the back of the Crillon when he heard Joshua and Fraser take off in the Model T. He hopped on the Triumph and hit the kick-start. Nothing. After a half-dozen tries, he dismounted. With fumbling fingers, he painstakingly went over the motorcycle's connections, its engine. Jesus, they were getting away from him. He would never catch them.

He couldn't find anything wrong. Desperate, he climbed back on the saddle and tried the kick-start again. The fool thing roared to life.

Goddamn the English and their crappy machines. How could mechanically savvy people like the Germans lose a war to people who produced engines like this?

Joshua and Fraser, the Dulles boys, all were long gone. Cook had to guess where they went. He considered the list he and Fraser had made of possible ways to get money or people to Germany. There were four train stations on the northern and eastern sides of the city, plus the Le Bourget airfield. Cook set off for them, starting with the train stations. He hurtled past three stations—the Austerlitz, the Lyon, and the East depots. Not a whiff of a Dulles, or of Joshua and Fraser.

Cursing, Cook opened the throttle for the run to the Le Bourget. He had to get there now, right now. Just let them all be there.

A lumbering delivery truck pulled out in front him. He hauled the handlebar left, nearly toppling over. The front wheel waggled while he strained to steady himself. The engine coughed. Then it came back. He straightened up and opened the throttle again.

When he neared the airfield, a parked car blocked the road. He slowed next to it.

Foster Dulles sat on the running board, a derby hat in his lap. "They have guns. There've been shots."

Cook reflexively reached to his waistband and pulled out the pistol. "How many?"

"Close to a dozen."

"Men?"

"No, shots."

"How many men?"

"I don't know. You don't have another gun, do you?"

Cook thought about telling Dulles to call for help but didn't. He and Joshua were fugitives from the law. No police.

He took off, steering the bike with one hand. Keep it simple, he thought. He was a surprise. The bad guys, whoever they were, weren't expecting him. He'd make the noisiest, most godawful entrance he could. One that would rattle the teeth of everyone there. Then he'd sort things out.

The first glimmerings of dawn spread before him, outlining two vehicles stopped near a shed. A lamp over the shed showed several figures. One stood next to a wagon bed, another was on it. He couldn't make out faces.

The figures in the clearing turned in his direction, reacting to the engine noise. He decided to jump off the bike, gun in hand, and run it into the center of the scene.

As he tensed for the jump, a shot fired, then another. The second one burst the shed light, plunging everything into murk.

Cook leaned left. He meant to leap off the bike but it was more like a tumble. He kept his left leg out from under the bike as it skidded ahead, but his elbow jammed into the ground first. His shoulder shrieked with pain. The motorcycle engine revved higher as it careened into the clearing toward the wagon.

The horse screamed. Eyes wild, the animal reared in its traces as the machine skimmed toward it. Cook heard a violent collision, but couldn't see it. His eyes were squeezed shut. He rocked on the ground, grabbing his elbow and moaning involuntarily. The gun was gone from his hand.

"Don't anyone move." It was Joshua's voice, strong and sure, coming from the direction of the airfield. "I've got the guns and the money, and I can see every last one of you."

Cook couldn't make him out, the pain of his shoulder defeating any attempt to focus his eyes.

The figure on the wagon jumped down and another shot came.

"Hold on there." It was Allen Dulles.

Cook ground his teeth, powerless to help, to do anything.

"Speed." Hands were on his chest. Fraser's hands.

"It's my shoulder. On fire."

"Lie back and breathe."

With a short cry, he lay back, Fraser's hands guiding him. He couldn't believe the pain, then it backed off a bit. "What's happening?"

"Your boy's saving our bacon."

Cook rolled to his side, meaning to stand. The effort made him dizzy. He rolled back with a gasp. His shoulder held hot lava.

Fraser, calm, spoke again. "For Christ's sake, stay put." He pushed Cook's left arm, the bad one, flat against his torso, then bent it at the elbow. "Just think about how proud you are of that young man. He's smarter than both of us put together."

"You're not helping," Cook said through tightly clenched teeth. "My shoulder. Pain."

"Damn, is that all the noise you can make? Shout at me!"

Cook roared, the sound reverberating into the sunrise.

Fraser rotated Cook's arm all the way out to the side. "Again. Another shout. Give it all you've got."

Cook roared again as Fraser rotated his arm back all the way across his body. Cook gasped. He could swear he felt a clunk inside his shoulder. The pain evaporated. His body went limp. Sweat broke out on his face. He started panting. "Sweet Jesus," he said.

Fraser smiled down at him. "Jesus had nothing to do with it." He helped Cook up to a seated position. The scene before them was confusing.

Joshua held a gun on one gunman and the man with the clipped hair. Both raised their empty hands in submission. Allen Dulles was straining to lift the burlap bag from the ground. Another gunman lay on the ground, moaning. Fraser went to see what he could do for him.

"Where do you think you're taking that?" Joshua called out to Dulles.

Dulles looked over his shoulder. "Why, Germany, of course." With a grunt, he got the bag up on his shoulder. "Hungry mouths to feed." From the relaxed sound of Dulles' voice, it almost seemed like he was the one holding the gun.

"Why should I let you take that?"

"Don't be tiresome, sport, not after the fine work you've done." Dulles grinned. "I can be grateful. You may have just purchased yourself a ticket home in the name of Joshua Cook."

"Can I trust you?"

"What choice do you have?" Dulles started to walk to the plane.

Joshua pivoted slowly to follow him with the gun, then turned back to Keller and the gunman.

Fraser tore his eyes from the spectacle and checked the gunman on the ground. He was shot in the chest. He wasn't going anywhere. This was Fraser's first time providing medical care directly on a battleground. He could use some supplies.

Dulles was up on a wing of the plane with Heinzelmann's pilot, the one in the peaked hat who first ran off into the night. They hauled from the cockpit the pilot who had arrived with Keller. He moaned in pain and confusion.

Fraser heard an engine behind him. The Peugeot was stopping behind the overturned Model T. Foster Dulles stepped out on the passenger side.

His brother shouted from the plane. "Excellent timing, Foster!" Allen's voice was even more jaunty. He and the pilot were lifting the burlap bag into the cockpit. Then both men pulled on flight helmets and goggles. "Back in time for dinner," he called with a wave.

The biplane trundled off over uneven ground, passing the shed to the field beyond.

"Here," Fraser said to Foster and his driver, pointing to the men on the ground. "They need to go to the hospital, and you seem to have the best means of transport."

They loaded three into the car, starting with Heinzelmann and the gunman with the chest wound, then adding Keller's pilot. Foster stood on the running board as the Peugeot turned in a wide arc and headed back down the road.

Fraser found Cook seated on the ground, leaning back against the shed and holding his injured arm. His son sat next to him. Four pistols lay on the ground before them. The wagon driver had come back from the field. He was talking softly to his trembling horse.

"We let the Germans go, the ones who could still walk," Joshua said, looking up. "We don't need to talk to any more gendarmes."

"Where'd they go?" Fraser asked.

"Out that way." Joshua waved vaguely at the field before them. "Don't much care."

Fraser turned to Cook. "We should probably rig up a sling for your arm, hold your shoulder stable."

Cook nodded. "Just a damned invalid, getting in the way, being looked after by my betters." He smiled and glanced over at Joshua.

"That," Fraser nodded to the milk wagon, "may be our best way out of here. Let me have a word with the proprietor." He walked off.

After a moment, Cook said to his son, "You shot that German."

"Not my first." Joshua looked out at the spreading rays of dawn. "Nearly bashed the other one's head in."

Cook shook his head. "I'm sorry, son. I shouldn't have put it on you, the army and all. It wasn't my place." His voice gave out and he shook his head, feeling battered by a wave of feeling.

Joshua looked over, then back to the horizon. "Don't take it on yourself, Daddy. I made up my own mind." One corner of his mouth curled up. "I would've been drafted anyway."

Cook drew a ragged breath. "Still, you could have gone into one of those support units, building roads or hauling stuff. Not the killing part." He picked up a stone with his free hand and jiggled it in his hand. "That would've been the smart play."

"The smart play? Nobody raised me to settle for the smart play."

Cook nodded, jiggling the stone.

"I need to do some thinking," Joshua started, then stopped.

Cook looked over.

"Some thinking about being home."

They both looked again at the horizon, now beginning to glow.

That's good," his father said.

THIRTY-FIVE

Monday morning, June 23, 1919

"Mr. Dulles." The president stood behind his desk as Allen Dulles entered his library. Wilson kept his hands clasped behind him.

"Mr. President," Dulles stopped halfway into the room. "Allow me to congratulate you on the new German government. We've been advised that they accept the treaty terms and will sign on Saturday."

"Mr. Dulles. It is splendid, yes. As the Duke of Wellington said, it was a near run thing. I can't imagine what those German politicians were thinking. They complained that the treaty blames Germany for causing the war in the first place, so to vindicate themselves, they threatened to provoke a second war. To show they hadn't caused a war, they proposed to start a war." He shook his head and gestured for Dulles to sit in a leather wingback chair that faced his desk. "For a race that prides itself on its rationality, the Germans can be most irrational."

"We can hope that Herr Bauer, who took over from Schneiderman on Saturday, will be different. His acceptance of the treaty was his very first act as the new *Reichsministerpresident.*"

Wilson came around his desk and sat in the other armchair that faced his desk. He gazed out the window, a small smile on his face. "I wonder if it's as simple as the language they speak. Such immense words the Germans produce: *Reichsministerpresident*. It seems a desperate effort to establish gravitas and importance, but comes off a bit ridiculous, like an army uniform with too much gold braid and too many medals." His skin looked gray and his eye twitch was back. He stopped it with his left fore-finger. "We're fortunate they've come to their senses, even at the last minute. What do we know about how Herr Bauer came to power? Your uncle Lansing has claimed not to know much about it."

"I'm in the dark, as well, Mr. President. It's internal German politics, you know. Perhaps my brother can explain it."

"Of course. Of course." Wilson pursed his lips. The Dulles brothers had proved so very useful, unlike their scold of an uncle. Wilson knew he didn't have to like the men who were useful to him, but he couldn't shake the feeling that the Dulles family had hearts unlike his heart. At least this one didn't patronize him.

"It takes a kind of courage," Wilson said, "to sign a surrender. Losing a war is no easy thing. I grew up in a country that had recently lost a disastrous war. It leaves scars that don't ever really heal. There's a lot of blaming."

Dulles was puzzled for a moment, then realized that Wilson meant his boyhood in the South after the Civil War.

The president rose and walked over to stare out his window, hands again gathered behind his back. Dulles judged that he shouldn't intrude on the presidential reverie.

After perhaps two minutes, Wilson turned. "Shall we review the logistics of the signing at Versailles? The ceremony must be seamless. We cannot abide any last-minute surprises, anything that might give the Germans an excuse for not signing."

"Yes, sir, but there is one thing if I might." Dulles stood and pulled a single sheet from the portfolio he held. He handed it to Wilson, who placed it on the desk and leaned over it.

"This paper is rather thin on details about this, ah, Sergeant Cook, is it? Can you enlighten me?"

Dulles gave a small shrug. "I really can't, Mr. President. In this instance, I am but the messenger for senior army officials. I'm told the initial verdict acquitting the sergeant—Cook, you said? — was a just one. There's speculation that General Parkman must have misread the file when he reversed it. But only presidential action can right this particular wrong."

Wilson reread the paper. "This says the good sergeant was in the 369th Infantry. Wasn't that one of our Negro units?"

Dulles' internal alert system began to sound. "I'm not sure, sir. I can never keep all those numbers straight."

Wilson stared at his young aide for just a moment. Based on close observation over the last six months, he knew there was very little that Dulles couldn't keep straight. "You know," the president straightened, "we've just had a riot in Charleston. The darkies were dissatisfied over something. And now we're sending home a great many of their sons and brothers after training them in the use of weapons. I don't wish to do anything that might stir them up even more."

"Naturally not, sir." Dulles shifted in his chair.

Wilson pursed his lips again. "Why is it you who is presenting this, Mr. Dulles? You're not part of the military. I have had that right all these months?"

"Certainly not, sir. But, well, sir, the army officers involved have left for Versailles or else they're pursuing demobilization now that the Germans have finally come to their senses. I was just asked to bring it in as a routine matter." He leaned forward for the paper. There had to be another way to skin this cat. Or else Sergeant Cook will just have to serve his sentence.

Dulles disliked injustice, but he didn't make a fetish about it. It's never absent from human affairs. "The military people will be back in a few days. They can deal with it then."

Wilson had resumed his study of the paper. "This Sergeant Cook, is he in prison?"

"He has, I understand, been denied his freedom." Dulles cleared his throat. "Really, though, I'm sorry to have brought it up, knowing so little about the situation."

Still staring at the paper, Wilson asked, "Did he fight?"

It was an opening Dulles decided to take. He did owe Sergeant Cook.

"I know that, sir. He was in the front line for several months and fought at the Argonne Forest. I understand he was gassed. His military records show that he was a brave and capable soldier."

"Some things you know and others you don't." The president looked directly at his young aide. "You are mysterious, Mr. Dulles."

"Sir, my line sometimes involves mystery."

"Can you assure me I should sign this?"

"I wouldn't bring it here under any other circumstances."

Wilson sat down with a smile. "Thank you, Mr. Dulles. It's always good to know what I don't know. That way I can remember not to know it." He picked up a pen, dipped it in an inkwell, and signed the paper. He handed it across the desk. "We must be sure that our brave men are treated fairly."

"Thank you, sir."

Wednesday evening, June 25, 1919

"With the whole world preparing to rejoice," Foster Dulles said as his brother approached, "and despite everything you and I have done to cheer him up, Uncle Bert has chosen this moment to become morose."

Foster and Lansing stood on the balcony of the Crillon suite. A sturdy breeze bowed the heavy drapes over the French doors. In their suit coats, with brandy snifters in their hands, the men didn't feel the chill that seeped in with the approach of night. Allen walked past them to a side table where a decanter stood amid several empty glasses.

"My mood," Lansing said, "has nothing to do with that excellent piece of business that both of you achieved." He lifted his brandy in tribute.

His nephews reciprocated.

"Your achievements, though, involved merely preventing a bad situation from becoming a catastrophe. I am afraid it remains a bad situation."

"We'll have peace," Allen said, joining the others. "The borders of Europe have been drawn in a more intelligent way than before."

"Really, Allen," his uncle broke in. "You believe that?"

"I didn't say they were intelligent, only that they will be *more* intelligent. Haven't you always lectured us that nothing built by man will ever be perfect?"

Lansing shook his head. "I fear I find the new arrangements only different, not even an improvement. The blunders are frightful. We have the Italians staggering over to the wrong side of the Adriatic, the Greeks pretending to be in Asia Minor again, the Poles in charge of Germans and poor Hungary wondering who has made off with the rest of it. Don't get me started on the lunacy of having French control of the Saar Valley. Under the old system, you couldn't seize land in Europe unless you actually conquered it. This is a new system, where you needn't conquer land so long as you say you are taking it just for a little while." He shook his head. "We've sowed the seeds for a dozen conflicts, and that's just in Europe!" He held his glass up. "Shall we salute the blunders?"

"Why not?" said Foster. He drained his glass. Allen finished his drink, then handed his empty glass to his brother, who walked to the side table for refills.

"Do you have no hopes," Allen asked his uncle, "that the League of Nations will succeed, that the silly quarrels over this border and that one can't be smoothed over peaceably?"

Lansing finished his drink and joined Foster at the brandy decanter to receive his own refill. "Very little hope, though the League is the only one of our employer's Fourteen Points to be even partly realized." He sighed. "You know how discouraging the word from home is. The Senate's in an uproar. I doubt America will even be part of the League." He dropped into one of the four large chairs before the empty fireplace.

Foster and Allen sat across from him.

"Even the president admits that ratification will be difficult. Devilishly difficult."

The men sat in silence awhile, sipping brandy.

"I suppose," Foster said slowly, "that Mr. Wilson might claim two victories here." He did not respond to his uncle's derisive snort. "He may have abandoned thirteen and one-half of his Fourteen Points, but he has changed the words we use to talk about the fate of nations. Clemenceau certainly won the battles over what he wanted right now, but Wilson's words may never go away. They may ultimately change everything."

"I hope," Lansing said, "that his second triumph was more tangible."

"Indeed, Uncle Bert. It will be a huge triumph if the treaty and the League actually succeed in stopping the spread of Bolshevism. That was really the only goal that all of the Allies agreed on. The rest of the last six months was just squabbling over spoils."

"Well," Lansing stirred himself, "be that as it may with the fate of nations, I have spent some time thinking of the fate of my nephews."

"Good old Uncle Bert," said Allen.

"I suspect that the final two years of Mr. Wilson's administration will offer few opportunities for advancement. The heady days, I'm afraid, are quite over."

"I agree," Foster said, "as does Mr. Cromwell. He's offered to take me back to the firm."

"As his partner?"

Foster looked uncomfortable. "He has dangled that before me rather crudely without actually committing to it. If he doesn't come through with it, I will go elsewhere. But I am very much inclined to accept for now."

"I applaud the move. I understand your misgiving, Foster, but it's an excellent opportunity. You'll have plenty of international work with him but won't have to carry the burdens of the peace conference's mistakes." Lansing turned to Allen. "I do have a notion for you, sir."

Allen looked at him inquiringly.

"You've demonstrated a flair for working with the Germans. How about Berlin?"

"Ah. And I would be in Berlin as…?"

"Allie," Lansing said, "I can hardly make you ambassador. You are twenty-six years old. It will be a suitable position, you may be sure."

"Actually," Foster said carefully, "Mr. Cromwell had some ideas for Allen, as well."

Lansing tried to conceal his annoyance. He waited for an explanation.

Allen began. "Cromwell's rather keen, as am I, on the Near East."

Lansing said nothing.

"This oil business is going to be a huge factor in the world, and the

Arabs, well, they're children about such matters. There's a vital role for Western nations to play there. And America must be part of that."

Lansing thought for a moment, then nodded his head. "Against my natural inclinations, I think that's rather wise of your Mr. Cromwell. The whole Arab and Jewish business will remain an open question for some time since the peace conference didn't resolve it."

"Exactly," Foster said. "It's only a matter of time until the French and British divide things up. Allen can be sure that the United States doesn't miss out when the dividing is done."

Lansing tapped his lips with a forefinger. "I imagine I can help with that, exactly as you were hoping I could."

The brothers smiled at him.

"Something should open up in Istanbul rather soon. I think Istanbul will continue as the place to be for that region. How does that sound?"

"Very good, indeed," Allen said. He looked down to form his next question. "What shall be done about Colonel Lawrence and his Prince Faisal, not to mention Rabbi Wise and Weizmann and so on?"

Lansing smiled his first smile of the conversation. "There's no need to do a blessed thing. It's a British problem. They made the mess. They can clean it up."

"This Lawrence fellow," Allen objected, "he seems pretty formidable."

Lansing retained his smile. "Oh, he's an impassioned amateur. The British Foreign Office has long experience with making short work of such men. Lawrence's day has passed, and I say Godspeed." He raised his snifter in salute.

Again, his nephews reciprocated.

THIRTY-SIX

Saturday morning, June 28, 1919

Even in late June, northern France was cool enough for the Frasers to wear coats. The three of them stood, arm in happy arm, before the royal palace of Versailles, the world's fullest expression of royal self-celebration. Violet had just finished reading from a guidebook about the palace's astonishing dimensions. Its sandstone walls enclosed seven hundred rooms. Its roofs extended for twenty-six acres. Its stables could accommodate two thousand horses. Its grounds covered almost twenty thousand acres and were dotted with some fifty fountains.

"It's an odd place to sign the treaty," Eliza said. "It's so grand. So contrary to Mr. Wilson's Fourteen Points."

"Ah, but where better to demonstrate France's majesty and greatness?" Fraser asked.

"I suppose," Violet leaned across her father, who stood between the women, "it's also calculated to irritate the Germans."

Eliza and Fraser exchanged a quick glance of pride. Violet had agreed that in the fall she would finish her studies at the Emma Willard School. She even said she was looking forward to it.

"You also can be proud," Eliza said, "that two of the men making peace are your patients."

"I can't help but think of my patients who didn't make it."

She squeezed his arm with her free hand. "But you made it. And we did."

The press of the huge crowd might have been frightening, but the day was too hopeful for that. Joshua stood on the other side of Violet, his Croix de Guerre pinned to his army topcoat, his infantryman's cap at a rakish angle. His father came next, left arm in a sling.

"Sergeant Cook," Violet said to Joshua, "my father says you've been quite the hero. I hope to hear about your adventures on our passage back to America."

He lowered his head, but smiled, too. "They might not be all that much to hear about, Miss Violet. Anyway, I'll be returning on a troopship with the other colored soldiers."

"Then I'll have to hear about your adventures before the crossing, or back home in New York."

Joshua added, with an eye to Fraser, "Perhaps not all of my adventures."

Violet tossed her head, causing her yellow hair to shimmer as prettily as when she practiced the gesture before the mirror. "I believe I've demonstrated that I can keep a secret, even very delicate ones."

Cook leaned forward to speak across his son. "Joshua and I won't forget that you folks stuck by us."

The crowd roared as the top-hatted leaders emerged from the palace. Clemenceau's white walrus mustaches were unmistakable, as was his old-fashioned high collar. His step was steady. Behind him, Wilson looked tall and solid, his spectacles reflecting the gray overcast sky. The other dignitaries melted into a mass of formally dressed men in late middle age.

Eliza and Violet hopped on their toes to see over the crowd. With a heroic groan, Fraser lifted Eliza by the waist to afford her a better view.

Joshua gestured to Violet and she nodded eagerly. He lifted her. "Now I can see the president but you can't," she shouted.

Joshua grinned up at her. "Don't you worry. I've seen him plenty."

The crowd started to surge toward the statesmen. Voices shouted and some threw their hats in the air in jubilation. With a broad smile that showcased gleaming teeth, Wilson doffed his hat to the crowd, which began to jostle him. He looked to be on the verge of tumbling into one of Versailles' majestic fountains when a company of soldiers pushed through the crowd, surrounded him, and escorted him to an open touring car.

When Fraser set Eliza back on the ground, he noticed Joshua holding Violet aloft. He thought to say something, but changed his mind. He looked back at the scene of powerful men climbing into fine cars.

"Look, Father," Violet cried, "it's Allen Dulles! Right there! Behind the president!" She looked down at her father. "He wasn't so bad as you thought, was he, Daddy?"

"I'm not sure that bad and good apply to young Mr. Dulles. I will say"—Fraser looked over at Joshua and Speed—"he's been a man of his word. I don't ask for more of him."

It was half an hour before the crowd's energy began to subside. As people drifted from the palace courtyard, Fraser and Cook fell into step with each other. The young people walked ahead with Eliza.

"Made my shoulder throb," Cook said, "just to see you and Joshua lifting those women up."

"Mmm," Fraser said.

Cook leaned closer and said in a lower voice, "I'll speak to him about that."

Fraser looked over, surprised. "I didn't mean that."

"Well, I did. Young people can be, well..." As Cook searched for the word he wanted, a short, sandy-haired man with a cane limped into view on their right.

"Colonel Lawrence!" Fraser called out. "I'm Major—"

"Yes, yes, I know you. Quite a day, eh? Not often one sees a catastrophe in the making. Those old men, they ruin everything they touch."

Fraser called the others back to meet to the hero. Lawrence barely acknowledged them, then began to edge away.

Fraser detained him with a hand on his shoulder. "Tell me, Colonel, did you end up with what you want?"

"Of course not. But there are no final decisions. We prolonged the game. We'll play a few more innings and hope for the best. I suspect we have the Dulles lads to thank for the absence of a decision, though by the end of the process I probably won't be feeling very thankful." He turned and limped off.

"That's one very strange duck," Cook said.

The two men started after the others of their party, who had already set off toward the army car Fraser commandeered for the trip to Versailles.

"I can't help but think about Wilson," Fraser said. "By rights he should have been in bed most of the last three months. I wonder how long he can hold up."

"Thanks to you, no one knows any of that."

"Thanks not just to me. Just think how many people know how sick he is—the people on his staff—why, there must be dozens. Then there are the dozens of people he negotiated with. They all could tell." Fraser shook his head. "It's surprising how the world chooses not to know something that's right there, clear as day."

"Well," Cook said, "if it was his sickness made him sign the order vacating Joshua's sentence, I say merci beaucoup and bon chance."

They were quiet for a few more strides.

"Jamie, are you feeling like telling anyone about all this?"

"Not a soul. How about you?"

Speed smiled. "Nah. Not this time."

AFTERWORD

Confronted with the prospect of writing a sequel to *The Lincoln Deception,* I could not resist the magnetic pull of the Paris Peace Conference of 1919. The decisions reached by the victorious Allies after months of negotiation determined the path of so much modern history: the rise of Nazism in Germany and World War II, the birth of the Chinese Communist Party, the mangled resolution of the Near East (perhaps unraveling right now as Iraq and Syria begin to dissolve). When historical fiction deals with real events, readers often want to know what really happened, so I offer some basic guidance.

The novel's timeline for the conference is based on history. Two surprising events are entirely true. First, an anarchist really did shoot French Premier Georges Clemenceau during the conference, and Clemenceau finished the conference (and the last ten years of his life) with a bullet in his back. In addition, there was a crisis at the end of the peace conference when the German government balked at signing the treaty. The risk loomed, though it seemed preposterous, that the war could be resumed after seven months of peace. In an overnight maneuver in late June, the German Cabinet was largely replaced and the new Cabinet approved the treaty, as did the German legislative branch.

The novel's cast of characters also is drawn from real life, beginning with the tragic central figure, Woodrow Wilson, and including Clemenceau, Lloyd George, and Lawrence of Arabia. As I set out to wrestle this sprawling story into some sort of shape—and to insert the fictional Jamie Fraser and Speed Cook into it—I made the happy discovery of Secretary of State Robert Lansing and his two nephews, future Secretary of State John Foster Dulles and future CIA Director Allen Dulles. All three men were in Paris for the conference. Lansing was almost entirely shoved aside by Wilson, which made him a natural commentator from the sidelines. The Dulles boys were intimately involved in the conference. Allen, who had spied for the United States in Switzerland during the war, became an indispensable staff support for Wilson. Foster Dulles led the American effort on the treaty with Germany. Many of the secondary characters in the novel—Chaim Weizmann, Rabbi Stephen Wise, W.E.B. Du Bois, Winston Churchill, Mark Sykes—were really there in Paris, though I may have adjusted the dates when they were in town to meet the needs of my story.

Similarly, I have sketched the events and characters of these historical figures based on what history tells us. The influenza epidemic of 1918-19 killed millions, including key British diplomat Mark Sykes early in the conference. Wilson had two health breakdowns during the conference; he did like to sing hymns, recite limericks, and tell "darky" jokes. And the US Army treated its black soldiers abominably. Joshua Cook's unit, which has become known in history as the Harlem Hellfighters, won a well-deserved reputation for discipline and courage, largely because it was assigned to the French Army, which treated them as men. All of these events, however, have been filtered through my unreliable imagination.

Those wishing to learn more about the peace conference might look at Margaret MacMillan's *Paris 1919,* Harold Nicolson's memoir *Peacemaking 1919,* and John Maynard Keynes' *The Economic Consequences of the Peace.* Fine recent biographies of Woodrow Wilson include *Wilson* by Scott Berg and *Woodrow Wilson: A Biography,* by John Milton Cooper, Jr. For a sense of the strange hero T.E. Lawrence, I turned to a work by his friend, Robert Graves, *Lawrence and the Arabs*. With the centennial of World War I upon us, we can expect many more excellent treatments of the war and the peace.

THE BABE RUTH DECEPTION

THE FRASER AND COOK HISTORICAL MYSTERY SERIES, BOOK THREE

Joshua burst through the door, throwing the trays against the wall to make maximum noise, their cymbal-like clatter both jarring and confusing. Cecil pushed the guard to the floor, then spun on another who sat inside the door, hitting him flush in the face with the pistol barrel. Joshua's voice rang out: "Hands on the table, chilluns!"

The cardplayers looked into the barrels of two German pistols. Cecil strode to the table while Joshua announced, "My friend here'll take your guns. If you sit nice and still, I won't shoot you." Cecil held out his sack. Some grudgingly, some quickly, the gamblers gave up their guns. Cecil carried the nearly full sack over to Joshua. He lifted the guns from the guards on the floor and added those to the sack, then left it at the door.

"Now the cash," Joshua called out. "Don't make us wait. My friend gets very impatient! Ain't nothing in your pockets worth dying over. Don't sweat the jewelry. Just cash."

Cecil grabbed the bills on the table and stuffed them into a second sack. Then he circled the table demanding wallets.

"I don't know who you are," Rothstein snarled, color flooding his usually pallid face, "but you're going to be one sorry son of a bitch."

Cecil backed toward the door, gun in one hand and money sack in the other. Joshua picked up the bag of guns and followed.

Joshua turned the lock, then they dashed to an open window at the end of the short hall. Joshua tossed out the sack of guns. Each man dropped from the window frame to the ground. Joshua held onto the bag of money.

They sprinted across the lawn, skirting lighted areas. Angry voices burst from the building.

In the ditch across the road, Cook heard the shouts. The men on the porch pulled out their weapons and jumped into the night. Muzzle flashes showed their progress across the lawn. Their chances of hitting something in the dark were close to zero. "They're going through the woods," Cook said to Fraser. "Let's go."

Cook and Fraser jog-trotted toward the Stutz as an engine roared in the woods on their left. "That's them," Cook said. A large car broke from the trees. Cook pulled Fraser into the ditch. He didn't want to spook the boys, draw their fire as they sped past. Fraser and Cook were gasping when they got to the car and got it running. Cook hopped in as Fraser started in the direction the boys were headed--north toward Canada.

"Follow them," Cook said, "but not fast."

"You're sure it's them?"

"Who else?" Cook craned his neck to look for the pursuit. "Get in the middle." Fraser did. "Weave, back and forth. You're drunk. Me, too." He pulled out a flask and splashed liquor on both of them.

The next seconds seemed to take forever. How could hoodlums be so slow? Finally, they heard an engine. No, several engines. "Okay now," Cook said. "We're still drunk."

A car roared up and tried to pass on the left. Fraser swung left to block it, then jerked right, as though recovering from a surprise swerve, then turned back left before the car behind could pass. The driver behind hit the horn, hard. Then again. Fraser turned the wheel in response, as if startled, holding the center of the road.

When the trailing car pulled right, Fraser slid that way. The honking was frantic. Fraser jerked the wheel from side to side, in no rhythm, as if in panic. "Good," Cook said. "Hang on."

Fraser veered left to block the second car, which was trying to pass both the Stutz and the first car. For a moment, the two pursuing cars advanced side by side. The second fell back. More seconds passed. Then Fraser heard tires squeal. An engine roared.

A car smashed into the Stutz's rear, heaving Fraser into the windshield. He didn't register the smack of skull against glass--it was the steering wheel in his chest that took his breath, then hurt like blazes. His brain shut down. The Stutz leaned right, then jammed itself into the roadside ditch, sending Fraser back against the windshield.

Dazed, a thought floated by Fraser -- cars explode in crashes. He should get out. He pawed his door, then heard noises behind him. He swiveled his head to see, which hurt like hell. He groaned. Men with pistols were running at him.

"Don't shoot! Don't shoot!" he tried to say. He lifted his arms in surrender.

Another engine blasted. A voice surged, indistinct, then faded. A flashlight blinded him, more shouts behind it.

Squinting against the glare, Fraser asked, "What's going on?" Cotton batting circled his head. The world was slow. "We, we..." The words were in his head. He had to catch up to them. "My friend," he got out, "my friend and I, we, you know, were in town." No one answered. "I'm a doctor," he said. Why did he say that?

A man screamed at him. Fraser couldn't make out words. When the flashlight moved off his face, he saw flashing circles. A face loomed up. There was a metallic taste in his mouth.

The shouts separated into words. "Stop screwing around! Get after those guys!"

Two gunmen started back. A third jammed a gun barrel into Fraser's chest. "Fucking civilians. You and your friend, count yourselves lucky we don't shoot you and leave you here to die. Goddamned lushes." He waved the gun at Cook. "Your nigger friend's way over his limit."

Fraser looked over. Cook had been quiet. That wasn't usual. He wasn't moving. Cracks spiderwebbed the windshield on that side.

"He's hurt," Fraser said. "Help us! Please! He needs a hospital."

"This is your friend's lucky day, Doc. I'm not shooting him and you're a doctor."

Available in Paperback and eBook from Your Favorite Bookstore or Online Retailer

ALSO BY DAVID STEWART

The Fraser and Cook Historical Mystery Series

The Lincoln Deception

The Paris Deception

The Babe Ruth Deception

Other Titles

The Summer of 1787: The Men Who Invented the Constitution

Impeached: The Trial of President Andrew Johnson and the Fight for Lincoln's Legacy

American Emperor: Aaron Burr's Challenge to Jefferson's America

Madison's Gift: Five Partnerships that Built America

George Washington: The Political Rise of America's Founding Father (to be released in February 2021)

ABOUT THE AUTHOR

After many years as a trial and appellate lawyer, David O. Stewart became a bestselling writer of history and historical fiction. His award-winning histories have explored the writing of the Constitution, the gifts of James Madison, the outrageous western expedition and treason trial of the mysterious Aaron Burr, and the impeachment trial of President Andrew Johnson. His *Fraser and Cook Historical Mystery Series* includes *The Lincoln Deception,* about the John Wilkes Booth Conspiracy, *The Paris Deception,* set at the Paris Peace Conference in 1919, and *The Babe Ruth Deception*, which follows the Babe's first two years with the Yankees.

www.davidostewart.com

facebook.com/david.stewart.5680

CPSIA information can be obtained
at www.ICGtesting.com
Printed in the USA
LVHW111604040720
659751LV00001B/42